DEATH AT GILLS ROCK

Terrace Books, a trade imprint of the University of Wisconsin Press, takes its name from the Memorial Union Terrace, located at the University of Wisconsin–Madison. Since its inception in 1907, the Wisconsin Union has provided a venue for students, faculty, staff, and alumni to debate art, music, politics, and the issues of the day. It is a place where theater, music, drama, literature, dance, outdoor activities, and major speakers are made available to the campus and the community. To learn more about the Union, visit www.union.wisc.edu.

DEATH AT GILLS ROCK

A DAVE CUBIAK DOOR COUNTY MYSTERY

PATRICIA SKALKA

TERRACE BOOKS

A TRADE IMPRINT OF THE UNIVERSITY OF WISCONSIN PRESS

Terrace Books
A trade imprint of the University of Wisconsin Press
1930 Monroe Street, 3rd Floor
Madison, Wisconsin 53711-2059
uwpress.wisc.edu

3 Henrietta Street, Covent Garden
London WC2E 8LU, United Kingdom
eurospanbookstore.com

Printed in the United States of America

Library of Congress Cataloging-in-Publication Data

Skalka, Patricia, author.
Death at Gills Rock: a Dave Cubiak Door County mystery / Patricia Skalka.
     pages   cm — (Dave Cubiak Door County mystery)
ISBN 978-0-299-30450-8 (cloth: alk. paper)
ISBN 978-0-299-30453-9 (e-book)
1. Door County (Wis.)—Fiction.
I. Title.   II. Series: Skalka, Patricia. Dave Cubiak Door County mystery.
PS3619.K34T48   2015
813′.6—dc23
2014038286

Maps by Julia Padvoiskis

Door County is real. While I used the peninsula as the framework for the book, I also altered some
details and added others to fit the story. The spirit of this majestic place remains unchanged.

For
Julia and Carla,
the diamond and the pearl . . .

Nothing is secret, that shall not be made manifest.

Luke 8:17

DEATH AT GILLS ROCK

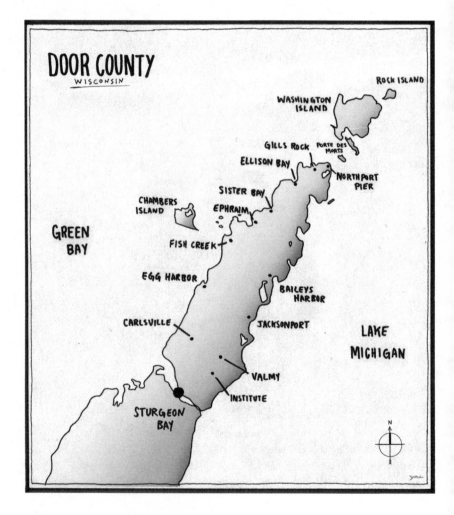

WEEK ONE:
SATURDAY
EARLY MORNING

1

Three of a Kind: Joined in Life, War, and Honor." Dave Cubiak skimmed the headline as he ran the water over the dirty dishes piled in the sink. The Door County sheriff was normally neat about his surroundings, but with one of his deputies out sick that week he'd been getting home barely in time to fix supper and rinse up afterward. Cubiak glanced at the mess in the basin. Cleanup duty called, but he knew that keeping up with local events was duty as well.

Cubiak brushed the crumbs from the table and sat down with the *Herald*. Braced for a piece of north woods fluff, he began reading. During his first year on the Wisconsin peninsula, he was often annoyed by the blur between hard and soft news, but gradually he'd come to understand that small-town reporting simply represented a different way of looking at the world. Where little happened, people were the news, and what happened to them mattered.

The story captivated Cubiak. The three boyhood friends were World War II veterans who'd fought together in the United States' only battles against the Japanese on American soil. They'd enlisted after Pearl Harbor and shipped out with the Sturgeon Bay coast guard contingent assigned to help the army pry the enemy from its foothold in Alaska's Aleutian Islands, staving off an invasion of the mainland. In 1943, American troops had ousted Japanese forces from strongholds on Amchitka, Komandorski, and Attu Islands. The trio—Terrence "Big Guy" Huntsman, Eric Swenson, and Jasper Wilkins—were to be honored at the commissioning ceremonies for a new patrol cutter named for the Battle of Attu, an eighteen-day siege that ended with a Japanese banzai, or suicide, attack.

Cubiak sipped his coffee and continued reading. He recognized the men. Huntsman, Swenson, and Wilkins were Door County stalwarts from Gills Rock, a blip of a town at the tip of the peninsula. After the bloody ordeal on Attu, the three friends served together for the duration of the war. Once peace was restored, they returned home to the isolated waterfront village of their childhoods. Two photos beneath the fold showed them before and after: first as gangly eighteen-year-olds in white coast guard uniforms, standing on the forward deck of the USS *Arthur Middleton*, and now as gray-haired octogenarians, scarred by time but still rugged and Viking-tall, framed against the steely waters of northern Door.

On the page 2 jump, the veterans were pictured with their wives. Three more of a kind, thought Cubiak. A smaller photo in the right-hand corner showed an army private named Christian Nils, also of Gills Rock. Just nineteen and newly married when he joined up, Nils died when his troop transport capsized in stormy seas during an ill-fated landing attempt. Huntsman, Swenson, and Wilkins were among the coast guardsmen cited for their heroic efforts to try to save Nils and the other 170 men washed overboard or stranded on the ice-coated, rocky shore of Amchitka Island.

The worst horror of war, Cubiak thought. Worse even than taking a life was the inability to preserve one. You killed your enemies but tried to save your friends. Everything surreal. Bombs and blood. The heavy silence of the dead and anguished cries of the dying. For him, sandstorms and strangling heat. For Nils and the three friends, impenetrable fog and frigid water.

Cubiak flinched. He rarely thought about his two closest army buddies: Tobias, a football player who'd left Kuwait without a leg, and Kenny, a drummer who went home in a body bag with only half a brain. The others were lost in a blur of confusion. Eager to forget, they had drifted apart. These three men, the trio that came back to Door County after the war, had stayed tight. Regular camping trips were made to Rock Island and weekly poker games took place in the log cabin Huntsman had built for that purpose.

Not long after Cubiak was elected sheriff, Big Guy had called and invited him to a Friday evening card tournament. "It'll give us a chance to meet and get to know each other," he'd said. Cubiak had grown up with a skinny kid tagged Fatso and had played high school basketball with a tall center nicknamed Shorty. He imagined his host as the antithesis of his sobriquet, and when the cabin door swung open he was surprised to find himself standing eye-level with the line of red reindeer that pranced chest-high across Big Guy's green sweater. Huntsman did more than tower in the doorway; he consumed the entire entryway, and for a moment Cubiak was reminded of the monstrous Kodiak bear frozen upright on its hind legs in the old Marshall Field's Men's Store in downtown Chicago.

"Hey, come on in, Dave," Big Guy said as he clamped a paw-sized hand on the sheriff's shoulder and pulled him across the threshold into the overheated cabin.

The phone rang, bringing Cubiak back to the early morning chill of his spartan kitchen.

He tipped the chair onto its rear legs, leaned back, and unhooked the receiver from the wall cradle.

"Chief?" There was no need to ask who was calling. Cubiak recognized the baritone voice of his deputy Michael Rowe. The officer was the youngest member of the force and the first person the new sheriff had hired after he was sworn in to office eighteen months prior.

"Mike, easy on the ears," he said.

"Sorry. I tried to raise you on the radio."

"It's Saturday. I'm in my kitchen. Just finishing breakfast."

"Right. Sorry. You see the *Herald* yet?"

"Reading it right now." As if to substantiate the claim, Cubiak dropped the chair back onto all fours.

"Yeah, something else, ain't it? Anyways, they're waiting for you to get up there and look around."

"Who? Where?"

"Huntsman's place in Gills Rock. Doctor Bathard called. There's been an accident."

Cubiak reached over his glasses and pinched the bridge of his nose. Evelyn Bathard, the retired coroner and the sheriff's first real friend on the peninsula, was not a man to make an unnecessary fuss. "What kind of accident?"

"He didn't say and by the time I'd asked he'd hung up. I tried calling back but the line was busy. Probably somebody calling the ambulance."

"How bad is it?"

"About as bad as it gets. Those men? Huntsman, Swenson, and Wilkins—they're all dead."

Cubiak looked at the paper again. In the photos, the men appeared vibrant and carefree. How could they be dead? They'd survived war and the near misses that life brings as a matter of course. Maybe Rowe was mistaken. "You sure?" he said, finally.

"I'm just telling you what the doc told me."

As he talked to Rowe, Cubiak moved to the window. The view opened to a patch of scrub lawn, a strip of rocky shore, and the lake. Four days of a northeast wind had churned up sand from the bottom and made the water dull and opaque. Whitecaps broke over the sandbar half a mile out and then flattened into soft, rolling waves. Approaching the table rocks along the shore, they reformed into curls of angry foam and hurled against the land. Lake Michigan had been ice-free for three weeks but the water remained frigid. Not as cold as the water in the Aleutians, he thought, but cold enough.

Cubiak finished with the deputy and then scanned the paper again. A map of the Aleutians provided a perspective on their value to the war

6

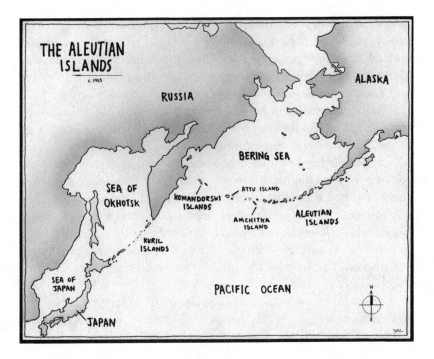

THE ALEUTIAN ISLANDS
c. 1943

ALASKA

RUSSIA

BERING SEA

SEA OF OKHOTSK

KOMANDORSKI ISLANDS

ATTU ISLAND

AMCHITKA ISLAND

ALEUTIAN ISLANDS

KURIL ISLANDS

SEA OF JAPAN

PACIFIC OCEAN

N

JAPAN

effort. Starting from the tip of the Alaska Peninsula, the island chain swept a thousand miles westward into the Pacific. That far? The dab of land at the very end of the archipelago was strategically positioned a mere 650 miles from Japan's Kuril Islands. That close? The Japanese threat had been very real, the service rendered vital.

The sheriff lifted his mug, anticipating a gulp of hot coffee. Affronted by the cold, bitter liquid in the cup, he spat the dregs into the drain and dumped the rest. Three men were dead, presumably the result of an accident. The day would not be an easy one.

Cubiak pushed aside a stack of unwashed dishes, maneuvered a large aluminum bowl under the faucet, and turned on the tap. As the container filled, he poured dry dog food into a second bowl and then carried them both out to the back porch. He'd already fed Butch earlier that morning, but she was nursing a litter of four pups and could probably use a little extra. Plus he didn't know when he'd get back. The round trip to Gills Rock took about an hour and a half even in spring before tourist traffic kicked in.

Butch lay curled up in the oval wicker basket that Cubiak had found at a resale shop and lined with a worn patchwork quilt for her. He set down the bowls and stroked the dog's head. Butch sighed and the puppies snuffled and squirmed, bending their soft sausage bodies to the contours of their mother's stomach. One of the pups was a miniature clone, a brown and white mutt with the hint of a spaniel's ears and a hound's sleek snout, but the others were a hodgepodge of mismatched colors and physical characteristics. There were two males and two females, but he didn't remember which was which. "Shush now," he told the dogs and opened the curtains in hopes the sun would emerge from behind the clouds.

Outside, the wind bit sharply. The arrow on the garage thermometer pointed to forty-eight, but the breeze made the temperature feel close to freezing. When he'd moved from the ranger station, several locals urged him to find a place in the interior, away from the windy shoreline. But Cubiak demurred. In his native Chicago, waterfront living had been beyond his means; even in Door County, he couldn't afford to live on a sand beach. Rocks made the difference. Rocks put lakefront property within reach, and not a day went by that he didn't gaze out at the water and appreciate its splendor.

Hunched into his collar, Cubiak hurried across the yard and climbed into his unmarked jeep, happy for the anonymity it provided. As a Chicago homicide detective, he'd grown accustomed to moving around undercover and was pleased to discover that in his new job he generally wasn't expected to wear or carry any identifiable paraphernalia associated with the office beyond his gun and badge.

As usual, Cubiak had nothing planned for the day. The middle school spring soccer meet was at the fairgrounds that weekend, and he knew that he'd want to avoid being anywhere near the games. Alexis had played youth soccer and had been pretty decent at it, for a seven-year-old.

Her last game, she'd even accidentally scored a goal.

"Did you see? Did you see me?" she'd shouted, her cheeks pink with cold as she raced toward her parents at the halftime break.

"Yes, honey, I did," he said, wrapping his arms around her slim, coltish frame. It was one of the little lies parents tell their children. Truth was he had a hard time distinguishing Alexis from the clump of kids that mindlessly chased the ball from one end of the field to the other.

"What a clusterfuck," he said when the second half began and Alexis again melted into the sea of green jerseys.

Lauren elbowed him. "It's cluster ball," she said, laughing.

Four years later, if Alexis were alive, she might still be playing, and he and Lauren would be shivering on the sidelines in the park near Wilson Avenue, shouting encouragement into the wind. If Lauren were alive as well. If he'd come home as he'd promised he would and they hadn't walked to the ice-cream store alone. If the maniac drunk driver hadn't barreled into them . . .

Guilt over the accident and grief over their deaths led Cubiak to drink himself out of his job with the Chicago Police Department and eventually brought him to Door County. He meant to stay for one year and was working as a park ranger when several people mysteriously died. After Cubiak tracked the killer, he was elected sheriff.

His newfound purpose helped ease him into the reality of life without his family. But just because he'd become resigned to the deaths of his wife and daughter didn't mean that the hours were less empty or their absence easier to bear. If nothing else, the trip to Gills Rock would fill the day.

Cubiak reached toward the dash for a cigarette and remembered that he'd quit four months earlier. He unwrapped two sticks of spearmint gum as he rolled down the driveway. Across Lake Shore Road, his nearest neighbor, Lewis Nagel, straddled the shallow ditch and trimmed weeds around the post that held a mailbox disguised as an ugly largemouth bass. The sheriff honked and Nagel looked up, raising a hand in a gesture that passed for a wave. Cubiak returned the greeting. A minute later, he was heading to Highway 42/57. Usually, he'd turn left and drive to the sheriff's headquarters outside Sturgeon Bay, but that morning, he went the opposite way, north up 42.

Traffic was sparse through the string of quaint resort towns that hugged the Green Bay shore. Cruising just above the limit, Cubiak wondered what sad circumstances he would find in Gills Rock. He'd been on the peninsula for almost twenty-four months and sheriff for all but the first seven, when he'd been employed at Peninsula State Park. How naïve he'd been. Hoping to escape death. But death offered no reprieve. Nasty and cruel, it materialized from a stew of old grudges and misdeeds, terrifying the locals and pulling him in.

Now more death, though accidental this time.

As sheriff, he'd learned from hard experience that most fatal accidents were associated with water mishaps or vehicular crashes. Could the three men have drowned? Such a fate seemed too unfair. And unlikely as well that all three would die like that. Only one, Swenson, had made a living as a fisherman but the other two were probably equally comfortable and savvy on the water. As far as Cubiak knew, there'd been no reports of isolated storms or sudden squalls, no missing boats in the past twenty-four hours. A car crash was no easier to contemplate. Bodies mangled and broken. Too often the stench of alcohol permeating the scene. But there were no vehicular accident reports either.

There were other ways to die, of course, and he'd find out soon enough what single incident or sequence of events had doomed the three friends.

Splotches of color—purple crocuses, yellow jonquils—jumped out from the drab landscape and helped take his mind off death. In Egg Harbor, a bright blue banner promoting the upcoming Spring Fest Weekend stretched over the roadway. Farther up, Fish Creek merchants arranged sidewalk displays for the town's annual Founders Fest. Spring was here, even if the weather didn't always match the change of season. If he concentrated, Cubiak could find hints of nature's rebirth in the budding leaves and the pale green whispers that quietly percolated across the forestland and countryside. These verdant traces were still largely overshadowed by a woodsy tangle of brown and black but presaged by an occasional splash of green so freshly vivid it seemed more like a flavor than a color.

Past Sister Bay, the promise of spring vanished under the lingering drabness of winter. Occasionally, mounds of snow hugged thick tree trunks, and as the last copse fell away, the village of Gills Rock emerged. Like a string of discolored pearls, its clapboard houses and shops clung to a sliver of rocky shoreline along the rim of Garrett Bay. At its northern end, the wide cove bled into Porte des Morts, a treacherous strait that connected the upper reaches of Green Bay to Lake Michigan and earned its name for the fierceness with which it had once swallowed ships and the crews and passengers they carried.

For decades, Gills Rock had been the jumping off point for the ferries that transported pedestrians and vehicles across Death's Door to Washington Island. With the ferry relocated to Northport Pier on the Lake Michigan side of the peninsula, traffic whizzed past the village and followed a picturesque winding road to the new terminal. Cubiak was uncomfortably familiar with that final zigzagging stretch of road.

He was still new to the area when he'd met Cate Wagner, a Milwaukee photographer, and ended up driving her back to the house near the ferry landing where she was staying with her aunt Ruby. He'd been instantly attracted to Cate but had tried to resist her out of loyalty to his dead wife. Cubiak had neither seen nor talked to Cate in a year and a half, not since he'd solved his first case on the peninsula, one that had given her reason both to leave the county and to despise him for his role in the events of that fateful summer. Cate had inherited her aunt's homestead as well as her grandfather's neighboring estate, The Wood. More often than he'd like to acknowledge, Cubiak detoured past the two properties, looking for a sign that she'd returned.

At the same time that he gave in to his yearning to reconnect with her, he dreaded the prospect. How could he make things right between them? Even worse, he'd been entrusted with the heart-wrenching secret about her past. "Are you going to tell her?" Bathard had asked once. "I don't know," Cubiak had replied. He still didn't know.

Distracted, the sheriff suddenly came upon a blue and white sign for Huntsman's Plumbing. He braked hard and swerved onto a stretch of rippled blacktop that hugged the low-lying, rocky shore. A bevy of gulls rose from the boulders. The birds were fat and speckled in shades of dirt and coal. As they dive-bombed the jeep, they screeched their annoyance and shattered the heavy morning quiet. Old and new came together along the lane, and the farther from the main road, the more elaborate the houses and the larger the lots. This bit of grandeur was followed by a long stretch of wild forest, trees so thick and tall that the jeep's headlights switched on. Without warning the forest opened to six small frame houses set in a jagged clearing and separated from each other by long, spindly driveways. Neatly aligned on narrow lots, the identical homes were painted a rainbow of pastel colors and looked like an experiment in community living. All but one were well maintained. The handyman's special was second from the end, tucked behind a massive weeping willow that nearly overwhelmed the front yard. A mangy German shepherd was tethered to the tree, and as Cubiak rolled past, the barking dog lunged at the jeep. The dog continued howling as the forest closed in again, yielding the faint odor of skunk that trailed the sheriff around a soft curve to a second notch in the woods and a pre-fabricated white metal barn emblazoned with the logo for Huntsman's Plumbing. A door marked Office and six blue vans in the small side lot carried the same emblem.

Big Guy's homestead was across the road, one of the last pieces of private, waterfront property this side of the county park. Cubiak steered between the two brick columns at the entrance. Twenty feet from the road, the driveway forked, with one narrow leg continuing on through the woods to the Rec Room cabin and the other wider branch bending back toward the yard and the house. The night he'd come to play cards, Cubiak had arrived in the dark and followed the cutoff to the cabin. This time he went the other way and coasted up to the two Door County ambulances from Sister Bay that were parked bumper to bumper in the drive. Cubiak pulled onto the grass alongside, leaving room for the third emergency vehicle, which had been dispatched from Sturgeon Bay.

The sheriff glanced at the house. Big Guy had done very well, he thought. The house, easily the largest in the area, was a handsome two-story structure built of fieldstone and topped with a slate roof. Several acres of carefully trimmed grass and bushes spread out like a collar around it. A gazebo overlooked the water at one end of the yard; at the other, a freshly painted dock with a power boat rigged for deepwater fishing was tied to the pier and a slick thirty-six-foot cabin cruiser named the *Ida Mae* hung in a sling alongside.

The opulence was dimmed by a gunmetal shroud of low-lying clouds, but Cubiak could imagine the splendor that a bright, sunny day would confer.

He turned his back on the residence and took a few moments to prepare himself before he joined the small crowd that huddled at the rear of the yard.

Against a backdrop of tall, bare bushes, Bathard and medical examiner Emma Pardy were conferring with Huntsman's son, Walter. A dozen men formed an awkward semicircle behind them. Probably fishermen and farmers from the area, they had the kind of tanned, leathery faces formed by decades of outdoor work. In a smooth continuous wave, they glanced up at the approaching sheriff and then down again at the three bodies laid out on the damp grass.

Shock and disbelief hung in the air.

As Cubiak neared, Walter drifted back toward the onlookers. Pardy said something to Bathard, who listened thoughtfully, nodding and tapping the bowl of a cherry-stemmed pipe on the heel of his hand. When she finished she knelt by one of the victims, notebook in hand, and the former coroner approached Cubiak. Unlike the other men, who were in jeans and faded work clothes, Bathard wore dark tan gabardine slacks and a navy duffel coat. "There was nothing to do. They were gone when I arrived," he said, slipping the pipe into his pocket.

"You got here first?"

"Yes. I was in Sister Bay, breakfasting with friends, when the ambulance went past. Old habits being what they are, I came to see if I could be of assistance. As it turned out, Emma was in Sturgeon Bay, at a soccer match, I believe. So at least one of us was able to get here quickly, not that it mattered in the end."

There was no rancor in Bathard's accounting. The retired physician recognized Pardy's competence and had supported her appointment to the post when the county shifted from the coroner to the medical examiner system.

As Pardy rose, the men fell back, one of them grumbling under his breath about how long it had taken her to reach Gills Rock. Pardy offered no sign that she'd heard the comment but Cubiak gave the man a sharp look. He'd seen a similar dynamic at play in the police department with men who couldn't handle the notion of a woman in a position of authority. Cubiak wondered if it had occurred to any of them that a male counterpart with school-age children would just as likely have been at the soccer games. That it had taken him, the sheriff, the same considerable amount of time to drive the length of the peninsula.

"Dave."

"Emma."

Pardy's firm grip matched her athletic look. She was tall and agile and, dressed in Lycra pants and jacket, looked more like a college student ready for a track meet than a mother of two with a degree in medicine. "So sad," she said.

Studying the three men, Cubiak considered both the sentiment and the truth of the comment. Huntsman, Swenson, and Wilkins. The victims were laid out in the same order as they had stood in the *Herald*'s page 1 picture.

"You've got photos of the bodies?"

"Bathard had already taken care of that by the time I arrived."

"They were in there?" Cubiak pointed to the log cabin barely visible behind a wedge of tall cedars.

"Yes."

"Who carried them out?"

A short, bearded man cleared his throat and cautiously flipped his right hand toward his shoulder. "Clyde Smitz. I live just down the road a piece." He nodded over his shoulder and then shoved his hand into his jacket pocket. "Ida called for help. She was upset, something about trouble at the Rec Room. When I got here, the men were all at the table. I was dragging Jasper to the door when my son Junior came." Smitz motioned toward a younger version of himself on his left and Cubiak recognized the man who'd uttered the disparaging comment about Pardy. "He got Eric and then between the two of us we got Big Guy out, too. We thought maybe we could revive them. Had to try, ya know. Couldn't just leave them in there. What if they were still alive?"

"You carried them all the way over here?"

"No." Smitz straightened in alarm. "We started working on them right outside the cabin. When we realized they were dead, it didn't seem right to leave 'em laying on the gravel, so we brought them here, to the grass." He rubbed his foot on the lawn as if to demonstrate that it provided a softer, more suitable resting place.

Cubiak nodded. "Of course."

Wilkins was nearest to him. The dead man's red flannel shirt hung free of his faded navy work pants, and the leather laces on his boots were untied. He was solid and broad shouldered, with a thick neck, thinning hair, rough hands, and a worn complexion. Cubiak squatted down for a closer look. Death was recent, judging by the skin tone. The same seemed true of the other two.

The medical examiner waited for Cubiak to stand before she spoke. "Looks like carbon monoxide poisoning. They had an old space heater in there, going full blast. Someone, maybe Walter, shut it off. I'm not sure he had much chance to look further, or if he should."

"Who found them?"

"Huntsman's wife, Ida." Bathard took up the story. "I left her in the house with the other spouses and a few of the neighbors. She seems quite stoic, though probably in shock. The other two were hysterical. I had to give them something to calm down. After that I talked to Rowe and called for the other two ambulances."

"Either of you have a chance to call Blackwell?" If no one had contacted the district attorney, he'd have to do it.

Emma looked up. "I did. He asked for an assessment as soon as possible."

As they spoke, the third ambulance coasted into the driveway. The EMTs who'd been first on the scene looked to the sheriff.

"Your call," Cubiak said to Pardy.

The sheriff left the two physicians to confer with the medics and went to offer his condolences to Walter. Despite the chill, the man's face gleamed with sweat, whether from nerves or the need for a drink, Cubiak wasn't sure. Three or four times during the past year he'd taken his car to Walter's shop for servicing and more than once had seen him fumble around in an alcoholic fog.

"Sorry about your father," Cubiak said, extending his hand.

Walter clung to the sheriff with the grip of a drowning man. He tried to speak but no words came from his open mouth.

"It's okay. We'll talk later," Cubiak said.

He escorted Walter to the gazebo and eased him down on the bench. "Sit here. Rest a bit," he said and then he waved over one of the EMTs and asked for a blanket.

As Cubiak draped the blanket around Walter, the medics pulled a gurney from the closest ambulance, secured the wheels underneath, and jounced the stretcher across the lawn. The crowd hushed and fell away. The EMTs took Huntsman first: body bag, zipper, and then the struggle to lift his great weight onto the gurney. While they worked, the silence deepened until the keening wind was the only sound to accompany the dead man on the short ride to the ambulance.

Cubiak stayed with Walter until the bodies had been removed. After the last ambulance pulled away, the sheriff retreated through the small crowd and walked down the narrow road to the cabin where the men had been found.

The cabin had a fresh coat of dark brown stain and a new roof with skylights. Just as on his first visit, Cubiak was struck by the unusual construction—rather than logs laid one on the other horizontally, the trunks were split and lined up vertically, a technique that Huntsman had told him allowed for easy expansion.

The door was open. Cubiak ducked beneath the varnished Rec Room sign over the entrance and crossed the threshold. On his first visit, the cabin had evoked happy memories of evenings spent with his former Chicago cop friends, drinking and watching football games through the haze of cigarette smoke in their paneled basements. This time around, the cabin felt cold and foreign, a room tainted by the chill of death.

The interior was as he remembered and expected it to be: a masculine enclave steeped in the north woods musk of booze, cigars, and Old Spice and hung with symbols of the outdoors. The head of a nine-point buck hung on one wall; fish of various shapes and sizes and vintage traps were mounted on another. As he looked around, Cubiak imprinted mental images of the room: a pool table and a cue rack on the wall; a pine bar with red vinyl stools, signs for Pabst and Schlitz, and shelves of hard liquor; nearby, a squat black space heater. In one corner, a large TV faced the two sagging couches, and opposite the door an oversize picture window opened to trees and water. A bulky, deer-antler chandelier hung from one of the cedar beams that supported the peaked roof. And dominating the space was an octagonal, professional-style poker table.

Cubiak pulled a digital camera from his pocket and slowly circled the room, further documenting the contents section by section. Strange, he thought, old friends gathered here regularly, yet the cabin seemed oddly impersonal. No photos, no magazines or books, no memorabilia, unless the stuffed creatures on the walls counted for something. No phone either.

At the poker table, where Smitz said the men had been found, there was ample evidence of the panicked rescue attempt. The playing table was shoved against the picture window and two of the chairs were overturned. An ashtray and several red plastic bowls lay upside down on the floor, amid a sprinkling of cigar butts, ashes, pretzels, and peanuts. An empty Jack Daniels bottle lay by the wall under the window. Poker chips littered the table and floor.

Drinks in the table's built-in holders indicated where the men had been sitting. The playing area stank with whiskey; there was amber liquid in the glasses and damp splotches on the felt surface. A copy of the *Herald* lay nearby, its front page with the glorious headline stained as well. One of the men had laid out a full house but the rest of the deck was scattered. The cards were decorated with a picture of a leaping stag. Cubiak counted two aces, a couple of sixes and fours, a king and a jack, three eights, and three jokers. The sheriff wasn't much of a poker player, but as far as he knew there were only two jokers to a deck and no versions of the game that involved jokers. He wondered if the three men made their own rules, if that was allowed.

When he finished with the rest of the room, Cubiak turned to the space heater. The portable unit was about four feet high and three feet wide and stood between the poker table and the bar, acting as a utilitarian room divider. Cubiak figured it was put there to keep the men warm when they were immersed in either drinking or playing cards. The heater was a heavy-duty, propane-fueled model built to take on Wisconsin winters. He touched the black metal top and sides. The surface was cool. He ran a hand along the pipe that extended from the heater to the wall. It felt solid. He sniffed for fumes. There weren't any, but with carbon monoxide, there wouldn't be.

At the table, Cubiak took the same seat he'd occupied the evening he'd played cards with the men. It'd been cold for days and the heater had been on. Bright orange flames had flickered behind the glass window, mesmerizing him and drawing his attention away from the game. If there'd been a malfunction that night? He grimaced.

Where had the three men sat? Huntsman, the host, was most likely pouring drinks. The seat nearest the discarded bottle was also the one closest to the space heater. Had Huntsman breathed more of the deadly fumes and been the first to exhibit signs of distress or had his bulk made him less susceptible to the effects of the poison gas? Wouldn't one of the men have complained of a headache or dizziness, a warning sign that should have caught their attention? Or did the three old friends just slip away, oblivious to the danger that stalked them? He hoped they hadn't suffered.

So sad, Cubiak thought, as he rose to his feet. Circling the room again, he closed the windows that had been thrown open to air the cabin. He found nothing out of the ordinary until he lowered the window by the door. One of the panes was smashed. Probably shattered in the confusion of trying to save the men. The hole was large enough for a raccoon to slip through and needed to be covered. Cubiak found an empty beer case and tore off a piece from the end.

As he jammed the square of cardboard over the opening, he noticed that the shattered pane aligned with the brass lock on the door. He toed the door away from the wall. A typical lock would be equipped with an interior latch; this one had a key. Cubiak turned the key, and a two-inch, steel shaft shot out from the mechanism. It was a dead bolt, the kind he'd often seen in high-crime urban areas.

No one lived in the cabin. As far as he could see, there was nothing valuable inside. Why a dead bolt?

Cubiak flipped the key to its original position, pushed the door closed, and reconsidered the proximity of the lock to the broken pane. Maybe the glass hadn't been smashed accidentally. If the door was locked maybe the window had been broken in the scramble to get inside and help the men.

Three men—old friends and war heroes about to be honored for valor exhibited more than a half century earlier—died playing cards in a private north woods hideaway. It made sense that the door would be closed against the cold night air but seemed odd that it had been bolted shut. Why had the men been sequestered behind a locked door? Cubiak wondered.

SATURDAY MIDMORNING

Cubiak followed the stone path across the yard to the back door of Huntsman's house. A stern, stout woman in turquoise sweats answered his knock. Her red hair was short and spiked and she stood arms akimbo, blocking the entrance.

"Yes," she said, and though her face was flushed, she spoke with a coolness that matched the weather.

Cubiak was puzzled. Then he realized she probably wouldn't know him without his uniform. "Dave Cubiak. I'm the sheriff," he said.

"Oh." Flustered and even more crimson, the woman stepped aside. "Esther Smitz. The neighbor. Clyde's wife," she said as she pressed into the wall of the mudroom to make way for him.

A corduroy barn coat and two rain jackets hung from hooks under a shelf piled with gloves and hats. An orderly row of rubber boots, clogs, and slippers hugged the baseboard; a stack of old newspapers nestled in the corner. Esther pointed the sheriff through a second doorway into the kitchen, a cheerful room painted a soft yellow and furnished with pale oak cabinets and white appliances. Two windows, a large one behind the rough pine table and a smaller one over the sink, looked out toward the water. Coffee was perking on the stove and a hint of cinnamon scented the air. Cubiak wondered if something wasn't in the oven. From deep in the house came the murmur of voices.

"This way, Sheriff," Esther said deferentially, leading him through a formal dining room and into the living room where a wall of windows revealed more of the bay. No doubt there were days when the view was spectacular, but that morning the vista was dark and somber.

Cubiak turned his attention to the interior. As much as the log cabin was a man's space, this room—like the rest of the house—was feminine by design: wall-to-wall white carpeting, a blond spinet piano, and a curio cabinet of small bird statues that looked fragile and expensive. Three large paintings of flowering gardens hung over a peach-colored sectional that ran along one wall and wrapped around the corner to the other. A woman sat on the sofa. She was in profile, before her a pink flowered cup and saucer on a low, glass-topped coffee table. The woman was slim and petite and dressed simply in a crisp white blouse and tan slacks. Posture erect. Skin smooth and clear. Head high and covered with soft blond-gray curls.

Cubiak crossed to her. "Mrs. Huntsman? I'm Sheriff Cubiak," he said.

She laid bright blue eyes on him and he saw immediately that she had been and still was, as much as age allowed, a woman of natural and uncomplicated beauty.

"Ida, please," she said with a hint of a smile, then gestured toward a high-backed chair. "I know who you are. Thank you for coming."

Cubiak always thought the hardest part of his job was dealing with the dead, until he had to talk to the living who mourned them. He never knew where to start or what to say.

"My deputy called. My being here is just routine."

She nodded and turned away.

Cubiak followed her gaze out the window. "I'm sorry about your husband," he said, sitting down.

She dipped her head again, still looking out over the water.

"And the others." In the overly warm room, a prickle of sweat rose on the back of Cubiak's neck.

"Yes."

There was an awkward silence.

"I know this is hard for you. But can you tell me in your own words what happened, starting with last evening?"

Ida brushed at a piece of lint on her knee. The nails were painted a delicate pink and her fingers displayed the beginning traces of arthritis.

"I don't know what happened last evening. My son, Walter, was here, you might ask him. I left around six for book group." She looked at Cubiak with a rueful smile. "It's just the three of us, Olive Swenson, Stella Wilkins, and me. Usually we meet here, but Olive was getting over a cold and wanted us to come to her house. We had dinner and talked, like we usually do. I helped clean up and then I drove home."

"What time was that?"

"Around ten thirty."

"Did you notice anything unusual when you got back?"

"No. Nothing. The lights were on in the cabin but they would be, wouldn't they?"

"And this morning, were they still on?"

"Yes. Maybe. I don't know. I'm not sure I even noticed. There were deer out back eating the hostas. I sent a few shots over their heads to scare them away. Then, as long as I was up and about, I decided to check on the boys."

"You weren't concerned that your husband had stayed out all night?"

"No. He and his friends did that every couple of weeks, up half the night playing poker, some kind of tournament they'd created. It was the boys' club night out. This morning, I knew they'd been celebrating and had probably had a bit too much to drink, so I went to offer them coffee and something to eat."

"You don't normally do that?"

23

"Oh, no. Poker nights and the morning after are sacrosanct with Terrence and his buddies. Usually they go out for pancakes and I don't even see my husband until noon."

"You're a tolerant wife. Most women . . ."

"I'm not most women," she said, cutting him off, "and Terrence isn't—wasn't—most men." She took a breath. "Sorry. It is difficult, more so than I'd imagined." She stopped to compose herself. "I saw them through the window by the door. They were slumped at the table, as if they'd fallen asleep playing cards. At first I wasn't going to disturb them, but I worried that they'd be all stiff and cranky from sleeping like that, so I knocked. But there was no response. I tried to open the door but couldn't. So I knocked again, harder, and called out, something stupid, like 'Yoo-hoo, I'm here,' but still they didn't budge. I started beating on the window and yelling and still nothing. That's when I realized something was terribly wrong.

"I ran back to the house and called Clyde Smitz, he's our nearest neighbor over there"—she motioned toward the road—"and my son, Walter Nils."

"You called the neighbor first?"

"Yes, I needed someone immediately. It would take Walter at least thirty minutes, maybe longer, to drive up here. When I got back to the cabin Clyde was already there, trying to force the door open."

"What was he doing exactly?"

Ida closed her eyes and was still a moment. "He was facing the path, gripping the knob with both hands and ramming his left shoulder against the door. 'It won't give none,' he said to me. That's when I picked up a rock and smashed the window. Then Clyde reached in and unlocked the door."

"The door was locked from the inside?"

"I guess. It must have been. What other reason could there be for it not opening?"

"And the key was in the lock?"

"Yes."

"You don't have an extra?"

"There's probably one around somewhere, but . . . I never looked. I never needed to."

"Is the door usually locked?"

"I don't know." The response was firm but Cubiak was sure she'd hesitated before answering.

"Do you have any idea why it was locked last night?"

She shook her head.

A phone rang in another room. Someone answered, and a rush of hushed chatter bloomed in the background.

"What happened then?" Cubiak said.

"I'm not sure. It was so chaotic. I ran to Terrence and started shaking his shoulders. Clyde tried to wake up Eric but couldn't. He stepped behind me to Jasper and tried to roust him. Just then Junior, Clyde's son, came running in. I don't know how he knew. Junior pulled Eric away from the table and dragged him toward the door. I don't think we were inside two minutes when my head started to hurt, like a vise clamping here"—she pointed to her temples—"and I understood. I told Clyde to turn off the space heater and I opened a couple windows. The door was already open and that may have been what spared us. Then Junior and Clyde carried the men out and laid them on the ground and I tried to do CPR."

Her voice caught. She looked up at Cubiak. "They were gone."

Cubiak picked up a box of tissues from the table and held it toward Ida. She took a sheet and pressed it to her eyes. When she'd finished, he went on. "You called your son Walter Nils. There was a man named Nils mentioned in the paper."

"Yes, my husband. My first husband. Walter is his son. I married Terrence after the war."

"You and Terrence had no other children?"

"No." She seemed about to say more, but whatever it was she decided to keep to herself. "Just Walter," she said.

They remained silent for a while.

"When you and Clyde and his son were trying to revive the men in the cabin was there any response, anything at all?"

She closed her eyes. "Nothing."

"Again, I'm sorry."

Out of respect, Cubiak waited another moment before he stood. When he rose, Ida offered him her hand. The skin was dry and the palm lightly calloused. He pressed it with what he hoped was a sign of reassurance. "One other thing. There's a copy of the latest *Herald* on the poker table. But the paper didn't come out until today."

Ida smiled. "Justin St. James, the reporter, drove up late yesterday afternoon with several copies of the early edition so Terrence and the others could see it. That's why they were together. They were celebrating."

"Of course." He paused. "Do you need anything? I could ask Esther to come in."

"No." She rested a hand on her collarbone. "I'm okay for the moment."

Esther Smitz rose from the kitchen table and started across the room when Cubiak reappeared in the doorway. He motioned her toward the back door, and she turned without hesitating, as if understanding that she was about to be questioned and that the conversation was to be private.

"Are the other spouses here?" he said.

"Stella Wilkins is in the guest room. Olive—Olive Swenson—went home. Someone drove her. She said she couldn't bear to stay."

"What about their kids or relatives?" He wasn't sure he should be directing these questions to a neighbor but didn't know whom else to ask.

"Olive is alone. She and Eric didn't have any kids and his one brother is long gone. She had a brother but he died a couple years back. I don't think she gets along with the sister-in-law. Stella's son, Martin, works on oil rigs somewhere. She made a call earlier, I guess to try and reach him with the news."

"You and your husband live nearby?"

"Yes, we're in the green house just up the road a ways, last one on the end."

"And you didn't notice anything unusual yesterday evening?"

"No. We had supper around five and then I did some mending while Clyde changed the oil in the truck. It was dark when he finally came in. After he washed up, I made popcorn and we watched television. Went to bed right after the news. There was a car went by when I was turning off the TV. Figured it was Ida coming home. I seen her drive out earlier." Esther's face clouded.

She's wondering what she missed, Cubiak thought. He needed to be careful and not let his concern about a locked door get out of hand. "Any chance of getting a cup of coffee?" he said to shift her focus.

As he slipped off his jacket, Esther set a mug of coffee and a plate of chocolate chip cookies in front of him. "I was thinking of making a fresh cup of tea for Stella. They drink coffee by the gallons here but times like this, tea seems more comforting."

"It does." Cubiak dunked a cookie. "I'll go with, when you take it to her."

Esther filled the kettle and fussed at the stove. She worked quickly and didn't seem driven by the need for unnecessary chatter, a trait he appreciated.

When the tea was ready, Esther filled a flowered cup, set it on a saucer, and put both on a small tray. With carefully measured steps, she led him back through the dining room and down a dim hall past two closed doors. Just short of a third that was open, Esther stopped and handed the tray to Cubiak. Knocking softly on the door frame, she spoke. "Someone to see you, dear," she said in a surprisingly gentle voice.

The bedroom had the same white carpet as the rest of the house and was infused with pale pinks. A spindly, forlorn woman sat on the bed, nearly lost in the battery of oversize, frilly pillows that were heaped against the carved oak headboard. With her dirty silvery hair and deeply lined face, she looked worn and frail. Despite the heat in the room, she huddled inside a red plaid mackinaw that was several sizes too large. Her legs were encased in cheap polyester pants and extended straight out, displaying the calloused bottoms of her bare feet.

Cubiak introduced himself and held out the tea. Stella Wilkins ignored the offering. He set the tray on the nightstand and pulled up a wooden rocking chair, balancing lightly on the edge of the padded seat. For the second time in less than thirty minutes he offered his condolences to a recently widowed woman.

"I can't believe they killed my husband," Stella said.

The statement and the bluntness with which she spoke surprised Cubiak. "Your husband is dead, but it appears to have been an accident."

"An accident?"

"Yes, looks like a problem with the space heater. Didn't anyone tell you?"

"They just said Jasper was dead."

"And you thought he'd been murdered?"

"Not murdered, just killed."

"Why would anyone want to kill your husband?"

"I have no idea."

"Why did you think your husband had been killed?"

"Because that's how people die. Something kills them. Heart attacks. Cancer. Accidents."

"But you said 'they' . . ."

She looked at him. "I did?"

"Yes."

She turned and stared at the door. "I don't know why I said that."

She's in shock, he thought. She doesn't know what she's saying.

After a while Stella Wilkins took a sip of tea.

"You called your son?" the sheriff said.

Stella nodded and told Cubiak that she'd left a message for Martin at the last number she had but it was months old and she didn't know when he'd get the news. Then she closed her eyes and sank back into whatever private world she'd been in when he'd disturbed her.

The kitchen was empty when Cubiak returned from talking to Stella. He filled a glass at the sink and drank it down. Pulling on his jacket, he stepped back out into the overcast day. The wind had picked up and the temperature had dropped. After the heat of the house, the cool air felt good and he left his jacket open as he crossed the yard. The ambulances were gone. The trampled patch of grass where the bodies had lain was given a wide berth by the neighbors who continued to mill around. Word must have gotten out. There were more onlookers than before, women as well as men and a few kids turning cartwheels in the tall grass near the shore. The adults gathered in small knots, talking and periodically squinting out at the bay as if answers to their questions could be found among the waves. Cubiak followed their lead and looked to the water. If only life were that simple, he thought.

Suddenly he felt cold. He zipped his jacket and continued on toward Walter, who remained at the picnic table, cocooned in the EMT's blanket.

The sheriff took the other end of the bench and leaned forward, his elbows on his knees, his head turned toward Walter. "I just talked to your mother. She seems to be taking things pretty well, considering."

Walter burrowed further into the wrap. "She's strong, not like she looks."

"Still, she'll need you to watch out for her. Must get pretty lonely up here."

"It does."

Walter shrugged off the blanket and looked up as if the expanse of empty sky confirmed this assessment of life on the outskirts of the small village.

"I'll take good care of her. And she has lots of friends. The other two especially. God, I can't believe it, all three of them in the same boat at the same time." He straightened his shoulders and pivoted toward Cubiak. "Big Guy wasn't my birth father, you know."

Cubiak nodded. He knew there was no predicting how people would react to the shock of death but still, it seemed an odd distinction for Walter to make under the circumstances. "Your mother told me," the sheriff said.

"Did she? Doesn't matter, really. He was the same as. Only father I ever knew." Walter stood and began folding the blanket. "Absolutely, the best, too. Scouts. Little League. Wrestling coach. The whole bit."

"You're lucky," Cubiak said, as a bitter childhood memory engulfed him. "Dad! Dad, get up." He was eleven and Davey to everyone who knew him. He saw himself in front of the meager building where he lived with his parents, three of them in three rooms. He was leaning over the prostrate figure on the parkway, trying not to inhale the stink of vomit and beer from his father's shirt. "Dad!" he begged, and while his two best friends watched from across the street, he wrapped his thin arms around his father and pulled him to a sitting position. "Dad! Get up, please. I have a game. I'm pitching. I'm gonna be late."

Walter tossed the wool throw on the table and dropped back onto the bench. He seemed exhausted.

"None of this seems real."

"It never does," Cubiak said. After a moment, he went on. "I hate to ask this: but do you know any reason anyone would have wanted to harm Big Guy—or either of the other two men?"

Walter jolted upright. "No! They were the guys everyone loved. Maybe there was a little envy, but to do something like this?" He jerked his head in the direction of the log cabin. "No way. You aren't thinking . . ."

"I'm not thinking anything, just following procedure. The questions don't always make sense. . . . You checked out the space heater?"

"Not really. It was already shut off when I got here. Then someone said you were on your way, and I figured I shouldn't touch anything anyway, that maybe you'd want to look at it first."

"I gave it a quick once over but wouldn't mind looking at it again."

Walter hesitated and then got up with the sheriff.

They remained quiet walking to the cabin. At the door, Walter stopped and let Cubiak pass.

"The window was broken," Cubiak said, indicating the cardboard, as he stepped inside.

"Yes," Walter said. His voice sounded hollow, as if he were speaking from a different part of the universe. Still outside, he peeked in and glanced around. "I don't know what we're going to do with this place now. Maybe tear it down."

"It's a nice cabin. Give it time," Cubiak said.

As the sheriff bent over the space heater, he realized that when Walter arrived that morning the bodies of the three men had already been carried outside. This was his first time seeing the scene of the deaths. No wonder he was reluctant to cross the threshold.

"Looks solid. Venting pipe seems fairly new. I don't see any cracks or holes," Cubiak said, as he heard Walter approach from behind. "Where's the tank?"

"In the woods," Walter said. He was ashen in the dim interior.

"And the vent?"

"Out back."

Cubiak led the way outside to the rear of the cabin.

"That's it." Walter stopped and pointed down. The small metal hood was low to the ground and painted black, making it nearly invisible against the dark exterior.

Cubiak knelt and ran his hand along the underside of the cover. "Not much room is there?" he said, squeezing his thumb and index finger into the narrow opening. "What should I be feeling?"

"Steel mesh. There's a piece covering the exhaust hole."

Cubiak felt a soft lump inside the metal hood. "That's not it. There's something else here," he said as he scratched at the obstruction.

A small clump of dried leaves and grass fell into his hand.

Walter leapt forward. "What the hell, those fucking squirrels," he said, tearing at his hair.

"Squirrels?"

"What else? Chipmunks maybe, but I'd lay odds it was squirrels. The little bastards build nests and hide shit all over the place."

Cubiak stood and brushed off his knees.

"Your father seems to have run a very successful business. Which would imply that he was conscientious and thorough. Wouldn't he be on top of something like that?"

"You'd think, but you know what they say about the cobbler's kids." Walter chuckled nervously, then abruptly turned somber again. "A handful of fucking leaves and three men die. And this weather, too. If it hadn't been so cold last night, they probably wouldn't have turned the damn thing on."

They stared at the vent and the pile of debris.

"You're mechanical, good with your hands," Cubiak said finally.

"Yeah, I guess."

"But you didn't go into business with your dad?"

Walter looked up. "No, I didn't. Guess I was always more interested in cars. And he didn't pressure me none, the way some might. Like I said, he was a good father, the best."

SATURDAY AFTERNOON  3

As they walked back to the yard, Cubiak nearly tripped over Walter's heels. Walter's pace had slackened through the course of the morning, whether weighted down by grief or slowed by age it was impossible to know. The low clouds had started to spit droplets of cold rain, and both men hunched their shoulders against the drizzle. It was just a few minutes past noon but the light had dimmed, as if time were trying to accelerate and push the day along.

At the gazebo, Walter halted.

Cubiak cupped his elbow. "Maybe go in, see how your mother is doing," he said.

"Good idea." But Walter didn't move. He seemed confused. Suddenly, he took a step back and extended a hand. "Thank you, you've been very kind." His face was sallow, his grip clammy.

Cubiak watched as Walter moved across the lawn, his head bowed and one foot dragging behind the other. The weather had driven away many of the onlookers. The remainder separated into two groups: those who deliberately drifted out of Walter's path, as if not wishing to intrude on his grief or fearful of it, and those who stepped forward to greet him.

Walter had grown up among these folks, and with words and gestures they let him know that he was among friends.

When Walter disappeared into the house, Cubiak returned to the cabin.

Bathard and Pardy huddled under the eaves.

"We were just discussing the postmortem," Pardy said, making room for the sheriff. "There's no need to autopsy the bodies since there's no sign of foul play. Blood tests will determine if the men died from carbon monoxide poisoning as we suspect. Evelyn and I will secure the samples this afternoon. I don't expect any surprises and should be able to confirm cause of death on Monday. Unless you have something?"

"Not really," Cubiak said, drying his glasses.

Bathard raised an eyebrow. "Meaning?"

Cubiak glanced toward the door and then told them about the broken window and the dead bolt.

Pardy frowned and brushed a tangle of damp ringlets off her forehead. She did not share the sheriff's concerns. "Three elderly men excited about the story in the paper, maybe half in the bag before they even meet up for the evening. They're all talking at once and the last one in absentmindedly locks the door. I don't see that there's anything to it."

Bathard nodded. "Precisely. Here are these three senior gents. They've got the paper and a bottle. They're reminiscing about the good old days and one of them happens to throw the lock." A shadow clouded Bathard's face. "My god, listen to me. I'm talking about them like they were frat boys reliving their glory days. They were young men fighting under god-awful conditions. Nothing but cold and fog and muck so slick a man could barely keep upright on his feet. They've got planes dropping bombs on them and a freezing ocean trying to suck them in. Most people don't realize, do they, what it was like?"

Pardy and Cubiak were both silent. Then the sheriff spoke. "Yeah. Most people have no idea." He looked at Bathard. "You were in the service?"

The physician's shoulders stiffened slightly, accentuating his ramrod posture. "Navy medical corps. Vietnam. Different—if one war can be different from another." Bathard cleared his throat. "As to the door, it's also possible that given the dampness and the proximity to the bay, the door was stuck and in the panic of trying to get in, Ida and Clyde assumed it was locked and smashed the window."

"Maybe."

"You're not convinced."

"I'm just wondering, that's all."

The locked door was just one issue puzzling the sheriff. Cubiak had grown up blue collar, with friends whose fathers were in the trades: plumbers, electricians, carpenters. Though they did well, none approached the level of prosperity that Huntsman appeared to have attained. He could have inherited the land and the business as well. But if he'd had to start from scratch, how'd he make enough to accumulate the sprawling waterfront property, the boats and cabin, and the huge house?

Cubiak finished with the doctors and continued around the cabin. Earlier, he'd noticed a faint path through the woods. Alone, he followed it. The trail cut through a grove of lush pines and ended at a small cove lined with smooth black rocks. The shallow inlet opened onto the bay but a curved slip of heavy forest blocked the view to the house and village, leaving the area completely isolated.

Three of a Kind, as Cubiak had already come to think of the men. They could have been doing anything here and no one would have known. Smuggling drugs or money. Or operating an illegal poker ring. He was the nearest law, and he was forty-some miles away in Sturgeon Bay.

"Jesus." Cubiak scooped up an ebony stone and skimmed it along the surface of the water. After nearly two years on the peninsula, he was still thinking like a big city cop. Life's different here, he told himself.

It was after one when Cubiak left Huntsman's place. Walter had remained inside with his mother, giving the sheriff a chance to question

Clyde Smitz privately. The neighbor more or less corroborated Ida's story about the door and sequence of events. Smitz got the call, ran over to the cabin, and was ramming the door with his shoulder when Ida arrived and smashed the window with a rock. Then he'd reached in and flipped the latch.

"So the door was locked?" Cubiak said.

"I guess. Yeah, sure, it had to be." Smitz massaged his left shoulder. "It was all so fast, you know. I didn't really know what the hell was going on. I could see them sitting there and I knew something wasn't right."

Did Smitz wonder why the door was locked? No. All he wondered was why three men he knew had to endure such a tragic, senseless death.

Cubiak left the neighbor to join the others on the lawn and quietly slipped away. There was no one else to talk with and no reason to linger. At Highway 42, he turned toward the heart of Gills Rock, hoping he hadn't missed lunch at the Sunset Café. The village's lone restaurant looked out over the small harbor and deserted ferry landing. From the lot, he climbed a flight of wooden stairs to the entrance. A bell jingled as he opened the door. A bald man at a corner table and the waitress talking to him looked up at the noise. The waitress said something to the patron and walked toward Cubiak.

"Anywhere you like," she said, gesturing toward the empty tables. She was square and stout with short wavy hair that was dyed fiercely black. The name tag on her ample chest read Mabel.

The sheriff took a stool at the end of the counter.

"We're out of the pork chops," Mabel said as she handed him the menu with a hand-printed list of specials paper-clipped inside.

He scanned the list, his mind still on Huntsman's yard. He'd asked Smitz if the three men ever played high stakes poker but the neighbor said no. And there hadn't been any money on the table. None that either Ida or Smitz mentioned.

"What do you recommend?"

"I like the chicken."

36

Cubiak ordered the roasted chicken plate. Watching Mabel push through the swinging doors to the kitchen, he wondered if she was going to cook his food as well as serve it. But she returned almost immediately with a thick ceramic mug of hot coffee.

"Cream?" She slid a small dish filled with one-serve containers of half-and-half within his reach and then looked past him toward the window. "You up at Huntsman's place?" she said.

There was no point denying it. Three ambulances racing along the lane at the bottom of the bay would have drawn attention to the drama on the other side of the water. And there'd been enough onlookers to ensure the story spread fast. Cubiak followed her gaze to the holster and sheriff's badge on his belt. "Yes," he said, stirring his coffee.

"Nice people. All of them. The women especially. Used to come in sometimes and order the Friday fish fry as takeout for their book club."

"You knew them well?"

The waitress lifted her chin. "Well enough. They were private women, Sheriff. Decent people who were friendly but not overly so."

"Did you do business with Huntsman?"

She chortled. "Sure. Half the peninsula did business with him. As if you couldn't tell. Big Guy did pretty good, that's for certain. But then they all did."

Mabel pointed toward the dock. "See those three charter boats? They're Swenson's. Three! Nobody up here's got three boats, and come the season they're out all the time." She spoke without envy, obviously proud of locals who'd prospered.

"And Wilkins?"

"You haven't noticed the name? Wilkins' Orchards. Wilkins' Farm and Garden Store. Wilkins' Dairy? If you came up 42, you went past the farm, the one with seven silos!"

"That was all Jasper's?"

"Mostly. His sister operates the store and maybe owns it, but he produces just about everything she sells. Runs what folks up here call the 'Three C Empire.' Cows, cheese, and cherries." Again, the same unmistakable tone of pride in her voice. Were some people really that guileless? he wondered.

A bell dinged. Mabel scooted to the kitchen and returned with a platter mounded with mashed potatoes, peas, and half a chicken smothered in gravy.

"This oughta hold you 'til supper," she said as she deposited the plate in front of the sheriff. "More coffee?"

Pie came with lunch, and again Cubiak cleaned his plate. He had a theory that sugar primed the senses but it seemed to have had the opposite effect on him that day. Leaving the diner he barely registered the stiff breeze that had come up. And he was at the bottom of the stairs before he noticed that the sun was out as well.

The resident gulls trailed him past the abandoned ferry landing to the village marina. The harbor was deserted but for a pontoon boat and Swenson's trio of swanky cabin cruisers. *Viking I*, *II*, and *III* were sizable vessels—Cubiak guessed about fifty feet—outfitted with impressive arrays of rigging. A discreet sign provided a contact phone number for Viking Charters; otherwise there was nothing to advertise the business and no indication of the cost.

Charter fishing was expensive. People went out for the bragging rights, the trophy fish, the experience of being on the water and pretending to work hard while others put forth the effort. Well, they were on vacation, and if they could afford to pay the tab, why not? For a man like Swenson, it was an honest way to earn a living, and Cubiak wouldn't begrudge anyone that opportunity.

Who would run the operation now? he wondered. The people of northern Door seemed like a rugged bunch, the kind who faced life without complaint and didn't ask for or expect special favors. Would Olive take over or would she sell the business?

Bathard had given him directions to Swenson's home in case he wanted to stop and talk with Olive. Not today, Cubiak decided. He'd faced two grieving women already and had learned all he could from them; he'd let the third widow mourn undisturbed.

The jeep was coasting into Baileys Harbor when the call came in.

"Chief!"

"Yeah, Mike. I read you. Go ahead."

"We got a problem in Fish Creek. Some kind of disturbance near the square. No details."

Cubiak pictured a party of inebriated tourists arguing over politics or golf. He couldn't imagine any other kind of dustup in one of Door County's flagship resort towns.

"Okay, I'll check it out. Anything special going on today?"

"Founders Fest."

"Right." Cubiak frowned. The street banners. He'd forgotten. In fact, he had trouble keeping track of the county's numerous celebrations. Founders Fest. Pioneer Days. May Crafts and Flowers Weekend. Summer Daze. Autumn Colors. Pumpkin Fest. Harvest Highlights. Wintery Wonders. Throw in the major holidays and there seemed to be something notable every other weekend—each event designed to showcase local artists and products and to pull in the tourists. The tourism board at work. Cubiak marveled at their imagination. It was no secret that tourist dollars drove the Door County economy. The heady days of the shipbuilding industry had faded to memory and dwindling jobs. Sturgeon Bay had been especially hard hit by the meltdown of the area's industrial base, but the economic ramifications reverberated throughout the peninsula. Even as cheap airfares and a burgeoning cruise industry lured visitors to other destinations, tourists were increasingly coveted. Although many were fiercely loyal to Door County, merchants and the local business associations had to be creative to entice new guests to the peninsula and to keep them coming back.

Founders Fest. Cubiak envisioned middle-aged men and women in period costumes strolling around the old square, posing for pictures with visitors amid stands selling hand-dipped candles and cherry preserves. In Fish Creek, more people than he expected wandered along Front Street and through the array of craft and food booths in the waterfront park. At the music stage, a local band covered "Proud Mary" for a mostly young audience that pulsed to the beat.

Martha Smithson's Bakery had a prime spot in one of the narrow streets leading up from the water. Martha, an eighty-year-old institution, waved Cubiak over and handed him a thick slice of cherry pie on a paper plate.

"Everything okay?" he said, watching her pour a cup of coffee for him. He knew it would do no good to protest.

"I'm down to three pies and a dozen oatmeal cookies. I'm not complaining," she said. "Cool weather makes folks hungry and that's good for most of us."

"No sign of trouble?" he said, holding out several dollars.

Martha scoffed. "No one messes with me," she said as she laid a gnarled hand on his and bent his fingers back over the money. "I'm keeping a running tab, Sheriff. One day you'll owe me a million dollars. That's when I'll come round and collect."

Cubiak winked. "I'm counting on it."

Up the lane, he passed a very tall blonde woman carrying an intricately carved, three-foot fish totem and stopped behind a middle-aged couple in Chicago Bears hats who were bargaining over a set of ceramic pickle crocks. Cubiak leaned in to the man. "You'd do better without the hats," he said quietly, and then he gave a salute. "Go Bears," he said.

From there, the crowd thinned quickly. Cubiak assumed they were scared off by the small mob gathered along the stone wall at the far end of the block.

The sheriff counted ten in the group, most of them teenagers: kids trying to look tough, dressed in black T-shirts and jackets and low-cut, frayed jeans. Several sported tattoos and all of them were smoking. Hardly the image Door County hoped to portray to the world.

It wasn't hard to pick out the main troublemaker. He was fat and greasy and looked older, maybe twenty-one, and sat on the wall as if holding court. A slim, pouty girl, about five years younger, perched on his lap. She had bobbed blue hair and heavily kohled eyes.

"Afternoon," Cubiak said as he stepped onto the curb and kicked aside a mound of cigarette butts.

The punk on the wall snickered, signaling the others to join in.

Cubiak stopped himself from laughing. Where he came from, they were nothing more than a bunch of wannabes but he knew that by local standards, they were a threat.

"Better move on, old man," the ringleader said, cradling his rough hands around the girl's buttocks, and the others again sniggered on cue.

Behind them, a woman watched the scene from the window of the Woolly Sheep Shoppe, one of the newer businesses in town.

Cubiak shoved his hands into his rear pockets and took them in, one by one, memorizing their faces. When he finished, he rubbed his hands together and then, as they looked on puzzled, he strolled off down the street to the end of the block.

At the corner he stopped, giving the group time to wonder what he'd do next, and then he sauntered back.

"Fucker." The taunt came from one of the boys sprawled on the grass. Cubiak shrugged and then circled around the gathering before going up the steps and entering the Woolly Sheep.

As he approached, the woman at the window darted behind the counter. She had a soft rounded body and curly black hair that made her creamy, pale complexion seem almost luminescent. "That was awfully brave," she said in a gentle Irish lilt that immediately melted his heart.

"You the owner?" he said.

"Yes. Kathleen O'Toole. Kathy," she said and extended her hand.

Cubiak introduced himself. "What do you sell?" It was an idiotic question, he realized. One wall held stacks of wooden crates stuffed with skeins of yarn. Books on knitting lined a shelf, and knitted goods—sweaters, scarves, and shawls—hung from several racks.

"Things woolen," Kathy said. She tried to smile. "Saturdays are usually my busiest. But I haven't had a single customer today. People walk up the sidewalk and look this way but when they see the welcoming committee out front, they turn and go away. The other shops have

41

entrances from the square as well as the street. I don't. The only way to get here is up those stairs and if this keeps up, I'll be out of business before the season is half over."

"How long has this been going on?"

"A week exactly. Three or four of them showed up last Sunday afternoon. It was cold, flurrying even, and I didn't pay much attention, but they were here again Wednesday evening. This morning they came back with the others."

"Did you say anything to them?"

"Sure. The first day after they'd been out there for about an hour, I asked them to leave, and they told me to go fuck myself."

"Do you know who they are?"

Kathy pressed her hands on the counter and leaned forward. "The large one is Tim Bender. His dad used to work in the shipyards with my ex-husband; they've both been out of work for several years. I don't know his girlfriend. The one to his right is Hillary Wozniak. Her mom's a nurse and a weekend cashier at the Piggly Wiggly in Algoma. Widowed. Four kids, two jobs. The boy next to Hillary is Roger Nils."

"Walter's kid?"

"Yeah. From his second marriage. Raised the boy himself after his wife split. You know Roger?"

"No, but I've heard of him." The young man was pale and sullen and lanky like Walter. His blond hair hung over his ears and neck like a Dutch boy cut gone wild. He didn't resemble the Roger Nils who'd been featured in the *Herald* the previous spring: that Roger was a good-looking honor roll student and champion wrestler who'd turned down half a dozen athletic scholarships for a four-year-ride at the University of Wisconsin–Eau Claire.

Kathy had kept on talking. "I don't know the names of the others but they're all local. Why are they doing this?"

"I don't know," Cubiak said. He fished for a card but his pockets were empty. "Anytime there's trouble, call me," he said, writing his number on the back of a store flyer.

42

With his badge and gun visible, Cubiak planted himself in front of the group and before any of them had a chance to react, he started in. "What I'm going to do right now is suggest that you all move on. Maybe wander across the street and buy a brat. Support the local businesses."

No one budged.

"Because if you don't leave, I'll run you in for disturbing the peace, and my guess is that for some of you it won't be the first time."

"You ain't got no right," the leader said.

Cubiak pressed the toe of his boot against the front of the punk's shoe. "I got every right. I've also got nowhere else to go, so I can just stand here all day, *Timothy*."

Someone in the group snickered and Tim reeled around. "Shut up." Turning back toward Cubiak, he slid the girl off his lap and pushed up from the bench. He was tall and carried muscle behind the fat. "Anything you say, Sheriff. Besides, I got shit to do," he said, sending a wave of sour breath toward Cubiak. He motioned to the others. "Come on. Outta here. But don't worry, we'll be back," he said.

The sheriff nodded. "You do that, and I'll be waiting for you."

As the group dispersed, Cubiak caught up with Roger Nils. "I need to talk to you," he said.

Roger took several more steps, and then he stopped and spun around. The stink of cigarettes and stale beer clung to him like an extra layer of clothes. His eyes were red and wary. A fine line of acne ran along his right cheekbone. "What the hell you want?" he said, looking past Cubiak.

"I want to know what the fuck you're doing here. Your grandfather's dead, your grandmother's up in Gills Rock, her world destroyed. Your father's there, too, beside himself and you're hanging out like some two-bit hoodlum."

"I heard about Big Guy, so what? He's not related to me."

Like Walter, Roger seemed eager to distance himself from Huntsman. Was it a defense against the pain of loss? "Maybe not by blood, but by adoption," Cubiak said.

43

The boy sneered. "Another of the family myths. Huntsman never adopted anybody, not legally."

The news momentarily stopped Cubiak. He could check it out easily enough. But should it really make a difference? he wondered. "Still no reason not to come by. It would have meant a lot to Ida. Instead of this shit. What's going on? Throwing away your scholarship and everything. Don't look so surprised. I read the paper. That's the thing about living in a small town. Everyone knows everything."

Roger cringed. "So now they know I'm a major fuck-up," he said.

"You're only as fucked up as you want to be." Cubiak gave him time to consider the idea before he went on, his tone softer. "Why are you messing up your life and ruining this woman's business? You probably know Kathy O'Toole, don't you? She's got two young kids to support, and she's poured her life savings into this store. You don't believe me, read the *Herald*. Then the likes of you come out here with your pals and scare away the clientele."

"Tourists!" Roger spat in disdain.

"That's right. People spending money where you live. You got a magic wand to revive the shipyards or the fishing industry, I suggest you wave it. Times change, my friend, and you learn to change with them or sink, and right now I'd say you're sinking fast. That's your choice. I really don't care—other than for how it affects other people like the woman who owns the Woolly Sheep. You don't have a right to ruin things for her."

"Oh, yeah, who's gonna stop me?" For the first time Roger looked straight at Cubiak.

The sheriff held his gaze and waited until the boy blinked. "I am," he said.

SUNDAY

In the soft light of dusk, they stood on the warm sand and listened to a barefoot, bearded old man who sat on a bleached log and played a drum. He wore a tattered shirt and pants and held the tall, narrow instrument between his knees, rhythmically slapping the stained drumhead with his palms. A breeze from the water wafted the sound toward a small grove of palm trees that shivered to the beat. Lauren sighed. She wore the same jasmine scent as the night air. When Cubiak stroked her hair she pressed into him. He kissed her neck. She tasted like the sun.

A bonfire blazed up the beach, and they began moving toward it, matching their steps to the drummer's languid beat. Voices erupted in the trees and from a large boat moored in the bay, singing and a different kind of music drifted toward them. Lauren twirled out of arm's reach and swayed to the water-borne samba rhythm. "Come dance." She moved her hips invitingly. "Come dance with me," she said again, her midwestern accent tipping into a heavy Irish brogue.

Cubiak stumbled on a piece of driftwood.

Lauren clutched his hand and spun toward him, smiling as her features melted into a stranger's face.

"No!"

He sprang awake, his T-shirt cold with sweat and the covers twisted ropelike around his ankles. His heart thudded as if he'd been running. Had he run from his wife?

The room was dim and strangely quiet, the way it was in the morning when the wind had died during the night. In a cruel mimic of his dream, Cubiak stumbled out of bed. He snatched a flannel shirt off the floor and shrugged into it. Pulling on his jeans, he padded into the kitchen. The *Herald* was still on the table, his green mug still on the counter, silent sentry to the sink full of dishes waiting to be washed.

Lauren would never leave such a mess for the morning. Taking in the sad domestic scene Cubiak wilted. This is my life? he thought.

"Yes," he said out loud in the empty room.

He glanced at the *Herald*. The paper was dated Saturday, making this Sunday morning. In a long-ago time he'd gone to church every Sunday, Saturday too. He'd been an altar boy. Costumed in a mini cassock and entrusted with the brass thurible, he'd wobbled behind the priest, heady on the smoke from the ornate incense burner. Dominus Vobiscum. Et cum spiritu tuo. The salutation and blessing echoed from his past, dragging in their wake the familiar words of the Confiteor Deo. That's what he needed. A good confession to wipe away his sins. The first year after he and Lauren were married, they had attended Mass regularly, each of them hoping to grab a last vestige of wonderment from the mystery of their faith. They even had Alexis baptized. They would not condemn their child to hell through ignorance or conceit. Dear god, if there is a god, save her soul if she has a soul. Had they?

He didn't believe in religion or ritual now. If Christ died to save humanity from sin, why did people keep sinning? Were they trying to entice him back?

Butch scratched at the door. She was probably out of food and water. Cubiak ignored the dog and stared out at the flat, dull water. If he concentrated, he could re-create the taste and touch of vodka on his tongue, but since he'd stopped his daily doses of the hard stuff, action was his only defense against melancholy, so he forced himself to move. He ran the faucet and poured water into the coffee maker. He measured out the grounds. On the porch, he filled a yellow bowl with food, set it down near the skeletal dog, and watched Butch shake off the blanket of puppies and shove her snout into the kibble. Inside, Cubiak picked the newspaper off the table, folded it, and carried it into the small back bedroom, his office, into the cascade of sunlight that flooded the bare windows. He tossed the paper on the desk. Somewhere he had a list of things to buy for the house; add *window blinds*, he thought, as he moved toward the living room. The parlor, as his mother called it, was darker than the office but barely better furnished and as impersonal as Huntsman's cabin. He pulled a pair of socks from under the sagging sofa and tugged them over his cold, calloused feet.

The aroma of fresh brewed coffee drew Cubiak back to the kitchen. He poured a cup and returned to the porch seeking the company of other living creatures. The week-old puppies were comatose, eyes and ears still sealed against the world. Butch lay motionless but for the occasional flickering of her tail. Her right front paw had been injured when he took her in and he'd been fooled by her lethargy. Once the paw healed, she'd revealed her true nature. She was a runner, a runner who gave up her freedom to care for her flock. Cubiak set his mug on the floor and rubbed her neck.

"Good girl," he said.

The dog nuzzled his palm and then sighed and laid her head down, drained by the ordeal of motherhood. Local vet Natalie Klein had been caring for Butch since that night a year and a half ago that the injured stray had wandered to the sheriff's door. She'd been out once to check the dam and her litter and to instruct him on the pups' care and feeding. In another week, he'd move them into the house. A month later, he'd take them to her office for their first vaccinations, a combo shot that would protect them against hepatitis, distemper, and parvovirus.

"You're not keeping them all," Natalie had said.

Of course not, he'd replied. But which to give away? And to whom?

"That one, Daddy. That one," he remembered Alexis saying as she pressed her forehead against the pet store window and pointed to the black and brown lump in the corner. "I'll call her Kippy."

It was a hot day and Cubiak had to stoop down to wipe the melted chocolate from his daughter's fingers. "You're not ready to take care of a puppy. Not yet," he said, looking for a trash container.

"But when? I'm almost six," she wailed.

"Not yet," he said again. He meant: not ever.

Butch quivered and the puppies rose and fell with the movement.

"Good girl," he said again.

Easing his hand under the heap of pups, he separated Kipper from the mound. The vet had given him strict instructions to weigh the puppies daily and to record their progress. She'd even loaned him a scale, which he'd put on the metal shelving unit. Boots and shoes lined the lower two tiers and the top two were a clutter of empty cigar boxes left by the previous owner. Cubiak had kept the boxes imagining that someday he'd fill them with nails and screws and other home-repair minutiae. The scale sat amid the mess. He lowered Kipper into the clear plastic bowl on top of the device and waited for her to settle in. Then he checked the digital readout and recorded her progress on the chart Natalie had tacked to the wall.

"They should double their weight the first week," she had said.

But Kipper's Sunday weight was the same as Friday's. Should he worry? He weighed the other three pups. Scout and Nico were on target, while Buddy had surged ahead an additional two ounces.

Cubiak left a voicemail message for the vet. He ate breakfast and was in the middle of washing up when she called back and advised him to start feeding Kipper goat's milk by hand.

"Get a nursing bottle, something small, the kind used for an infant," she said.

"I've got an eyedropper."

"Don't use that! She can't close her throat yet. With a dropper, you could accidentally fill up her stomach and esophagus. If that happens the milk will flow to her lungs and she'll drown."

"Okay. I'll get a bottle."

An unexpected errand. For him that morning, a small blessing. Forty minutes later, Cubiak was back. He measured one ounce of goat milk into the tiny bottle and set it in a pan of warm water. While the milk lost its chill, he carried Kipper into the kitchen and nestled her on a towel on his lap. What if she refuses the bottle? he thought. But he needn't have worried. Kipper sucked greedily at the nipple. "That's a good little girl," he said, stroking the top of her head with his thumb.

By noon, Cubiak had fed the pup a follow-up snack and finished cleaning house. By twelve fifteen, he'd emailed Rowe and the traffic deputies about the situation in Fish Creek, requesting they make their presence known as frequently as possible. He wasn't due at Bathard's until three thirty. Time enough for a Sunday afternoon drive. He liked to cruise around the peninsula, taking in sights and learning the back road shortcuts. Today, he would drive with a different purpose. The previous morning, three old friends had been found dead, the result of a tragic accident. Although there were no loose ends to tie up, he needed to satisfy his curiosity about plumbers and squirrels.

The local phone book listed six plumbing businesses in Sturgeon Bay. A quick survey would indicate how they compared with Big Guy's enterprise. The first, Pristine Plumbing Inc., was on the other side of the canal in a blue-collar neighborhood near the city limits. The area looked recently hatched; trees were spindly, houses fresh-scrubbed, pavement smooth and unblemished. Cubiak was looking for 145 Spinnaker, and found the address attached to a corner, pink stucco ranch framed with rows of green hedges. An empty clothesline and a homemade swing set filled the area out back. The only indication that this was the site of a business was the yellow van parked in the short asphalt driveway; the sign on the side read Pristine Plumbing: Service with a Smile.

Wellington's Water Works was six blocks away. The setup was almost identical but instead of a swing set, the backyard held an above-ground pool and the van in the driveway was blue.

Five of the enterprises on Cubiak's list were nearly clones of one another. The only one that was different was Peninsula Plumbers, which provided both plumbing and septic services. In addition to the obligatory van, Peninsula boasted two tank trucks that were parked in a small gravel lot behind the attached garage.

He wondered if the half-dozen companies combined equaled Huntsman's Plumbing in volume of business and income. If they took in more work, he didn't figure it was by much. Why? What made the difference between Koch Industries and the neighborhood hamburger stand? Ambition, luck, timing, hard work? Or something else?

From the plumbers, Cubiak turned to the issue of squirrels. Larry Myers was the local expert on all things natural, and on Sunday afternoons, Myers ran the information desk at The Ridges Sanctuary. The preserve, which was located along Lake Michigan north of Baileys Harbor, was a local treasure that chronicled the natural process by which the shoreline had evolved over some fourteen hundred years. During that time, the ebb and flow of lake water had created a series of swales and ridges, hence the name. Similar patches of ecologically sensitive land with the rare flora they supported had existed in several different regions along the Great Lakes, but over time the plots had been used for parks or residential development or allowed to erode, leaving the parcel in Door County as the only existing example of the phenomenon.

Even in conservation-conscious Door County, the area had nearly been sold to a developer as a trailer park site. After word of the pending sale got out, an ad hoc group of citizens launched a successful attack against the project. Cate Wagner's wealthy grandfather had been part of the fledgling organization. The group eventually became the Door County Nature Conservancy, which Cate's late aunt Ruby headed when Cubiak arrived on the peninsula. He'd liked Ruby. Against her family's wishes, she'd married Dutch Schumacher, the son of a grocer who became the county's most legendary sheriff, and then gone on to make a name for herself as a fabric artist. But it had all ended badly.

The memory of Ruby's final days lingered with Cubiak as he trailed the boardwalk to The Ridges' nature museum. Pushing through the door, he was grateful to see Myers at his desk.

"Sheriff," the slim, rugged man said, getting to his feet. "Something I can do for you?"

Cubiak put aside his brooding about Ruby and stifled his big city urge to start in with his questions. He'd learned by past mistake that Door County residents preferred a circumspect approach to business.

"Nice day," he said.

"It is. We've had quite a batch of visitors this afternoon."

After a couple minutes of polite banter, Cubiak mentioned the space heater and the vent hood stuffed with leaves and twigs. "I was told squirrels were the culprit."

"Squirrels, huh?" Myers led the sheriff to an exhibit of four stuffed squirrels.

"We got red, brown, black, and gray. They're all native to the county and any of them would be capable of such behavior."

"But no way of knowing for certain?" Cubiak said.

"Not unless you saw them in action. Adult squirrels are more likely to be concerned with food storage. The younger ones are mischievous and could have jammed the vent with twigs or whatever for no logical reason."

So Walter was probably right, Cubiak thought, although the notion of killer squirrels still sounded to him like a headline from one of the tawdry rags at a supermarket checkout counter. As for Huntsman and his friends, he still wasn't sure if his concerns were legitimate or echoes of the petty prejudices his long-suffering parents had embraced, that success was birthed by luck or connections and had nothing to do with effort. To them, hard labor was the price exacted for breathing.

Cubiak liked to believe that work could bring its own rewards. Look at Bathard. Retired and well off, he could sit and read all day if he wanted. But a year after his wife died, he unpacked the woodworking tools he'd inherited from his father and starting making birdhouses and bookcases in the old horse barn behind his house. One day over lunch in town, Bathard told Cubiak that he had decided to take on a bigger project and planned to refurbish a wooden sailboat. "You want to help you can, as long as you're willing to listen to my music," Bathard said. "And when the vessel is seaworthy, I'll show you how to handle it."

Thus began Cubiak's introduction to opera and sailing.

Eight months later, after futile visits to nearby marinas and harbors, the sheriff knew the names of many famous musical compositions and could identify several singers by voice. But Bathard had yet to find his boat.

The coroner was lecturing about knots on the Saturday they visited the Olson Orchard outside Juddville. With the owners dead for ten years, their farm had taken on the sad countenance of a failed dream, one becoming increasingly common across the rural landscape: a vacant house holding up a thin coat of chipped paint, a garage leaning sideways off its foundation, a weathered barn with caved-in roof. On land that hadn't been worked for a decade, rows of wizened fruit trees lined up in strict formation, like silent sentries sprung from the weed-choked soil. A hand-lettered sign announced the date of the upcoming auction that would determine the orchard's fate. "More condos," Bathard said as they stepped into the sharp cold air.

The previous evening he'd gotten a call from a former patient who'd relocated to Arizona and was back in Wisconsin for a funeral. The caller had once been an avid sailor and the coroner told him about his quest for a salvageable wooden boat. They're hard to come by, the doctor lamented. But there was one, the former patient told Bathard, probably long gone, that had been dry-docked every winter at Olson's Orchard. It had belonged to the couple's only son, who'd died. The parents had been unable to part with it and it could be that the boat's still there, he said.

Under January clouds that threatened snow, Cubiak and Bathard searched the grounds and trekked down a rutted path to a narrow barracks once used to house migratory cherry pickers. The front wall had imploded around the door; the rest of the structure framed a hodge-podge collection of broken camp beds and splintered crates. Behind the old home away from home, they discovered a battered metal road trailer, and strapped inside was the Olson boy's prized sailboat. Pulling off the shredded tarp, they got their first full look at the vintage vessel in its incongruous setting. The thirty-two-foot boat towered over the two men and looked as far beyond hope as its surroundings. The lead keel bubbled with rust, and the years out of water had shrunken and separated the hull's wooden planks. On board, there was more damage to tabulate: a deck soft with rot, a cracked mast, and a cabin infested with mold and mildew.

"Forget this one," Cubiak said.

"Certainly not. It's a Stout Fella, made right here," Bathard said, as if that simple fact trumped all. "My neighbor had a boat like this. He'd take me out with his kids. This is the kind of boat I learned to sail on."

Bathard called the auction company and five days later, the boat was trucked to his homestead. A crane hired for the day gently lifted the newly christened *Parlando* into the custom-built wood cradle that would be its new nest until it was made water ready.

Listening to Bathard rattle through the long list of items that had to be repaired or replaced, Cubiak was sure the doctor had made a mistake. But he never wavered and by the time Cubiak arrived that day, he'd absorbed his friend's infectious optimism. As the sheriff rolled the door open, music swept over him. Dust motes danced in the beams of sun that flooded through the skylights. The horse stalls and hayloft had been long removed from the barn, but the sweet scent of hay lingered and mixed with the perfume of fresh wood shavings.

Bathard futzed at the workbench. "You're late," he said, reaching up to hang a pliers on a wall filled with tools: hammers, clamps, rasps, and others that the sheriff had yet to learn to identify.

"I was running errands."

The doctor turned down the volume and Cubiak repeated himself.

"Working more likely," the coroner said as Cubiak helped himself to coffee from an old-fashioned aluminum percolator.

"I removed all the fittings." Bathard pointed to a shelf lined with neatly labeled plastic bags. "If you're up for a couple of hours of hard work, we can start on the keel. You know how to use one of these?" He held up an electric grinder.

"I've used a sander."

"Close enough."

They began on the port side, Cubiak at the prow with the grinder and Bathard near the stern with a cold chisel.

"Don't spare the elbow grease," the coroner said.

It was a nasty task, harder than the sheriff had imagined. Earplugs couldn't block the screech of metal on metal. Dust thickened the air, sparks popped, and his hand ached from the steady vibration of the grinder.

"Makes you appreciate people who work with their hands," he said when they stopped for a break.

Bathard wiped his brow. "A lesson, I'm afraid, I learned rather late in life," he said, surrounded by the tools of his father's trade.

The coroner was quiet for a moment. Then he grabbed a broom and began sweeping up. While he worked, Cubiak described his encounter with Roger Nils.

The doctor leaned on the broom. "It's true that Huntsman didn't formally adopt Walter but that never affected how he treated the boy. Raised him like his own from what anyone could see."

"Roger said it was 'another of the family myths.' What do you think he meant?"

"Probably nothing. He may have been agitated talking to you and simply misspoke. Then again, all families have secrets. Usually they're private matters that don't have any significance beyond the family circle."

"In other words, keep my nose out of it."

"Not exactly, but try not to overthink everything. Three men died. An unfortunate incident that could have been and most likely was an accident. Emma will give you the official test results tomorrow, but I can tell you now that what we initially suspected as the cause of death was verified."

"Carbon monoxide poisoning."

"Yes, sadly. Something both simple and preventable." Bathard looked at the sheriff. "I realize this is your job, but you need a life beyond work, give yourself something else to think about."

Cubiak pulled the safety glasses on over his lenses. "I've got the dogs."

"The dogs."

"Better than nothing."

"Well, that's true. Natalie helping you out?"

"You know she is."

"Good, given what you don't know about animals." Bathard chiseled at a lump of decay along the bottom edge of the keel. "Still thinking about that locked door?"

Cubiak shrugged and ran the grinder for several minutes. "I am. Something else, too." He laid the grinder down near the bandsaw and explained his concerns about the men's extensive holdings. "I wonder if they didn't have another source of income. Gambling, maybe."

Bathard looked amused. "You think they were running a north woods poker ring in Gills Rock?"

"It's possible."

"Lots of things are possible but that sounds doubtful to me. Consider, for example, that the men who made up the usual crowd of players don't enjoy a level of income that would allow for high stakes gambling."

"You ever asked to play?"

"Once or twice, years ago. Anyone elected to office or considered prominent for whatever reason gets invited, more a courtesy than anything. As I understand, the weekly games—the ones that mattered—were limited to a close circle."

Bathard brushed bits of rust off the keel and then went on. "Nothing unusual about that, really. The regulars are men who have much in common. I may be a local and a native to the area but I'm not accepted as one of them. Whether it's because of education, profession, or day-to-day routines, the difference is that some people are automatically part of the group and others are the odd men out. I'd attribute it to the classic town-versus-gown mentality rather than to anything sinister."

The doctor's assessment made sense to Cubiak. He turned his attention back to the boat and cleaned another square foot of the pitted keel before Bathard signaled an end to the day's work.

"No way you're taking a honeymoon voyage on this," Cubiak said as he stepped back from the vessel.

Bathard had been seeing Sonja Anderson, a widow from Washington Island, for nearly twelve months and would marry her in another two weeks.

The physician chuckled. "Even shooting for a first-year anniversary sail might be overly ambitious. But it will be worth the wait, I'm sure." Bathard paused. "Dave, I invited Cate to the wedding."

"I thought you might." Cubiak stopped to inspect one of the new planks in the hull. "Is she coming?" he said finally.

"She hasn't responded. It's possible she's traveling and hasn't had her mail forwarded."

"Or she doesn't want to come back."

"Indeed. It can't be easy for her."

A sliver of moon hung over the lake when Cubiak pulled into his driveway. He was full from the pot roast Bathard had prepared and tired in a good way from the work. He fed Butch and fixed another bottle of goat milk for Kipper, and then he cracked a beer, his drink of choice now that he was pretty much done with the hard stuff. A six-month-old copy of *National Geographic* lay on the counter. Cubiak subscribed to the magazine because Cate freelanced for it, and he'd kept that issue because she was one of the month's featured photographers.

Did she ever think about him? he wondered as he looked at her picture on the contributor's page.

Cubiak often puzzled over his continuing interest in Cate. They'd known each other for only a couple of weeks and hadn't talked or seen each other in nearly two years. They came from startlingly different backgrounds and had little in common. Yet he found himself drawn to her perhaps in no small part because she reminded him of Lauren. Attractive, though in a different way, and sensitive like his late wife.

He missed Cate. But he missed Lauren, too, and didn't know what was fair or right. Perhaps he should ask Bathard, but even that seemed like the first small step toward betrayal.

Cubiak finished the beer and opened another. He was halfway through when one of the puppies yelped, and he remembered that he had meant to call Natalie that evening.

He felt a stab of guilt about the vet. They'd been going out, off and on, for more than a year. He liked Natalie. She was clever and fun. But he sensed a coolness about her as well, and he missed the warmth he had known with Lauren. When he was dating Lauren, he'd known what to say when her father had asked what his intentions were. He wouldn't know how to respond if asked the same question about Natalie. Unsettled by this uncharacteristic indecision, Cubiak poured the rest of the beer down the sink, tossed the magazine on the pile by the door, and went to check on the dogs.

MONDAY

5

The wall clock in Cubiak's office ticked toward eight thirty as he flipped through the stack of weekend incident reports. The familiar litany of offenses was numbing: the usual drunken assault at the Rusty Scupper Tap, domestic violence that varied only by address, a half-dozen fender benders, and a plethora of speeding tickets. Did people never learn?

The red light on the phone console flashed.

"Yes?"

"Morning, sir." Lisa's cheerful greeting broke the spell. Despite working for the sheriff's department, where the base side of humanity paraded in constant display, his young assistant exuded a never-ending aura of optimism and grace. "How are you today?"

"Fine, thanks." Did she believe him?

"Good to hear. Doctor Pardy's on line one."

"Thank you." He took the call.

"Emma." Cubiak liked the name, the old-fashioned ring of integrity it conveyed. He liked saying it out loud.

"Dave. Just getting back to you with the official test results on the three gentlemen at Gills Rock. No question, carbon monoxide. Blood levels for each came in around seventy-two hundred ppm. You'll have the paperwork later this morning."

"How long . . . ?"

"No way of knowing. If the concentration of CO in the room was low, up to half an hour. If the concentration was high, they would have died within two or three minutes."

"There was nothing obviously wrong with the space heater."

"Well, something caused the buildup of carbon monoxide."

Squirrels, thought Cubiak.

Pardy went on. "I've got a call in to the DA as well. Bathard says Blackwell will want an inquest if only to make the cause of death official and rule it an accident." She hesitated. "Do you want me to call the families or shall you?"

Cubiak heard chatter in the background. Someone trying to get her attention. "I'll do it. Thanks."

"Any time."

Pardy hung up. Cubiak gave a half smile. The coroner was not from Door County and like him lacked the penchant for filling time with niceties. The sheriff held the receiver and fished Ida Huntsman's contact information from his wallet. He was punching in the number when the intercom button flashed red again.

"Urgent call for you, sir. Line two." Lisa was uncharacteristically terse.

Cubiak jumped to the incoming call.

"Sheriff, Walter Nils . . ."

"I was just phoning your . . ."

Walter cut him off. "You gotta get up here, Sheriff."

"Where are you?"

"Gills Rock. At my mother's place."

"What's going on?"

"Come see for yourself. It's just hateful. How could anyone do this?" Walter's voice was thick, as if he'd been crying. "Hurry, please."

For the second time in three days, Cubiak made the drive north. Nature had not wasted time extending spring's verdant hue up the peninsula. Grass and trees were kissed with a rich halo of green. In Ephraim, golden forsythia bloomed alongside the crocuses and daffodils. Even the landscape past Sister Bay had shed its gloomy mantle. Only the farthest tip of the land retained winter's somber tones.

The last mile to Huntsman's home was almost a repeat of Saturday: the statue-like gulls perched on the rocks, the barking dog still tethered to the willow. The only difference was the clothesline behind the Smitz house. Before, empty; now, laden with laundry: yellow checked sheets and pillowcases, two faded pink towels, several blouses, and a pair of men's long underwear, dingy from overuse and stiff with frost.

Cubiak started the turn into Huntsman's driveway when he braked and stopped. Something was different. On the other side of the road, three of the plumbing vans had been moved from the lot and parked bumper-to-bumper along the front of the building, obscuring the company logo. That's odd, Cubiak thought. As he walked over for a closer look, a woodpecker started hammering into the trunk of a nearby tree. Although the sheriff couldn't see the bird through the foliage, he sensed that his every move was being telegraphed through the forest. Leaning around the hood of the first van he discovered what was hidden behind the lineup of vehicles—a white wall defaced with angry strokes of red paint that spelled out a nasty farewell: Good Riddance.

Cubiak whistled quietly. The bird's staccato concert paused but began again when he picked up a stick and poked at the crimson streak that underlined the message. The paint was fresh. He looked around but the hard ground yielded no footprints.

The vandals hadn't stopped with defacing the shed. At the Rec Room, they'd dislodged the cardboard from the broken window, smashed several other panes of glass, and made deep scratches in the picture window. The woodpecker transmitted a flurry of reports.

Two for two. Had the house been vandalized, as well? Had Ida been harmed? Cubiak was sure Walter would have said something if his mother had been injured. The sheriff passed the area where the bodies had been laid out the previous Saturday. The gazebo was unscathed but splotches of red paint bloomed like algae on the pier and the side of the power boat. The most spiteful damage was to the cabin cruiser in the sling where large red *x*'s crossed over the name *Ida Mae*. Again the paint was still wet. And again there were no tracks in the damp grass. Had the vandals been so bold they'd used the brick walkway rather than cut across the lawn?

The yard and dock weren't visible from the village or any of the waterfront homes. This early in the season, there were probably few people out and about anyway. Perhaps the woodpecker had been a witness but the bird had taken its secret language and flown away. Had Ida heard or seen anything?

Walter waited at the back door. Like Esther Smitz, he blocked the sheriff's way.

"This was in the mail," he said, jabbing a white envelope at Cubiak.

The envelope, a standard number ten, was unstamped, the address typed: Ida Nils Huntsman.

"It was in the box with the rest of the mail. My mother thought it was a sympathy note."

Cubiak pulled a sheet of pale blue paper through the slit in the top of the envelope. THEY GOT WHAT THEY DESERVED. Typed. All caps.

"Someone must have put it there!" Walter said, twisting his hair.

"Do you have any idea who . . . ?"

"No." Walter slumped into the door jamb and rubbed a jagged thumbnail against his teeth. "Why would anyone do this? I don't understand."

"How's Ida?"

"I don't know, she's . . . she's acting pretty strange. You'd better come in." Walter stepped aside and let Cubiak pass. Big Guy's jackets and boots had been removed from the mudroom, replaced by a petite, yellow plaid coat and a pair of black clogs.

"In here," Walter said, leading the way through the kitchen and dining room, past the living room and into the first doorway on the right.

They entered the master bedroom, with its sprawling king-size bed, flanked by matching nightstands; two flowered reading chairs by windows that faced the water; a fireplace with a built-in alcove that was neatly stacked with wood; His and Her dressers made of a light wood, pecan maybe; a luxurious en suite bathroom; and a walk-in closet, one side hung with dresses, skirts, blouses, the other empty.

Ida looked up from where she stood on the other side of the room, separated from them by an ocean of mattress. Dwarfed by the bed, she seemed more fragile than when Cubiak had first met her. She held the sleeve of a brown gingham-checked shirt that lay front-side down in front of her.

"Morning, Sheriff," Ida said as she draped the sleeve down the length of the shirt, aligning the edge with the side seam.

"Mrs. Huntsman," he said, watching her fold her husband's shirt. In three quick movements, she packaged the piece of clothing into a neat rectangle, the same way his mother had folded his father's shirts.

"Ida, please," she said, as she inspected her handiwork and added it to the pile at the foot of the bed. The bedspread was covered in stacks of clothing: pants, shirts, sweaters, ties.

"I've finished with the socks and such," she said, pointing to a black garbage bag by the wall. "Catholic Charities is coming this afternoon. I didn't want to keep them waiting."

After his father died, Cubiak thought his mother had acted precipitously, waiting only two months to empty his side of the closet. When Lauren and Alexis were run down, he'd been unable to part with anything of theirs for more than a year.

Ida's haste was difficult to comprehend. Was she in shock? Did she realize what she was doing?

"Walter's told you?" she said, reaching for another shirt.

Her son stared at the floor.

"Yes, he's told me. But I'd like to talk to you about it. Perhaps in the kitchen?"

"Of course." Ida laid the shirt down and dusted off her hands.

Cubiak waited until Walter had poured the coffee—mugs for the two of them and a cup and saucer for his mother—then he pulled the envelope from his pocket and set it on the table.

"Tell me in your own words what happened," he said to Ida.

The color in her cheeks rose as she stirred her coffee. She took a sip, carefully set the cup down, and looked up at Cubiak.

"Nothing happened. I came out this morning to see if the deer had returned and noticed what looked like red smears on the boat. It was early, just past dawn, and I thought the light was playing tricks on me. You know the way clouds sometimes catch the sunlight and reflect it back? I thought it was sunlight bouncing off the clouds and then off the water and the stern. Anyway, I came outside for a closer look. It was upsetting at first to see my name defaced but I thought it was just kids, you know, being stupid and mean the way kids sometimes are. I didn't notice the company shed until later, when I went out for the mail. So there it was again, more ugly red paint saying that hurtful stuff. And in the box, the envelope."

"Was it mixed in with the rest of the mail or lying on top?"

"It was right on top, the first thing I saw."

"And you brought it into the house and opened it?" As he talked, Cubiak extracted the letter and laid it flat on the table, turning it toward Ida.

She blushed again. "Yes."

"But you didn't call me? Why?"

"I told you, I thought it was kids."

"You mean teenagers? Punks?"

"Yes."

"Ma!" Walter leaned forward as if reaching for the note. Then he fell back in his chair and grabbed at the corners of his mouth.

Cubiak wondered if Walter had come to the same conclusion he had: that teenagers pulling a prank wouldn't bother typing and printing out a note; they'd scrawl their nasty message without thinking.

"My son disagrees, but I still believe it. Terrence sometimes had to shoo them away, not just boys, girls too. They came down from the park and snuck around the cabin. There was nothing in there worth stealing, but they wouldn't know that and he thought they might break in."

Cubiak glanced at Walter. "But you don't think it was kids responsible for the vandalism and the note."

Walter rubbed his hands together. "At first I didn't. But now, I don't know. Maybe my mother's right."

Cubiak reached for the note. "You don't need to have this around," he said.

Ida and Walter watched him fit the letter back into the envelope.

"Doctor Pardy called this morning. Tests confirm that the deaths were caused by carbon monoxide poisoning."

Walter cleared his throat and stared at the table, but Ida met the sheriff's glance. "They didn't suffer, then," she said.

"Very little. If at all."

"I see." She sat still for a moment. Then she scooted her chair away from the table. "May I, Sheriff? I have work to do."

Outside, both men glanced at the water as if to confirm that the damage to the pier and the boats hadn't been something they'd jointly imagined.

"You got someone to help with the cabin windows?" Cubiak said.

Walter shook his head. "I don't want people coming by. You know, gawking. I'm just putting up plastic anyhow, from the inside, and I'll put a tarp over the back of the boat so my mother doesn't have to look at it. At least she can't see the company shed from here. I moved the trucks so no one driving by can see the shit on the wall but I won't be able to do anything more until after the funeral." There was bitterness in his voice.

"You staying up here awhile?"

"Yeah, at least another couple of days."

They walked side by side across the yard, having to talk over the sound of waves crashing onto the shoreline rocks. "Roger come by?" Cubiak said.

Walter stopped and Cubiak saw the worry about the boy layer over the worry about Ida and the grief about his father. "Roger? How do you know Roger?" He tried to make his voice light.

This was not the time to bring up the incident in Fish Creek. "I saw the article in the paper last spring."

Walter started down the path again. "Yeah, that was nice, wasn't it? Roger was here last evening. Came to see his grandmother."

"He'll be back for the funeral?"

"Sure. Why wouldn't he?" Walter spun around. "You'll be there, won't you?"

"Of course."

"You think it's okay, having the one funeral for all three of them? It's the same people coming for each of them. Be too hard to make them come for one and then another and then again. Better this way, wouldn't you say?"

"Yes. I'm sure. It makes sense."

Good people, Mabel had said of Terrence Huntsman, his wife, and the others when she served him lunch on Saturday. Clearly, the waitress hadn't spoken for the entire community or the peninsula. Someone resented the three men enough to try and dirty their reputation. Why? The graffiti on the plumbing office looked like the cheap-shot work of kids who didn't like being bossed around. *Good riddance* to whom? Presumably to Huntsman, the one who got on the wrong side of the marauding teenagers. Same with the vandalism on the cabin and dock. The property belonged to Big Guy and was easily accessible. But the note to Ida was cruel. Not the kind of thing a bunch of kids would write. And, the message didn't apply just to Huntsman. *They got what they deserved* meant all three men.

He needed to learn more about them.

At Sister Bay, Cubiak turned inland and hopscotched down a network of back roads to the Woodlands Sawmill.

The mill was a relic from a time when the peninsula was heavily forested. In that not-so-distant past, dozens of mills operated at full capacity, slicing tree trunks into the boards that would help build the cities and towns of the Midwest. All were silent now, except for the circular, jagged-tooth blade at the Woodlands mill. The monster saw sat under the sloped roof of an ancient lean-to in the center of a wide clearing. The structure was open on two sides to disperse the noise and dust and to accommodate the gigantic tree trunks that were once milled there. Even now the ground was covered with fresh sawdust from the trees that locals brought in to be custom cut for home remodeling jobs, a small business but enough to keep the facility going.

A half-dozen pickups stood at the rear of the clearing, alongside a wooden shack rimmed with racks of antlers. A single stream of gray smoke shimmied from the chimney and the rumble of voices could be heard from within.

". . . not a fucking dime," a gruff voice barked as Cubiak walked in.

"Shut the damn door," another man yelled from the back as the sheriff stepped into a cloud of hot, dry air.

Cubiak pulled the door closed and a silence fell, thick as the smoke in the room.

In the dim light he made out a row of hazy silhouettes along the cluttered work counter and back wall. In the middle of the room, a hefty man bent over a woodstove.

"Sheriff." The large man at the stove spoke.

Someone coughed. "Sorry 'bout that, Sheriff."

Cubiak shrugged as Henry Fielding, the proprietor, grabbed a Jim Beam bottle between two fingers and poured something red out of it into a tumbler. "Here you go, Dave," he said, shoving the glass at Cubiak. "We're just drinking to the three old gents who died," he added.

The toast echoed from the corner and all but one of the men raised their glasses. They were a wizened bunch in overalls and flannel shirts, old enough to be nursing home escapees.

Cubiak tossed down the drink and inhaled sharply as a ribbon of sour cherry wine burned a ditch along the back of his throat. He swallowed a cough. According to Bathard, Fielding produced a fresh crop of wine every year and was as proud of it as he was of the lumber he cut on the monster saw. "It's sometimes fit to drink and sometimes fit to use for salad dressing and sometimes fit to pour down the drain, but if you want to be included in the club and privy to the gossip the members generate, it's always fit to be praised," Bathard had told him.

Fielding eyed Cubiak expectantly.

"Your best yet," the sheriff said.

The miller brandished the bottle again but Cubiak put up a hand. "Sorry, can't. On duty." He set his empty glass on a windowsill and moved down the counter. He knew the men were watching him and so made a show of dropping two fives into the kitty. In keeping with local custom, he coated a saltine with a thin layer of fish spread. He didn't like fish and would have been happy to forgo the ritual. But that would be rude.

"Don't let me interrupt anything," he said around a mouthful of cracker.

"Nothing to interrupt. We're talking about those three men, the vets, y'know. What tough luck," said a jowly man at his elbow.

Cubiak glanced down the row at the members of the "Woodlands Social Club." All but one clutched an empty glass. The man who had boycotted the toast scowled at the floor.

"Guess you all knew them," the sheriff said, setting off a chorus of comment.

"Sure did."

"Good men."

"Yeah, a damn shame."

Then silence again. Was it because they had nothing to say about the dead men or because they were of an age when death loomed large, not as an abstract subject but a real threat. Had they heard about the vandalism? Not a whisper.

"I was just up there checking on Ida," Cubiak said finally.

"Heart of gold, that Ida."

"All three of them ladies."

Amid the chatter about the widows, Cubiak watched the abstainer weave his way toward the door. He resisted the urge to follow him.

"I guess you'll miss the poker nights."

There was no response. Another man edged toward the exit.

"What did you play? Texas Hold 'em, Seven Card Stud, or some kind of local variation with jokers," he said.

"Jokers! That some kind of city poker?"

Two of the men snickered and made as to leave.

"Truth is we didn't spend all that much time up there playing cards," said the stout man in the corner.

"Stakes too high?"

"Nah, just not convenient."

"Most guys only went once or twice. It was kind of clubby, you know what I mean? Don't get me wrong, they were good guys, the three of them. Just kind of had their own thing going."

The last man drifted out the door, as the sheriff helped himself to a piece of cheddar. "Something I said?"

"Folks have things to do," Fielding said. He began cleaning up. "There's been talk time to time about the poker games, nothing specific, just a word or two people'd mention about not being comfortable. Don't mean nothing really. And no one wants to think badly of the dead." The sawmill operator dumped the leftover crackers and fish spread into the trash. "These men were veterans. Heroes. That means something to folks here. How they played cards, who they played cards with don't matter. Ain't no one's business but their own and now they're gone it ain't anyone's business."

Cubiak let the comment slide. "Did you know them well?"

Fielding seemed to shrug inside the heavy jacket he wore despite the heat in the shed. "I knew them. Wouldn't say well," he said lowering his gaze. "Milled a couple of black walnut trees for Big Guy when he built the addition to the house. He was very particular about how I treated the wood, and I respected him for that."

"I hear he was pretty generous with his money."

Fielding gazed at the cobwebbed ceiling. "He was. Could afford to be, as I understand it. Don't get me wrong. He was a good citizen, but the type who liked to run things, too, kind of a bully peacock, full of himself and all. Course, he had a lot to be proud of, can't begrudge the man what he accomplished."

"You didn't care for him then?"

"I didn't say that. Man was a hero, after all. He just had a different way of doing things. I like to look at people eye to eye, you know, on the same level. Big Guy seemed to prefer people looking up to him."

"Like his old friends, Swenson and Wilkins."

"Maybe. Yeah, I guess. Few times I saw the three of them together, it was clear Big Guy called the shots. In fact, he pretty much always called the shots."

That trait may not have sat well with others. "Who was the man who ignored the toast earlier?" Cubiak said.

Fielding snorted. "Him! Bruno Loggerstone from down near Peninsula Park. From what I know, he's still mad about something that happened thirty years ago."

"That's a long time to hold a grudge."

"A talent some people have."

"I guess. They all seemed to think highly of Ida and the other two, Olive and Stella. Funny, though, no one mentioned Walter Nils or Wilkins's son."

"Walter's okay. Guess we just take him for granted. Marty Wilkins ain't been seen around here for years. Don't even know if he's still alive!"

"That leaves just the one grandkid. Roger."

"Looks that way. Unless Marty went out and multiplied. Might have a crop of offspring circling the globe for all anybody here knows. Suppose we'll find out eventually. There's money involved and people'll come crawling out of their hidey-holes for that." Fielding looked at Cubiak. "I just hope Roger uses his share to go back to school. Don't know what got into that boy."

"Any idea why he quit?"

"Not a one. Damn shame, you ask me. Smart kid. Good athlete, too, and here he's working at the coast guard station. Don't make sense."

"He's a civilian. What's he doing over there?"

"Last I heard he got a job helping paint the place to get ready for the big celebration. Now look what's happened." Fielding tossed a chunk of wood into the stove, sending a spray of orange sparks into the room. "Ain't life a bitch," he said and slammed the metal door shut.

TUESDAY
MORNING

It was still dark when Cubiak stumbled into the kitchen. The cold tile floor pricked his bare feet, and he shifted from one to the other as he poured the usual eight cups of water into the coffee maker, an amount that filled his favorite mug exactly three and a half times. Someday, he'd do the math. In the east, a narrow streak of blazing light sliced through the black sky, heralding the dawn that would evolve into the morning of the funeral. Cubiak hated funerals. He couldn't look at a coffin without seeing his wife laid out in her teal dress and his daughter in her orange polka dots, a fuzzy pink teddy bear in her arms.

Walter told him they were anticipating as many as six hundred people. Whoever had vandalized Huntsman's property and sent the cruel note to his widow would likely be among the mourners. But who could it be? Who would have done anything so ugly and mean so soon after the three men died? Was it just a prank, as Ida insisted? Or an act of vengeance? Judging from what Fielding had said the day before, it seemed Big Guy was the kind of man who could make enemies as easily as friends. Did old grudges diminish or fester with time? Would someone dare try to disrupt the funeral?

While the coffee brewed, Cubiak fed Butch and weighed the puppies. Kipper had gained one ounce. "Good job," he said, rubbing his thumb on her lumpy head. He brought her into the kitchen for her bottle and then tucked her back into the basket with the others and covered the squirming heap with an old towel.

Outside, his breath formed a vaporous cloud. It was colder than he expected and he wasn't properly dressed, but he had no time to change. Hood up, he loped down the driveway. He ran to forget and to ready himself for the onslaught of emotion he knew would come. At the halfway mark, he stopped to catch his breath. A trickle of sweat ran past his ear onto his cheek. He swiped it away and then pulled off his hood and started back.

The puppies were comatose when Cubiak slipped into the house. He put out extra rations for Butch, filled his mug, and spread peanut butter over two pieces of wheat toast. He ate standing up, taking in the full bloom of the sun over the water. When he finished, he whisked the crumbs into the sink and rinsed up. Time to shower and dress.

Attending Catholic schools, he'd worn uniforms—life simplified. As sheriff he put on his uniform only for official functions. But showing up at the funeral in full dress might make people wonder about the nature of the deaths, something he wanted to avoid. Instead he shrugged into his one good shirt, looped a dark burgundy tie under the collar, and pulled on a pair of black wool trousers. With his charcoal herringbone jacket, it was the closest he came to a suit.

Like Cubiak, the deceased veterans were Catholic. Unlike him, Huntsman, Wilkins, and Swenson had been practicing Catholics. As active members of Our Lady of the Lake parish in Ellison Bay, they attended Sunday Mass, made it to services on the Holy Days of Obligation, confessed their sins to the priest, and wrote generous checks to the annual building fund.

The parish church was surprisingly grand, given the town's small year-round population. Brilliant white and set on a low rise south of the village, the building sounded a clarion call to believe in something more than pure humanity. That sad morning, against the bright blue sky, the steeple acted like a magnet, drawing traffic up the peninsula. At the intersection of Spruce and Highway 42, a traffic deputy directed vehicles off the highway. By the time Cubiak found a parking spot, the processional had begun and the giant wooden doors were swinging shut, muffling the dirge of the organ and choir.

He followed a narrow sidewalk into the courtyard between the rectory and the church and entered through the side door. The sheriff had stationed Rowe in the rear of the church so between the two of them, they could keep watch over both entrances. Cubiak was nearer the service itself. From his vantage point, he had a clear view over the mound of flower arrangements and through the decorative plumes of the Knights of Columbus to the altar, the two celebrants, and the three caskets. The priests wore ceremonial purple vestments. The coffins were draped in white palls and arranged in the shape of a truncated cross: one lengthwise in the main aisle and the other two placed perpendicular to it along the altar railings.

The parish of Our Lady of the Lake served the Catholic community of northern Door, and the church had been constructed when membership had been at its zenith. Although Sunday attendance had fallen off steadily, that morning the sanctuary was full. This was no ordinary funeral and the packed pews reflected the fact. The mourners were mostly middle-aged and older, but a notable number of younger men and women, entire families even, were squeezed in among them. The congregants rustled and whispered and by their demeanor generated both a sense of solemnity and an air of excitement. An event of this magnitude assumed a historic significance and would not be repeated.

The widows were in the first pew on the left, joined together in the place of dubious honor. Ida was nearest the main aisle, Stella in the middle, and then Olive. They were three women in black but the similarity ended with their attire.

Ida appeared rested and almost serene, as if she found peace and solace in the familiar setting and the unfolding ritual. Her softness accentuated Stella's bony sharpness, hard fixed gaze, and rigid upright posture. The third widow, Olive, was noticeably younger than the other two. Flashing pink nails and lipstick, she seemed nervous and uncomfortable in her role.

Walter and Roger, the nearest living relatives, sat behind the women. Pale and wearing dark glasses and black suits, they appeared to be two versions of the same person, separated by both a handful of decades and demeanor. Roger fidgeted, restless and uncomfortable in the face of so much death, while Walter lolled against the hard bench, cheeks sunken and eyes downcast, looking either drunk or hung over or a combination of both.

Across the aisle from the bereaved were the eighteen pallbearers. Six men for each coffin, four coast guardsmen and the neighbor Clyde Smitz among them. Esther sat several rows back, her red hair a glowing torch in the sea of black. Cubiak scanned the rest of the crowd. Among those he knew were Pardy and Bathard; Justin St. James from the *Herald*; Henry Fielding, owner of the sawmill; Gary Dotson, the coast guard director; Mabel, the Gills Rock waitress; and various business owners and county and town officials. Most of the others, he didn't recognize: pews filled with fishermen, farmers, and neighbors. Half hidden behind a rear pillar was an elderly man in a wheelchair, head down and hands clasped on a fringed lap blanket. Nothing untoward.

The priest had a rich, warm voice, and his lavish remarks during the homily matched the dead men's prominent stature in the county: pillars of the community, decorated veterans, loving husbands, generous supporters of the church and local sports teams, role models for the younger generation. Stella, who earlier seemed the most stoic of the three widows, sobbed. But Ida and Olive did not cry.

"These good decent men have gone to their heavenly reward," the priest said.

In the moment of silence that followed the pronouncement, Roger began coughing. A baby wailed. As the mother carried the infant out, the priests motioned the mourners to stand. Amid the noise of kneelers being kicked upright and shuffling feet, the celebrants began to recite the creed. "I believe in one God, the father Almighty," they intoned as a chorus of voices joined in.

The funeral Mass unfurled with practiced pomp until it culminated in a sense of finality that was as palpable as the cloud of incense that hung over the room. This was good-bye. The congregants were somber as they watched the three coffins being rolled back down the aisle. There was no escaping bitter reality: the men were gone and all those present would one day meet the same fate.

At the church door the palls of Christian baptism were replaced with America's Stars and Stripes. The Knights took up positions on either side of the stairs and raised their swords. Beneath the arch of sacred steel, the three veterans were carried down the stairs.

After several minutes' confusion and milling about, a military honor guard led the mourners to the small, hillside cemetery behind the church. In the sacred ground, three freshly dug graves waited, like wounds in the earth. The pits were blessed and the Lord's Prayer recited in a murmuring wave of voices. But as the priest talked of ashes to ashes, Cubiak retreated into himself. This was an image he could not bear.

The sharp retort of rifle fire brought him back to the gravesides. Three men in dress blues had raised their weapons and fired off a three-volley salute. The deafening sound stunned the onlookers and then slowly faded into an unearthly silence that was disturbed only by the faint whisper of wind through the surrounding trees. In the uneasy quiet, a lone soldier raised his trumpet and played Taps. When it seemed there were no more tears to be shed, no more emotion left to be wrung from the mourners, a contingent of bright young navy officers stepped forward and in a mesmerizing, synchronized motion lifted the flags from the coffins and folded them in half lengthwise, and then in half again, and then again and again. A triangle of cloth and memory for each widow, presented "On behalf of the President of the United States and a grateful nation . . ."

Mercifully, the service ended. The mourners were released to drift away, the widows left to bid their private farewells. The women were quick about it and soon walked down the hill to where the crowd had gathered. The people were hungry, and it was time to eat. Good plain food cooked by neighbors and served in the church dining room was the reward for sorrow.

In the dim basement hallway, Ida, Stella, and Olive took up their positions in a shoulder-to-shoulder receiving line, greeting friends and neighbors as they entered the church hall for lunch.

Cubiak lingered outside. He was looking for Roger when Gary Dotson, the coast guard station chief, approached.

"This certainly changes our plans," Dotson said.

"You heard about what happened at Huntsman's place?"

The chief nodded. "You wouldn't mind coming by tomorrow to go over things again?"

"Course not."

"Good." Dotson frowned.

"What else?"

"Nothing."

Cubiak was sure there was something more bothering Dotson. He started to ask again when a woman in a threadbare brown-plaid coat hurried toward them clutching a casserole dish. She averted her face as she passed the men but the sheriff remembered seeing her in church. She'd sat directly behind the pallbearers, amid the closest friends and neighbors.

Seconds later, there was a crash in the church basement, followed by a scream.

Cubiak hurtled through the open doorway and down the stairs. In the cramped foyer, he collided with the woman in brown, who stood facing the three widows. The trio's black dresses dripped with red wormy strands and bloodlike splotches. Pieces of crockery lay in a pool of red at their feet.

Cubiak grabbed the woman in brown by the shoulders and spun her around. Her hands were smeared red as well. An ugly yellow bruise spread above her right eye.

"Who are you?" he said.

She blinked and said nothing.

Several men rushed from the dining hall but Rowe and Bathard elbowed past them into the entryway.

"Keep everyone inside. And close the doors," the sheriff told the deputy.

While the doctor tended to the three stunned women, Cubiak propelled the assailant up the stairs into the church. The aroma of incense lingered in the air. Sunlight filtered through the stained-glass windows and lit the funeral flowers on the altar, creating an air of softness and peace.

"Who are you?" he said again.

"God's servant." The woman's voice was hard and defiant.

"What's this all about?"

"Justice. I killed the son-of-a-bitch."

"What do you mean? Who did you kill?"

"My husband. The man who ruined my life." The woman held her hands out as if expecting him to cuff her. "He got what he deserved. They all did."

"Who?" Cubiak said.

The woman spat on the floor. "All of them—four of a kind."

While Cubiak questioned the woman, Rowe ducked into the nave. He motioned the sheriff aside. The red liquid was beet juice. The wormy threads, sliced beets. Ida, Stella, and Olive were upset but unhurt.

"Who are you?" Cubiak said for the third time when he and the woman were alone again.

She crossed herself.

"Where is your husband?"

She said nothing.

"Where do you live? What's your address?"

Silence.

Hurried footsteps approached from the side door. The priest had changed into his collar and black suit. He seemed diminished and confused but enveloped the woman's hands in his.

"My dear, are you all right? I overheard your questions, Sheriff. What is going on here?"

"I killed Joe," the woman said.

Whatever the priest had intended to say next went unsaid. He stared at her. "I will hear your confession when we finish," he said after a moment. Then he turned to Cubiak.

"Her name is Agnes Millard. She lives in Gills Rock. I don't know the exact address but the house is on the road along the bay, not far from Huntsman's place. There's a German shepherd tied up out front." He hesitated. "I assume you'll need to go there. Will you allow Mrs. Millard to stay with me?"

"I will, but I'll leave my deputy here."

The priest laid a hand on Agnes's head and blessed her. "Of course," he said, and led her to the confessional.

Downstairs, Bathard waited.

"I phoned Pardy. She was halfway to Sturgeon Bay. I told her that you might be calling," he said.

"Right, thanks."

"The luncheon was canceled. Everything's going to be put away and served Sunday after the eleven o'clock Mass. Can't let the food go to waste."

"And the women?"

"Several of the neighbor ladies helped them clean up. Walter took the three of them back to Ida's house. It seems they all wanted to be together. I promised to come out and check on them later."

"Good."

"What will you do now?"

"Go see if a dog knows anything about a dead man."

TUESDAY
NOON

The road to Gills Rock was deserted. Tourist traffic this far north hadn't started up yet, and most of the locals were probably still at the church. Holding the gas pedal to the floor, Cubiak pictured the crowd at the parish grounds, picking up pieces of gossip, and wondering when it would be polite to leave and get back to their daily routines. The sheriff was still on 42 with the heater on and the windows up when he heard the German shepherd howling. The sound was an amalgam of despair and rage, as if the beast had a preternatural understanding of the morning's events.

Along the empty lane, the dog paced under the willow, straining at the chain that anchored it to the gnarled trunk. The sight of the sheriff's vehicle ignited a new burst of fury, but when Cubiak turned into the driveway and cut the engine, the animal fell silent. With its huge head thrust forward and threads of saliva hanging from its mouth, it trained its hooded yellow eyes on the jeep.

Rather than incite the animal further, Cubiak turned his attention first to the bay where the water lay flat as granite under a looming sky and then to the neatly kept, frame cottage next door where Esther and

Clyde Smitz lived. The green house stood in sharp contrast to the one he was about to enter. The house the dog guarded, the house where the priest said Agnes lived, was sadly worn by time and weather. All trace of color had eroded, leaving the shell something less than white but without enough pigment to be called gray. A section of rusty gutter hung alongside the side door, and the front porch roof was caved.

Cubiak looked at the dog, which despite its thick coat appeared half starved. The animal remained locked in position. The sheriff cracked the door open and inhaled the fishy air.

"Good dog. Nice dog," he said.

A low rumbling vibrated deep inside the dog's throat.

Cubiak's feet hit the ground and the German shepherd lunged, snarling its fangs and ugly raw gums, thrashing to get free. With each movement the chain sliced deeper into the trunk, but the metal links held.

"Good boy," Cubiak murmured as he picked up the empty water dish that lay overturned just out of the animal's reach. He carried the bowl to the faucet on the side of the house, filled it with fresh water, and then brought it back and set it on the stubby grass. Wary of the angry mutt, he toed the bowl forward far enough that the dog could drink without sinking its teeth into his foot. The animal growled in response.

With the dog still protesting, Cubiak made his way down the cracked asphalt driveway. A late-model brown pickup was parked outside the garage, a metal shed almost as big as the house. Limp arbor vitae ringed the deep yard, and a sliver of grass ran under the clothesline, but most of the area had been plowed for a garden plot. In the back, smoke rose from a trash barrel. The sheriff knocked at the side entrance, but there was no answer. When he tried the knob, the door swung inward.

"Hello."

No answer.

He entered a narrow, dim utility room. Several vintage denim jackets and two pairs of patched bib overalls hung along the wall. A small laundry tub took up one corner and next to it was an old-fashioned wringer washer. A mop and broom stood in a blue bucket beneath a single clothesline hung with a half-dozen rags. Cubiak opened a second door and stepped up into the kitchen.

The room was a neat square, so antiseptically clean that he imagined a hint of ammonia in the air and so outdated that he half-expected to find a hand pump at the cast-iron sink. A metal camp-style percolator sat on the stove. Cheap linoleum covered the floor. A narrow pine table next to the sink provided the only counter space. A smaller square table under the window was set with two plates, two mugs, and two forks. There were no cupboards on the walls. The only refrigerator was a small, dorm-style appliance shoved into the rear of a narrow pantry. A fifty-pound sack of dog food and bins of potatoes and apples lined the floor of the storage area. The shelves held basic foodstuffs: flour, rice, sugar, oatmeal, molasses, coffee, and bags of dried beans. There were no packaged foods and even fewer pots and pans than in his kitchen.

Beyond the kitchen, a hallway led to the bathroom and two tiny bedrooms. There was a sewing machine and rolltop desk in one, and a tall dresser and full-size bed in the other. Cubiak doubled back toward the kitchen and paused in front of a doorway covered with a long piece of unbleached muslin.

The barking stopped. A clock ticked.

He pulled back the modest drapery and took in the compact living room, instantly recording the details. The woodstove and wooden rocker. The frayed rug and worn armchair. The television and VCR player. The shotgun on the floor. The twin spider webs of blood on the wall. A man in a navy blue suit sprawled across the sofa in a small ocean of red and worse. Joe Millard was bearded and hefty, his face frozen in surprise and his chest blown open.

The sheriff closed his eyes a moment and then looked again. He recognized the dead man as one of the onlookers at Huntsman's place on Saturday and one of the pallbearers that morning. Cubiak had seen him carry one of the caskets to the cemetery, but for which of the deceased he wasn't sure. Why had Millard gone back to his house instead of staying for lunch? Why had his wife followed him home? Or had she returned to retrieve the forgotten casserole and found him there? What had provoked her to kill him that morning? Cubiak could imagine the kind of life she had with the man. Why not take her vengeance a year ago, or next month? Why today?

Cubiak radioed Rowe from the jeep and asked him to call Pardy as well. He read the faded house number over the front door. "Can't miss it, second to last house on the strip. Big willow and dog out front."

The water dish was empty. The dog hunkered near the tree, its head on its paws and its eyes squeezed into two black slits.

Cubiak got a fistful of dog food from the panty and tossed the kibble into the dish. "You're not fooling me, buddy. You're watching my every move, aren't you?" Cubiak said.

The dog twitched.

While he waited for his deputy, Cubiak hooked a hose to the outside faucet and dragged it to the smoldering trash barrel. There wasn't much inside but kitchen garbage. With the fire out, he checked the garage. An upright freezer was stuffed with packages wrapped in butcher paper and marked Venison and Squirrel. Expensive hand tools and fancy fishing gear were neatly stored along one wall. In the truck he found a CD player and GPS. Joe Millard liked his toys.

Cubiak was cordoning off the buildings with police tape when Rowe turned in the drive.

The dog exploded. Rowe went white.

"He doesn't cotton to strangers."

"No shit."

The sheriff walked his deputy through the crime scene. When they got back out front the dog's dish was empty again.

"Good boy," Cubiak said. Then he told Rowe, "You wait here for Pardy. I'll be back."

"Where you going?" Rowe said as the sheriff maneuvered the jeep around the deputy's patrol car.

"Over to Huntsman's. I got some unfinished business there."

Cubiak had the Rec Room sealed off when Walter came up, a lit cigarette in hand.

"What're you doing?" he said.

"Something I probably should have done before."

Walter took a drag and tugged at the tape. "This 'cause of Agnes?"

"Yes."

"Is Joe dead?"

"Yes."

"She shoot him?"

"Someone did."

"What's that got to do with anything here?"

"I don't know. Maybe nothing, but I intend to find out." Cubiak double-checked the door. "Your mother home?" he said, motioning toward the house.

Walter nodded. "They're all here."

Cubiak heard the buzz of conversation from the mudroom, but when he appeared in the kitchen doorway the chatter stopped. Still in their sullied black, the three widows ringed the pine table. They were drawn and pale, their eyes red-rimmed, and their mouths pinched shut. A portrait at odds with the soft comfort of the room. Coffee cups and a plate of sandwiches were set out before them; the food was untouched, the cups half empty.

Cubiak took the chair at the head of the table, aware that he was usurping Walter's place. "Ladies, you've had a very trying day," he said.

Olive and Stella stared at their hands. Only Ida met his gaze. "Mr. Millard?" she said.

"Joe Millard is dead, shot. Presumably murdered."

Ida inhaled sharply but said nothing. The other two women slumped farther into their seats, as if trying to distance themselves from the news.

"You all heard what Agnes said at the church about the men being four of a kind." Cubiak spoke slowly, giving them time to reflect. "Do any of you know what she meant?"

"No." Ida's response was quick and firm.

Stella stifled a sob.

"Mrs. Wilkins?"

She lowered her head, refusing to meet his glance.

He turned toward Olive. "No," she said in the whisper of a frightened child.

Cubiak waited a moment. "I'm sorry to have had to intrude on this of all days. But if you think of anything that might be helpful, I'd appreciate hearing it. For now, I won't take any more of your time this afternoon. Thank you," he said as he stood.

At the back door, he shook hands with Walter. Following the brick path through the manicured yard, Cubiak ran through the encounter again: the women had stopped talking when they saw him and then avoided looking at each other when he asked about Agnes. They had lied to him. But about what and whether to protect themselves or their neighbor he didn't know. One thing he was sure of: they were hiding something.

TUESDAY AFTERNOON

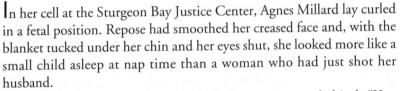

In her cell at the Sturgeon Bay Justice Center, Agnes Millard lay curled in a fetal position. Repose had smoothed her creased face and, with the blanket tucked under her chin and her eyes shut, she looked more like a small child asleep at nap time than a woman who had just shot her husband.

Cubiak watched her from the hall. Rowe came up behind. "You gonna book her?"

"I have no choice."

"Well, I got a call in to the judge about bail. Probably won't hear anything back until tomorrow."

"What about a lawyer?"

"She doesn't have one and says she doesn't need one."

"You told her I was coming to talk to her?"

"Yeah. This morning. She said that she expected as much."

Behind the one-way glass, Agnes shuddered and popped to a sitting position. Clutching the blanket, she opened her eyes and stared directly at the two men.

Rowe took a quick step back. "You know, sometimes I wonder if they can't really see us. You ever think that?"

More often than not, Cubiak thought. Not that he'd admit as much to his deputy. "You're imagining things," he said.

Agnes's hands fell to her lap. Instead of the blue cotton pants and top issued by the county jail, she wore the starched dress she'd had on at the funeral.

"What's that all about?" Cubiak said, trying to keep the criticism from his voice.

Rowe gestured helplessly. "I told her she had to change but she wouldn't. Said she won't wear pants. I ordered up a smock thing, you know, kinda like a dress, but it'll take a couple days. I didn't know what else to do."

"Okay, but send someone to bring something else down from her closet. The dress is evidence."

Through the intercom Cubiak gave Agnes five minutes' notice and then asked Rowe to bring them coffee.

"She drinks tea."

"Tea, then. And one coffee," he added, straightening his collar.

Cubiak took Agnes to the interview room and left her alone. While he waited for the deputy to return, he watched her through the remote ceiling camera. She exhibited none of the signs of nervousness and anxiety he would expect but sat motionless behind the speckled, vinyl table, almost catatonic in the small, windowless room. Nor did she react to the abrupt click that signaled his entrance.

As he sat down opposite her, Cubiak recited the time and date, and his name and that of the suspect for the recorder.

"I brought you something to drink," he said, sliding the cup of tea toward her.

Agnes looked up. Her eyes were a dull, flat green.

"I was out to the house. Your husband is dead."

"I told you that before," she said, tracing a circle near the cup with her finger. "I shot him."

"With the rifle I found lying on the floor?"

"Yes."

"Was it your husband's rifle or is it yours?"

"His. I don't own a gun."

"Why'd you shoot him?"

Agnes pried the lid from the cup and tented her fingers over the vapors. "I had my reasons."

"Would you care to share them?"

"No." She sipped the tea.

"If you tell me, maybe I can help."

Her nostrils flared. "I don't need your help."

"You'll have to tell your lawyer."

"I don't have a lawyer."

"The court will appoint an attorney. You need someone to represent you."

Agnes laid her palms flat and leaned toward Cubiak. Her skin was pallid and parchment thin. In the harsh lighting, spider webs of red veins spread across her cheeks. "I won't talk to any lawyer. There is no one on earth who can represent me to the true judge." She glanced at the ceiling. "You know who I mean?"

Cubiak had a good idea. "Then you may be facing two judges."

Agnes snorted.

"Were you just trying to scare Joe?"

She blinked. "No. I wanted to kill him."

"I see." Cubiak took a swallow of coffee and then set it back down. "Was your husband kind?"

Agnes almost smiled, as if he'd told a joke. "No. But that don't matter."

"You're a delicate woman . . ."

She looked flustered. "Ain't anyone ever called me that before . . ."

Cubiak went on as if he hadn't heard. "Joe looks like he was a pretty strong fellow. Did he abuse you? 'Knock you around' as people like to say?"

"No." She stiffened again, all hint of softness banished.

"How'd you get that?" The sheriff indicated the bruise over her eye.

"Feeding the dog. I was in a hurry to get away from the beast and forgot about the low branch by the porch."

Agnes spoke forcefully, daring him to dismiss her account, but Cubiak said nothing. Given what he'd seen of the dog, her story sounded credible. He'd check with Esther Smitz and the other neighbors about indications of other incidents, broken bones, loud arguments.

"You ever have to call the authorities?"

"The authorities?" She seemed genuinely puzzled.

"Dutch Schumacher or Leo Halverson, the former sheriffs."

"Why would I do that?"

"If things ever got out of hand at home."

"I take care of things myself."

Cubiak nodded. "Not much in the way of conveniences in your home. That Joe's idea or yours?"

"We considered ourselves sensible people."

"No phone."

"No one to call."

"Didn't even have a proper refrigerator."

She bit her lip. He'd hit a nerve.

"You must have known how easy some of your neighbors had it. You don't look like the kind of woman who gets jealous over nothing, but that was a pretty harsh existence you and Joe had."

"We lived according to our means."

"You worked?"

"Some. What I could get cleaning at the school and around."

"And Joe?"

"He did odd jobs here and there."

"He ever work for Huntsman's Plumbing?"

"One time or other, he would've. Worked for anyone who had a job and money to pay him."

"Including Eric Swenson and Jasper Wilkins?"

"Probably, I don't remember for sure."

"Are you from Gills Rock?"

"Yes, born and raised."

"And Joe?"

"He was born on Washington Island. His mother moved to Gills Rock with him and his brother after their father drowned. Went down on the *Steinbrenner* in Lake Superior."

"Must have been hard for her with two sons."

"Not for her it wasn't. Married again in a couple months."

"For the boys then."

Agnes shrugged. "Could be. Joe didn't like to talk about it."

"He wasn't the talking kind?"

"Not at home."

"What do you mean?"

"He never said much at home. What he said anywhere else I wouldn't know because I wasn't there."

Cubiak settled back and let Agnes enjoy her small victory.

"Gets lonely up there, I imagine," he said after a moment.

"For some maybe."

"Not for you?"

"I ain't complaining."

"Are you friends with any of the other women in the area? Ida Huntsman, for example. She lives right up the road."

Agnes pursed her mouth. "I cleaned Ida's toilets. I wasn't her friend."

"What about Olive Swenson and Stella Wilkins?"

"I cleaned for Olive, too, not regular, just sometimes. Not for Stella though. Stella does her own work." Her tone let him know that she thought better of Stella for that, money notwithstanding.

Why hadn't one of the three widows mentioned this to him? Did they consider it irrelevant or didn't they think of it?

"You didn't socialize with the ladies?"

"No. I said as much already." She tugged at the loose hairs on her neck, more dismayed about her relationship with the other women than with the killing of her husband.

"You're not a member of the book club, then?"

Agnes harrumphed. "I ain't never been asked. And wouldn't join if I was," she added.

"Why not? It's something to do."

She lifted her chin, defiantly. "I got plenty to do. I don't need that trash."

"Books are trash?"

Agnes ran her hands along the edge of the table as if searching for crumbs to brush off. "The kind those women read are. Romance novels." Disapproval in her voice. Agnes shifted her weight, and for a moment Cubiak thought she might stand and start pacing. Instead, she reached for the tea and drained the cup. "Bunch of nonsense, makes people want what they can't have."

Cubiak pictured the covers of the one or two romance novels he'd ever seen. He couldn't argue with her assessment. "How long were you and Joe married?"

"Thirty-nine years."

"Do you have any children?"

"No."

"May I ask you a personal question?"

Agnes made a harsh sound like a laugh. "Seems they're all personal."

"Did you love your husband?"

For the first time, the prisoner faltered. "I tried," she said finally, collapsing a little into herself.

"Why did you marry him?"

"Why? He asked me."

"Do you think he loved you?"

She mashed her lips into a thin line. "No. I know he didn't."

"Was he unfaithful?"

She closed her eyes and inhaled sharply.

"Why are you so certain your husband didn't love you?"

Agnes crossed herself and drew her folded hands to her flat bosom. "Our father, who art in heaven, hallowed be thy name . . ."

"What did you mean when you said Joe and the three men who were buried this morning were 'four of a kind'?"

The prisoner lowered her head, leaving Cubiak to stare at the cap of white hair and the even whiter ribbon of scalp that ran through the middle. "Thy will be done on earth as . . ."

"Is that what you were doing, Agnes, the will of God? Is that what you believe?"

"Give us this day . . ."

Cubiak got to his feet. "This interview is over," he said.

Rowe was waiting in the sheriff's office. "Doctor Pardy called, sir. Asked you to call her back."

"Sir?" Cubiak raised an eyebrow.

Rowe shrugged. "Something about funerals makes me mind my manners. Sir."

Cubiak waved the deputy out the door and phoned the medical examiner. The way Agnes had linked her husband to the other three men made him wonder if Millard hadn't been a frequent visitor to the Rec Room. Perhaps he'd even been at the cabin the night the others died.

"Dave, nothing you didn't already know. Joe Millard was killed at close range. Died instantly. I'll do the autopsy tomorrow but I don't expect to find anything of interest."

"You might."

"Really! Such as?"

"An unusually high level of carbon monoxide in the blood."

"You don't think . . ."

"I don't know what to think yet. Earlier at the church, his wife called Joe and the other three deceased men 'four of a kind.' I'm wondering what she meant."

WEDNESDAY  9

A two-masted schooner with a bottle-green hull sliced through the bay outside Cubiak's kitchen. Serene. Silent. Driven by the wind.

"Sir?"

Cubiak sighed. The sight of the large vessel so close to shore had distracted him from his conversation with his deputy. "Don't *sir* me," he said, pulling the phone cord along the wall.

"Yes, sir . . . Sheriff."

The day was magnificent, and the sloop's fore and aft sails billowed like artful clouds piled against the slate blue of the sky. Blue was the color of hope, Cubiak thought, and he hoped that his intuition was wrong.

"What are we supposed to be looking for?" Rowe said.

"Whatever there is to find. I went over the space heater with Walter but I'm no expert and as far as I can tell, neither is he. Maybe we missed something."

Cubiak reached for his coffee.

"That's why I want it checked out by people who know what they're doing. Get two men from the oldest heating companies in town and take them up to Huntsman's cabin. Not some junior flunkies. The head guys, the ones who've been around for a few years. Have them try and figure out how the cabin filled up with enough carbon monoxide to kill three men. Maybe it was squirrels, but if it was something else we need to know and soon." Cubiak gestured as he talked, dribbling coffee on his boots. "Dammit."

"What?"

"Nothing." The sheriff put the cup down and checked his shirt for stains. "And not a word to anyone. They report back to me."

"Yes, sir. Anything you say, boss."

Cubiak hung up and glanced out the window again. The boat was gone, leaving only sky and water. Either he'd imagined the sloop or it had moved on to the next dip in the scalloped shoreline. How easy it would be to maneuver up and down the coastline unseen. If he hadn't been home or the captain had kept to deeper water, the boat could have sailed past unnoticed.

Refilling his mug, he thought about the roll call of victims in Gills Rock. Huntsman. Wilkins. Swenson. And now Millard.

Four deaths. Three presumably accidental. The most recent deliberate, with the killer confessed. It could be unhappy coincidence that Joe Millard was shot dead three days after the others breathed the poisoned air, but Cubiak considered coincidence facile and likely to provide a simplistic solution to what was usually a complex situation. Even if the autopsy revealed traces of carbon monoxide in Millard's blood, what would that prove? That Joe had been in the cabin Friday night and had asphyxiated the others, or that he'd been lucky and left before he, too, succumbed to the toxic gas? Only to be shot by his wife the day of the funeral for reasons she wouldn't reveal. By itself, a measurable level of carbon monoxide in Millard's body wasn't enough to place him in the cabin the fateful night. It might just be an indication of a leaky exhaust system on his truck.

The phone rang.

"Yes?"

"We're leaving." It was Rowe characteristically reporting his every step.

"Good."

"Sir—I mean, Sheriff—why am I doing this?"

"To be thorough."

"Okay. Got it. Good. Later."

Cubiak didn't really expect the expedition to learn anything that would alter the circumstances in the Rec Room on the fateful night. Once the experts announced that they'd found nothing amiss, the blame for the first three deaths would be laid on the squirrels. And with Millard's death attributed to his wife, the matter would be shelved. In the meantime, the sheriff had other business to attend to that morning.

In a packed meeting room in Fish Creek, angry merchants demanded that Cubiak arrest the loiterers at Founders Square. The business owners did not take kindly to his explanation of why he could not. Merely sitting around in a public arena is not illegal, he told them. Nonetheless, he'd beefed up car and foot patrols and encouraged the shop owners to do their own positive loitering.

"If you get there first, they're not going to come and sit on your laps." A ripple of laughter. "And one more thing," Cubiak said. "Has anyone talked to them? They're all locals, the sons and daughters of people you've known your entire lives. Don't you wonder why they feel so alienated from the community?"

"Does it matter?" said Kathy O'Toole. The owner of the Woolly Sheep looked faint with fatigue; the dark circles under her eyes popped against the backdrop of her pale skin.

"I believe it does," he said.

Later, at the Sturgeon Bay Coast Guard Station, Cubiak met with Gary Dotson, who was almost as agitated as the Fish Creek shop owners. The chief didn't waste time on preliminaries.

"Everything's fine for the actual launch itself. I talked to the general manager at Palmer Johnson this morning and the cutter will be ready on schedule. Senator Adamas will be here—he sponsored the ship's commissioning—and his wife will do the honors with the champagne. Standard protocol. There's some talk the governor might attend as well. And why not? Sturgeon Bay is up to be designated a Coast Guard City, a first for Wisconsin. We'll have the mayor and all the local dignitaries. The shipyard will be open to visitors, and people will also be able to watch from the other side of the harbor. It's the ceremony here," he said, pointing out the window toward the lighthouse and the station grounds at the entrance to the canal, "that's got me worried."

"You don't have room for everyone?"

"No, that's not it. We had three thousand people here for the Tall Ships, so that's not the problem. Come with me."

Dotson led Cubiak to a small workroom where a couple dozen photos and several yellowed copies of *Stars and Stripes* lay on a table. "This is all we've got. I was told that there were boxes of material from the Aleutian Campaign in our storage room but we haven't found much. Either someone was mistaken or the stuff has been misplaced. We looked everywhere. It's been a long time and things can go missing. This photographer Charles Tweet was up there shooting for a while and he sent me some stuff, and I'd planned to ask the three old gents themselves for any souvenirs, letters, et cetera that they might have. Now I'll have to ask their widows, but I hate to impose at such a time. The folks at the Maritime Museum are doing their best to help out as well, and of course eventually the exhibit goes on display there. I'm just worried that the overall effect is going to be far less impressive than what we'd hoped for and what the men deserved."

Dotson turned toward the window and stood at parade rest, his legs apart, his shoulders tense, and his hands clasped waist-high behind his back. The station was eerily still but for the muted crash of waves against the concrete pier that ran out into the lake. Cubiak waited.

"Yesterday at the funeral you asked me if there was something else going on," Dotson said after a pause. "I told you there wasn't, but you were right, Sheriff. In fact, there's something I need to show you."

Back in his office, the chief pulled a manila folder from a locked file drawer and scattered the contents on his desk.

"They're all addressed to me," he said, surveying the six small envelopes that littered the blotter. He handed one to Cubiak. "Here, read it."

Inside was a handwritten message scrawled in a mix of crude penmanship and printing and spelled out on a sheet of coarse, lined tablet paper. "No honor for dishonorable vets. Fuck all three."

"And the rest?" Cubiak said.

"They're all pretty much along the same lines. Mean and nasty and aimed at Huntsman and his pals."

"They come from all over the state," Cubiak said, checking the postmarks.

"Yes. Some from towns I never even heard of."

"When did this start?"

"First one came in September. Last one in November."

"You have any idea what this is about?"

The chief returned to the window but this time stood with his back to glass. "No idea. I've never heard a word uttered against any of those three men. Someone's got a grudge, but who or why, I don't know."

"You think it's linked to the missing archives?"

Dotson shrugged. "I don't even know that there's anything really missing. Someone could have been cleaning up twenty years ago and thrown the stuff away." He tapped the desk. "Funny thing, they almost always arrived on a Monday."

Cubiak looked at the envelopes again. "None of them were posted in Door County."

"No, nothing closer than Stevens Point."

"You mind if I take these with me?" the sheriff said, gathering up the letters.

"Be my guest. I'd rather never see them again if you want to know the truth. It's just . . . I wonder what this means for the ceremony."

"Probably nothing. But if it does mean something, whoever sent these did you a favor."

"A favor? Sheriff, I . . ."

"We'll both be on guard, and that's better than being caught unaware."

On the way out, they passed the dining room where two men were busy with rollers and paint. "Didn't Rogers Nils work here, helping with the painting?"

"He did. Started sometime after Christmas. Then one day in February, he left and never came back. Too bad. He's a hard worker. Nice kid, too."

It was ten past three when Cubiak got back to headquarters and found Rowe in the conference room with the two HVAC installers. The men, thick bodied and ruddy, were drinking Cokes and bantering back and forth with the deputy. When Cubiak entered the room, the men both stopped talking and sat grasping the soft drink cans in hands that were rough and discolored by their work. Rowe introduced them and explained that they'd spent nearly an hour inspecting Huntsman's space heater. "They went over it inch by inch, Sheriff," the deputy said.

"And?"

The bearded man, who looked the older of the two by a few years, spoke up. "It's an old unit. Not up to code. It looked alright when we checked it out but I'm guessing Huntsman had trouble with it at some point 'cause he replaced the vent pipe with his own jerry-rigged system."

Cubiak remembered that the vent pipe had looked new. "What do you mean 'jerry-rigged'?" he said.

"The valve or damper has an external control. A knob on the underside of the line, down near the floor."

"Was the valve open or closed?"

"Oh, it was open."

"You're sure?"

The second man cupped his chin and nodded.

"Any chance the valve could have closed by itself?"

"I don't know, Sheriff. The wing nut that holds the knob in place is kinda loose but not really likely. Anyways, it was open. And if it had closed then how'd it open up again?"

"Maybe someone kicked the knob when they were trying to get the men out."

The bearded man shrugged. "Anything's possible, Sheriff."

Cubiak looked at the second installer. "Maybe," he said, skepticism evident in his voice.

"And the pipe itself was clear?"

"That's right, no obstructions. We checked that first thing," the younger man said.

Cubiak figured the men had heard about the leaves in the vent but he repeated the story. "So you think it could have been squirrels?" he said.

"Yeah. Could be."

"Happens."

"An accident then?"

The installers nodded in unison.

"Can't see it any other way," the older man said. "Damned thing is, if they'd had a carbon monoxide detector in there this never would have happened."

"So, it's squirrels then?" Rowe said when he came back from seeing the men to the door.

"We can't rule out problems with the valve, and the possibility that it was deliberately closed and then reopened. Which means we need to identify everyone who had been there Friday night or who might have had a key to the cabin. Ida claims she didn't but she could be lying. Same goes for the other two women. And then there's Walter."

"But motive, sir? For murder?"

"I don't know. But if the unit was deliberately tampered with, it had to have been done by someone with access to the cabin."

"That makes all the card players suspects, too," Rowe said.

"Especially someone who lost big. There's Agnes as well. We have nothing to connect her to the deaths of the three vets. But she's admitted to killing her husband and she referred to them as a unit—four of a kind. Why? If she had reason to murder one, would she have had motivation to murder all of them? Or the means? Like the other women, she says she didn't have a key but if Joe did, she could have found it."

Rowe tugged at his cuffs. "Right. So what do I do?"

Cubiak looked at his deputy. Rowe was a good cop who knew the rules and was fierce about enforcement, but he lacked the experience and instinct to follow a trail of clues, especially one so fractured and disjointed.

"I'll be out of the office a lot the next few days. I'll need someone to tend the store," he said.

Rowe nearly saluted. "You got it, sir."

Heading home, Cubiak detoured to Walter Nils's garage. A-One Auto Repair was on the city's west side, sandwiched between a self-service laundry and a hardware store. Walter conducted business far from the waterfront and trappings of a resort community, and business looked good. Several cars and an SUV crowded the small lot. Three more vehicles were lined up inside the dim interior, a high-ceilinged room piled with tires and smelling of axle grease and cigar smoke.

"Anybody here?" Cubiak called out.

A pair of scuffed work boots emerged from beneath a black Volvo as Walter rolled out from under the carriage. When he was free of the vehicle, he scrambled to his feet. Grime streaked his coveralls.

"Sheriff," he said. The mechanic wiped his hand on a frayed rag and started to extend his hand and then thought better of it. "Sorry. Goes with the territory. One of the reasons my second wife left. Said she hated dirty fingernails."

Walter laughed but Cubiak wasn't sure if he was joking.

"I'll be quick."

"This still about what happened up there, at the cabin?" Walter said. He didn't clarify if he meant the deaths or the graffiti and Cubiak didn't ask.

"Right. Routine business. I need the names of the men who were regulars at the poker games. Not going all the way back but the recent players."

"Oh god, Sheriff. I don't know. They come and go. Besides, I'm hardly up there. You'd have to ask my mother and even then, I'm not sure she'd be able to tell you. What's this about anyways?"

Cubiak ignored the question. "Another thing: who would your father call if he needed any work done around the place?"

This time Walter's laugh was genuine. "No one. He did everything himself. Prided himself on self-sufficiency."

The sheriff studied the array of tools above the workbench. "He installed the space heater?"

"No doubt."

"And he'd take care of any repairs?"

"Probably."

"He never thought to update it? Get a newer model?"

"Big Guy prided himself on keeping things running. As long as the heater worked, he'd use it. Why?"

"Nothing particular. Looks like you got your hands full here. Roger ever help you out?"

"He comes by every once in a while, but only to work on his old junk."

"Does he live with you?"

"Used to. Got his own place in Valmy this winter. He'll sleep upstairs if he's been out with the boys and doesn't want to make the drive." Walter rubbed his dirty hands on his soiled pants. "What's all this about Roger?"

"Curious, I guess. I like him, just trying to figure out why he left school."

"Yeah, well, I sure as hell don't know. We had plenty of arguments about it, too. But he's a good kid. Just a little lost. Don't worry about Roger. He'll be okay."

THURSDAY  10

Under a leaden sky, the air was chilled and the grass blanketed with a heavy dew that sent its cold wetness seeping through the soles of Cubiak's shoes as he crossed the Huntsmans' lawn in midmorning. A vast emptiness prevailed over the estate, mirrored by the flat open reaches of the wide bay. The gazebo furniture was stacked in a heap. At the dock, the vandalized boats were shrouded in ghostly off-white tarps. The only sound was the distant drone of a boat motoring north into deeper waters.

Approaching the house, Cubiak caught the faint aroma of cinnamon. Ida was waiting in the mudroom. Her manner was cheerful, and in contrast to the gloomy outdoors, she wore lipstick and a bright flowered bib apron over a pink shirt. "Come in, Sheriff. You're just in time. They've cooled off enough to eat," she said as he dropped his jacket over an empty peg. In the kitchen she motioned toward the table and then set down a mug of steaming coffee and two pastries layered with a thick coat of icing.

"They're messy, you'll need this," Ida said, handing him a napkin and fork. She waited until he took a bite before she lifted her apron over her head and claimed her spot near the window.

"Good?"

"Delicious," Cubiak said around a mouthful of viscous sugar. He felt like a kid again, sitting at a chipped red-and-gray formica table dunking one of his mother's brittle peanut butter cookies in a glass of milk while she argued with his father in the next room.

"You said you needed to tell me something," Ida said, bringing him back to the cozy yellow kitchen.

"Yes, about the space heater."

"Oh." Her spirits seemed to sag.

In vague terms he explained what he'd learned from the furnace installers. "It may not mean anything but I need to look into this further."

"Of course," she said.

Ida tried to sound complacent but a thin worry line creased her forehead, and Cubiak remembered that her brow had been similarly furrowed the morning he'd met her, the morning her husband and his friends had been found dead in the cabin. "Have you had any more trouble?" he said.

"No. I told you, it was nothing. Just some kids." Again Ida pretended nonchalance but there was something guarded in her tone.

"It's possible someone had a grudge against your husband or one of the other men," Cubiak said.

"They were good men, Sheriff. Civic leaders. They won awards for their work in the community. Why would anyone have a grudge?" Ida's voice was fueled with indignity.

"Even good men have enemies," he said. Then, after a pause, he added, "Perhaps one of the men who played poker with them. Do you know who they were?"

"Lots of men were invited to the games." Ida carried the empty cup and plate to the sink. "Big Guy would mention a name now and then but it wasn't something I paid much attention to."

"Not even the regulars?"

"I'm sure I can come up with a name or two, but it won't be much," she said.

"I'd like a list of clients, as well." Cubiak spoke over the sound of the running water.

Ida abruptly shut the faucet. "What in heaven's name for?"

"Routine. Maybe there's a disgruntled customer."

"I don't see the point of it. Big Guy didn't have disgruntled clients." She dried her hands on a striped dish towel. "Eric and Jasper were independent businessmen, as well. I assume you're following the same line of reasoning with them." She tossed the towel on the counter, not waiting for an answer. "You realize you're not making this any easier for me. For any of us."

Cubiak started to apologize but Ida cut him off.

"I'll have the names for you this afternoon, card players and customers." She smiled, but he thought the smile was forced.

As he pulled away, Cubiak thought about Ida's reaction to her husband's death. Her apparent calm acceptance, her alacrity in removing his clothing from the house, her lack of concern about the graffiti and the disparagement of Huntsman's name and reputation. She seemed to have readily accepted his death. Was it her age or religion that comforted her in the face of loss? Perhaps she was in shock or denial. Or the pain of loss was too intense to confront directly. People grieved in different ways and were not to be judged by anyone, certainly not by someone like him who'd made of mess of his own mourning.

The road leading away from the Huntsmans' estate was deserted. At Esther and Clyde Smitz's tidy house, the shades were pulled against the larger world. Next door, the Millards' rundown cottage was ringed by yellow police tape. In the front yard, the willow tree looked barren without the heavy chain that had encircled its trunk. What had become of the dog? It was hard to imagine anyone wanting that nasty creature.

Cubiak followed the long curve of the highway through Gills Rock and east toward the ferry dock. The Swensons' driveway appeared a quarter mile after the bend, allowing him to turn off before he reached the elaborate Bavarian lodge that Cate's grandfather had built for the family. Would Cate stay at The Wood if she came up from Milwaukee for Bathard's wedding? He couldn't imagine her returning to Ruby's house. Did she still blame him for what happened to her aunt? There was so much he needed to know.

The lane to Olive's house wound through thick woods like the entrance to Cate's grandparents' grand summer home. And just as The Wood spoke of money, so, too, did the Swensons' residence, though the structure of steel and glass was as strikingly modern as the other was old-fashioned.

A red Mercedes convertible sat outside the garage. Cubiak rang the bell and Olive opened the door immediately, as if she'd been standing inside, waiting.

"Sheriff, how nice of you to come," she said. She wore intense makeup and a dark purple tunic over flowing black trousers. Her thick, smoky perfume stung his eyes. She held out a hand and in the other grasped a blue tumbler half full of a pale yellow liquid. The ice cubes in the glass tinkled as she led him from the vaulted entrance and through a wide hall hung with yellow and red tapestries. Her stiff, studied steps indicated that this wasn't her first drink of the day. Past a gourmet kitchen they went down two steps into a room that overlooked a copse of firs and the waters of Death's Door. Olive waved Cubiak toward a low, leather chair angled toward the massive windows. From one of the trees, a hawk flew up on silent wings.

"Anything for you, Dave?" she said as she refreshed her drink at a liquor table along the far wall.

"No, thank you. I'm on duty."

"Of course." Olive floated past him and dropped into an upholstered love seat. "I had an early appointment at the hairdresser's in Green Bay. Can't get anything decent done around here," she said as she ran her fingers up the side of her neck and into the soft folds of her fresh cut.

"I wouldn't know."

"Of course not. Men." She tried to sound nonchalant. "You're here to talk about Eric."

"All three of them, actually."

Olive set her glass on a low table. "Ida called and told me about the space heater. But that doesn't mean anything, does it? It was still an accident, right?"

Cubiak wondered if her urgent undertone stemmed from concern about the nature of her husband's passing or the disposition of an accidental death insurance policy. "Most likely, yes."

"Most likely? But maybe not?"

"There's the possibility someone wanted to harm Eric and his friends."

Olive dismissed the notion with a quick shake of her head. "You wouldn't say that if you knew Eric. He was a complete milquetoast, always anxious to please. Everyone loved him. My husband was the ultimate Mister Nice Guy, Sheriff. The only one with reason to hate him was me."

She challenged him with a look but he said nothing. Death sometimes prompted people to open up about circumstances they would normally not reveal, and Olive seemed ready to talk. In one sweeping movement, she grabbed her glass and rose from the couch. Cubiak waited. At the window, Olive threw her head back and shivered. Then she took a long pull on the drink and began to pace.

"You wouldn't know it to see me now, Dave, but I was quite the looker. I could have had any man on the peninsula."

"And you chose Eric," Cubiak said, his tone encouraging.

"Why not? Why wouldn't I? I was the prom queen one year and Miss Door County the next. Eric was eleven years older than me and the best-looking man on the peninsula. Unlike the silly boys I'd known in school, he was sophisticated and charming. A war hero. Handsome in his uniform. When he smiled, the world stopped just to take it in. He was the most fun and the best dancer, too. I thought we'd have a wonderful life together, like his parents and mine. They were happy here. Eric knew I wanted children, but he'd been hurt in the war and the odds were against his ever fathering a child. When things between us got serious, he told me about the injury and what it meant—he gave me a chance to back out but I wouldn't hear of it. I was headstrong and naïve. I thought he was being noble! I thought we'd figure something out, I thought that if we loved each other enough, nothing else mattered."

She hunched her shoulders and began to cry.

"You don't have to . . . ," Cubiak said, hoping she would.

Olive straightened, defiant again. "I want to. I've kept quiet about things too long. With a little help." She swirled her glass, the ice cubes clinking, and then turned to the window again as if telling her sad story to the trees was easier. "There was more to it, however. The injury also affected his ability to perform." She almost choked on the word. "For a long time we got by on hand holding and hugs. Innocent kisses and sweet endearments. He called me 'Doll' and was gallant, to a fault, especially in public. All the women adored him. My friends burned with envy. After a while he stopped bothering with the niceties when we were alone. At home I became as invisible as air. He spent most of his time working or out with his friends, came and went as he pleased. So I started to do the same. Eventually, I learned to get by with the occasional lover, the casual affair. I'm not proud of what I did but not ashamed. It was either that or go mad, and I was halfway there already."

The silence of the confessional pulled the walls in. Cubiak lowered his eyes, like a priest burdened with heavy secrets. "You never discussed the situation with anyone?"

"No."

"Not even your mother?"

Olive sniggered. "My mother would have told me to bear my cross with dignity and the love of the Lord."

Which is probably what the priest would have said, Cubiak thought. "Your friends?"

"Never! *That* wasn't a topic of conversation for any of us. We talked cookies and diets, drapery fabrics and chicken recipes, what we were giving our husbands for Christmas."

"Your physician? There may have been alternatives . . ."

"That dear sweet man who sometimes went fishing on Eric's boat? How could I? At first, I didn't want to embarrass my husband or make him feel lacking. For god's sake, he was wounded defending his country! After a while, after all those years, who cared anymore? I read silly romance novels with Ida and Stella and waited for time to take its toll. We all wear down eventually, Sheriff."

Olive poured another drink. She seemed distracted, and Cubiak sensed that there was more she wasn't telling him. If he was wrong, she'd sit down and the conversation would be over. If he was right and the alcohol was liquid courage, she'd remain on her feet and keep talking.

Olive sucked greedily at her drink and then walked back to the window. She stood motionless for a long while, her forehead pressed to the thick pane. Suddenly she straightened and whirled around. "Damn that Agnes," she said, flinging the empty tumbler to the floor. The glass thudded and for several seconds the walls echoed the sound of the cylinder rolling across the wood.

"Agnes Millard?" Cubiak couldn't help himself.

"Yes, Agnes, that dried up old hag."

"What did Agnes do?"

"She opened her big mouth and spoiled everything. It was last December, two weeks before Christmas. Ida, Stella, and I were listening to carols and baking cookies at Ida's house. She and Big Guy hosted a community party every year on Christmas Eve, and Agnes was there cleaning. Ida had packed up a tin of cookies for her. There were some books on the counter that we'd read recently and when Agnes was finished, Ida asked her if she'd like to take them as well. Agnes got all huffy. She said that the books were nonsense and that she didn't need any of that stuff. 'Joe don't bother me none, because of the war injury,' she said, 'and I don't need to be teased into wanting something I can't have.'

"When she left, the three of us stood there in our silly red aprons trying not to look at each other—the cold ugly truth staring each of us in the face. Ida spoke first. I remember her voice being very quiet. 'Terrence's got one of those, too,' she said. Then Stella started laughing almost as if it was some kind of inside joke. I wanted to laugh, too, but Stella was already shrieking, almost hysterical. 'Yes, yes, the war injury,' she said. And when they finally looked at me, all I could do was cry."

The color had drained from Olive's face and she swayed, steadying herself against the wall.

Cubiak helped her back to the sofa and poured a glass of water from a pitcher on the tray. Then he took his seat and waited again.

After a while, Olive clasped her hands and leaned forward, pressing her balled fists between her knees. "We're not stupid women, Sheriff, but we sure were naïve. One man, yes. I'm sure it happened. But three—four, if you include Joe—all with the same story? We tried to rationalize that this lie, this excuse, was cover for interest in other women, but we didn't get very far with that argument. Suddenly, everything that had been going on for all those years made sense. The overnight poker games. The camping trips. The fishing expeditions to Canada. For a while it seemed they went moose hunting every winter.

"That afternoon, over cookies, I think we all figured out the truth. Again and again, the three of them plus one. Joe wasn't the first, that's for sure. Seems there was always the extra. But ultimately to have to settle for Joe Millard? Couldn't they do any better than him?"

She looked at Cubiak defiantly. "What they did was wrong but, well, at least it's not a crime, is it?"

"No, it's not a crime." Not now. But there was a time . . . Cubiak was stunned. The pieces were falling into place but not the way he'd expected. He waited and then he asked the question he couldn't avoid. "Did you kill your husband and his friends?"

Olive looked up, astonished, and shook her head. "I wish I had. Eric used me. I was his cover, his façade. I gave him the respectability he craved and needed. He stole my life so he could have the life he wanted. If you want to know the truth, I'm glad he's dead. I only wish he'd died sooner."

Cubiak wasn't sure he believed her claim of innocence. Of the four women, only Agnes could have killed Joe. But any one of them, including Olive, had enough motive and possibly the means to kill the other three.

Olive stood. "I need some coffee," she said.

The Swensons' kitchen gleamed with stainless steel appliances and ceramic tiles of slate and white against oyster-colored walls. Cubiak sat on a high stool at the island and watched Olive work. She was efficient and calm; he took a cue from her demeanor and continued his questioning in a businesslike fashion.

"How long was Joe the fourth man?"

"Two or three years."

"And before him?"

"I don't recall. It started with just the three of them, and I thought it was so sweet the way they stayed together. Childhood friends, war buddies and all. Then the fourth man started appearing. I don't know when, twenty years ago, probably more."

He'd have to ferret out the names. If Huntsman, Swenson, and Wilkins had been murdered, all their close male acquaintances were potential suspects. "Your husband's business, how did he get his customers? Through advertising?"

Olive sat down across from him. "Most of the clientele were referred by the owners of the big resorts." She named a dozen prominent businessmen.

Cubiak recognized them all. Civic leaders, like the three dead men, and potential suspects, as well.

Half an hour and half a pot of coffee later, Cubiak left Olive to her memories and misery. In Gills Rock, he called Bathard. It was going to be a longer day than he realized, Cubiak explained, and he needed someone to look after the pups. Especially Kipper. He started explaining how she needed to be fed when Bathard interrupted. "I'm a doctor. I think I can figure it out," he said.

Stella Wilkins lived two miles south of the fishing village, and the farm she'd operated with her late husband took up a generous portion of the landscape along the way. Cubiak passed carefully tilled fields waiting to be planted and herds of Holsteins and sheep grazing in separate pastures. A long gravel driveway ran between a stretch of low white wooden fence to the farmstead where a new metal barn and seven sleek silos caught the rays of the late-appearing afternoon sun. A neatly landscaped yard surrounded the old red brick farmhouse, and on the front porch Stella waited, hugging a long brown cardigan to her rigid, slim frame. Her mouth was set, and deeply chiseled lines laced her face like roads on a map.

"Olive called," she said as Cubiak made his way up the stone walk. Before he could respond, she turned and entered the house. With quick, stilted steps she led the sheriff through rooms filled with Shaker furniture and into the kitchen to a round oak table in the corner where two large windows met to offer a nearly one-hundred-eighty-degree view of the garden and the rolling countryside beyond.

"Please," she said, nodding to an empty chair. Despite knowing the nature of his visit, she served slices of pumpkin bread and poured coffee while Cubiak took in the fine-crafted cherry cabinets and designer appliances, the kind he and Lauren had coveted but couldn't afford when they'd talked about remodeling.

"You know about the potential problem with the space heater?" he said.

Stella nodded.

"That morning when your husband and his friends were found dead and you said, 'They killed him,' you meant Olive and Ida, didn't you?"

Stella's eyes grew moist. She nodded again.

"Why?"

"Because of what we learned from Agnes last Christmas," she said, turning her head away.

"Do you still think Ida and Olive killed your husband?"

"No. I think Agnes did it." Stella's composure crumpled as she looked back toward Cubiak. "She's a murderer, isn't she? She's confessed to shooting Joe, and if she killed him then she probably killed the other three as well. She started all this!"

"With her talk about Joe's war injury?"

"Yes." Stella flushed with anger.

Cubiak sipped his coffee. When Agnes threw open Pandora's box, he was sure she didn't realize what she was doing. Based on what he knew, Joe's killing was a spontaneous act of rage. From the beginning, he'd assumed that Agnes didn't understand the true nature of the men's involvement until the day of the funeral. But what if he was wrong and she'd known all along? Stella could be right, but he remained unconvinced.

"There are other possibilities," he said finally.

"What do you mean?"

"It seems that none of you three women knew much about the card games at the cabin. Your husbands could have been running a high-stakes poker ring and been killed by someone who'd lost big and owed more than he could pay back."

Stella scorned the idea. "Impossible. None of them were any good at cards. Poker was just an excuse for their parties and get-togethers."

The sheriff made a point of surveying the room again and studying the landscape outside the window. "You live well and own a lot of prime farmland. It takes a considerable amount of money to support this kind of comfortable lifestyle."

Stella glared. "We worked hard. We were lucky."

"Luckier than most."

She shrugged.

"Olive said that the three of you women never discussed the intimate details of marriage."

"That's right, we didn't. Not like these women who go on television and blurt out the family secrets. We weren't like that. For us, it was just too private. The one time I asked Ida if she wanted another child, she got flustered and said that she and Terrence couldn't have kids. I was pregnant at the time and it seemed cruel to ask why. Neither of us ever brought the subject up again."

Stella fell silent, as if debating how much more to reveal. Finally she continued. "I was the eldest of six girls, Sheriff. Five beauties and me. I was the one who wasn't supposed to get married, much less have a baby, so you can imagine that I was immensely grateful when Jasper asked me to marry him. After a while, things between us became intermittent and eventually tapered off. Jasper blamed residual trauma. I remained quiet about the whole business and gave thanks for what I had."

"You didn't kill your husband or join in with the other two women in murdering the three of them?"

Stella inhaled sharply. "No. I have an alibi. We all do!"

"Indeed, but it's one you provide for each other. I assume no one else was at book group that evening?"

"No, but Olive ordered our dinner at the Sunset Café."

Cubiak nodded. "And when she picked up your order she probably told Mabel or whoever waited on her that you ladies were meeting that evening."

"I'm sure she did. We had nothing to hide."

Cubiak let the comment be. "Were you ever able to reach your son?" he said.

"Martin? Yes, he left a message saying he'd be here as soon as he could."

"When he gets back, tell him I'd like to see him."

On the way out Cubiak led the way and Stella followed. As he passed the family room, a large photo of a young man in cap and gown caught his attention. "Martin?"

"Yes."

Alongside the portrait hung dozens of other photos that documented the early years of the Wilkinses' only child. Martin had been a high school wrestling champion. In one picture, he and Walter Nils stood side by side clutching twin trophies. "Martin and Walter are the same age?"

"Walter is three years older than our son." Stella looked at Cubiak. "Martin *is* our son. It's possible, you know." Chin up, she laughed bitterly. "We were a family. The ultimate sham."

By the time Cubiak made his way back to Ida's house, heavy cloud cover blotted out the sun and the air smelled of fish, not cinnamon rolls. Ostensibly he'd come for the two lists of names she'd promised, but more importantly he knew the three women would have talked by now and he was anxious to see if Ida's demeanor had altered.

"Come in," Ida said when he knocked.

Big Guy's widow sat at the kitchen table, her hands folded on top of a typed sheet of paper. The morning's warmth and sweet aroma had seeped from the room just as the softness had vanished from Ida's face. Her mouth was set and her eyes hard.

"Now you know," she said.

Cubiak lingered inside the doorway. She had not invited him to sit down.

"Why didn't you say anything about Agnes when I was here after the funeral?"

"It didn't seem relevant."

"Even after she accosted you and Olive and Stella? Even when you knew that she'd shot Joe?"

"It was her place to say why she did those things, not mine to speculate."

"You may think that, but in a murder investigation information of any kind can be useful." He took several steps into the room. "May I sit down?"

Ida dipped her head slightly.

In the heavy silence, Ida uncurled her hands and laid them flat as if bracing herself for what was to come. "Do you think Agnes killed my husband and the others?" she said after a moment.

"No."

"I see."

He waited. "Do you think Olive or Stella could have done it?"

Ida looked up. "I can't speak for my friends. You'll have to ask them yourself, Sheriff."

"I did, and they both denied any involvement. What about you, Ida? Did you kill Big Guy and his boyhood friends?"

Ida smirked. "Why? Because they were homosexuals? No, I did not."

"You weren't angered then, by what you'd learned last December?"

"Surprised, yes, but not angry. I had long suspected that something was going on."

"But you said nothing to your closest friends?"

"I couldn't have imagined doing so. What if I was wrong? Think of the embarrassment."

"You and Big Guy were married for more than five decades. That's a long time to go without physical intimacy. Didn't you resent all you'd missed?"

The familiar softness returned to Ida's face as she relaxed against the back of the chair. "I can see where you might think that but it wasn't like that at all. I have my memories and a good imagination, and I used them both when I had to. Sex isn't everything. And I had Walter to care for. You don't understand, Sheriff. You can't begin to know what it was like for me. I was just seventeen and pregnant when my husband was killed in the war. In the government's eyes I was a widow entitled to a few dollars, but in reality I was a scared kid with nothing. I had no education. No job. And no place to call home."

"You had your family. Couldn't you . . ."

"My family! They were the worst. I'm not going to sit here and resurrect my childhood nightmares for you. But I will tell you this: Christian Nils rescued me from my family, and I couldn't—I wouldn't—crawl back to them, not even with a baby. I had no one and no decent options. Terrence marrying me was like a miracle, an answer to all my prayers. He saved us, me and Walter. That's all I cared about."

Ida looked at Cubiak. "You don't believe me?" She pulled a small notepad and pencil stub from her pocket and scrawled something on the top sheet. "Here's your lists and an address. Take a good look where I live now and then go there and see what I came from."

Cubiak folded the paper. "You were his cover."

"Yes, and he was my salvation." She frowned and then brightened. "Maybe Agnes didn't kill them. Maybe no one did. Accidents do happen."

Cubiak blinked back vivid memories of the hit-and-run that had killed his wife and daughter. "I know," he said.

FRIDAY

11

Cubiak walked into headquarters balancing three large lattes on a cardboard tray. A chai tea brew for Agnes, vanilla for Lisa, and plain for himself. In exchange for her drink Lisa handed him four messages. Two complaints about barking dogs, a dispute over a backyard fence line, and a reminder from the local crackpot that the end was near. Cubiak tossed the last note in the trash, put the others on Rowe's desk with a Post-it that read "Look into. No rush," and carried the remaining two cups through the lobby to the cellblock.

Door County treated its incarcerated guests well. Prisoners ate nutritious meals, slept on firm mattresses, and lived in freshly painted and tidy quarters. They had access to television, playing cards, and counseling services. Some even commuted to local day jobs. In Cell 6, Agnes Millard perched on the edge of her bed wearing the orange shift that Rowe had special-ordered. The garment hung from her shoulders as she hunched over the Bible that lay open on her lap. She'd asked to be allowed to have the book and Cubiak had seen no reason to object.

"Good morning, Agnes."

The prisoner continued reading.

"Morning," Cubiak said again.

Agnes put a finger on the page to hold her spot and looked up. "Sheriff."

"I have hot tea waiting. I thought we could talk a little more this morning. You can bring that with you," he said, indicating the Bible.

In the interview room, Cubiak held the chair out for Agnes and then slid the chai toward her.

She glared at the drink as if it were toxic.

"Go on."

After a moment's hesitation, she took a sip. Her eyes widened. "This ain't tea. What is it?"

"It's a special kind of tea. There's steamed milk in it."

Agnes pressed her mouth to the lid. "I ain't never had one of these," she said, almost smiling.

Cubiak gave her time to enjoy the hot, sweet drink before he activated the video recorder and announced the formal start of the interview, identifying date and time and those present.

His actions startled the prisoner. She set the cup down and looked at him as if he'd betrayed her by ending the party.

"Last week you confessed to killing your husband but you refused to give a reason for your action. I believe I have a clearer understanding of the situation now," Cubiak said.

Agnes bristled.

"Joe was sexually involved with other men, specifically with your neighbor Terrence Huntsman and his longtime friends Eric Swenson and Jasper Wilkins. When I got here this morning, you were reading the Bible. There are some who believe the Good Book condemns homosexuality as an abomination." He paused. "I feel I have reason to count you among them."

Cubiak reached for the holy book. "May I?"

She let him take it.

"You know what I'm looking for, don't you?" he said as he turned the tissue-thin pages. "The book of Leviticus. Chapter eighteen, verse twenty-two." He paused and waited for a reaction but Agnes remained stoic. In the best preacher's tone he could muster, he read, "'If a man also lie with mankind, as he lieth with a woman, both of them have committed an abomination: they shall surely be put to death; their blood shall be upon them.'"

Cubiak set the Bible down, open to the page. "I don't imagine you have to look, do you? That's one passage you know by heart. In fact, you probably know a large portion of the Good Book by heart."

He nudged the tome toward Agnes but she continued to stare past him.

"You shot your husband because you thought you were fulfilling the scriptures. You thought you were doing the work of the Lord.

"I saw you in church that morning, sitting a couple of rows behind Joe. Everyone in the church went to communion, including the two of you. I was raised Catholic. I know how it goes. You can eat the consecrated bread and drink the blessed wine only if you're in a state of grace. So both of you had been to confession beforehand."

Cubiak stood and leaned forward, towering over the prisoner.

"You shot Joe to save his soul."

"Yes," Agnes screamed, her spittle hitting his chin. "I shot Joe to save him from temptation. I shot my husband to save him from sinning again."

"And by doing so, you sacrificed your own soul."

Agnes grabbed the Bible and clutched it to her chest.

"Or has God forgiven you?"

She snatched his wrist. "You understand!" she cried, her eyes pleading with him.

"I understand the laws of men," he said, loosening her calloused grip.

"The laws of men!" she said and kicked at the floor.

"They are based on God's law." Cubiak sat down again and gentled his voice. "'Thou shall not kill.'"

Agnes looked at him, and then she turned away and lowered her head. "I will pray for you."

For several minutes her soft whisperings were the only sound in the room.

When Cubiak interrupted, his tone was firm and official. "Did you kill Terrence Huntsman, Eric Swenson, and Jasper Wilkins?"

Agnes wheeled toward him. "No!"

"But you wish you had."

"They got what they deserved." Her face flushed with anger.

The exact words used in the hateful note to Ida.

"You sent the anonymous letter."

"What letter?"

Her puzzlement seemed genuine.

"You defaced the shed."

"No. I didn't do that! I heard it was kids. You know, being mean. Kids are nasty these days, Sheriff, not like before."

"Something I don't understand, Agnes. When exactly did you discover the nature of the relationship between Joe and the other three men?"

"The morning of the funeral." Agnes yanked the lid off the cup and picked at the rim. "When we came back from the cemetery I didn't see Joe anywheres and figured maybe he was in the church basement helping set up for the lunch. I'd forgotten the salad I'd made for the luncheon so I went back to get it. When I walked into the house, I heard men's voices in the living room. They were talking dirty and laughing. I knew one of them was Big Guy. It didn't make sense. He was dead. I tiptoed through the kitchen to the doorway and saw my husband sitting on the couch watching that filth on the television. The four of them."

Her voice caught. "Joe was crying, sobbing like a baby."

The shards from the paper cup were scattered across the table. Agnes gathered them into a neat pile and nudged it over the edge, waiting for the pieces to settle on the floor before she went on.

"I ran to the VCR and pulled out the tape. Joe tried to get it away. I shoved him and we started fighting and he punched me in the face, here"—she pointed to her bruised eye—"and I fell into the couch. I must have laid there a minute or so, and when I sat up he was kneeling in front of the VCR player trying to put it back in. That's when I went and got the rifle and shot him."

"And the tape?"

"I burned it."

Cubiak blinked and remembered the thin plume of smoke rising from the trash barrel behind the garage. "Were there more tapes?"

"No."

"You looked?"

"Yes."

"Joe didn't hear you drive up?"

"No."

"The dog didn't bark?"

"He knows my car."

"Did you try to help your husband after you shot him?"

Agnes pulled her hands into her lap and clasped them contritely. "He was dead. There was nothing more I could do for him."

"Why did you go back to the church?"

"I didn't know what else to do. I thought maybe I should tell the priest what I'd done, that I'd sent Joe to heaven. And I'd made the salad. I couldn't let it go to waste. I figured they'd need it for the lunch."

Cubiak looked at his cup of steamed milk and coffee. He'd yet to have a swallow. Waste not, want not, his mother had always said. Even under the most extreme circumstances he could imagine her doing just as Agnes had. "I see. Then why throw the beets at the three women?"

"I had to, Sheriff. Joe wasn't a nice man but I thought he was a decent person. Only he wasn't. He was filthy and I'd been living with his filth. I couldn't bear the shame and when I saw the three of them— Ida and Olive and Stella—standing there all proper and ladylike and holier-than-thou, I filled up with some kind of awful fury. I wanted them to feel dirty like I did. Ida especially. All those years, cleaning the mud off her floor, scrubbing the toilets for her and that man."

As if offering proof of her humiliation, Agnes held out her rough, red hands for the sheriff to see. He'd already realized that her life had been unduly harsh, especially compared with those of the other three women. But Joe had denied her far more than material comfort, and in that she was not alone.

"For years, you'd accepted your husband's excuse about a war injury to explain the absence of physical relations in your marriage."

Agnes started. "How did you . . . ?"

"Olive Swenson told me about the confrontation between you and her and the other two women last December. According to Olive, you said you had no use for the books they read—trash, you called them—and that you'd made your peace with your situation and didn't need to fantasize about something you couldn't have. You told the three widows that Joe didn't bother you, 'because of the war injury,' and that you didn't need to be teased into wanting something you couldn't have. Is that correct?"

"Yes."

"What did the other women say to you?"

"They didn't say anything. They looked at one another and then stared at me like I was a freak."

"You had no idea that their husbands had also claimed to have similar war injuries?"

Agnes gaped. "What?"

"They had never confided in each other. Sex was something they didn't discuss, so each of them thought it was her own burden to bear, until you brought it out into the open."

"I'll be damned." Agnes blushed and crossed herself. A quick laugh escaped her lips. She brightened and then laughed again. "The princesses didn't know!"

"Princesses?"

"That's what they acted like. That's what I called them."

"You didn't like them, did you?"

"Had no reason to."

121

"Just the women or their husbands as well?"

"I had no use for any of them. Especially Big Guy. You have to understand, Sheriff, that nobody ever cared much for Joe. He wasn't a likable person, but Big Guy? Everybody liked him. He made sure of that." Agnes picked up the Bible again. "It just all seemed so unfair, you know? I hope him and the other two rot in hell."

It was nearly noon when Cubiak finished with Agnes. He escorted her back to her cell, where a tray waited. In town, he picked up two turkey sandwiches, chips, and water and drove to Bathard's. The doctor was in the boat barn. Perched on a board that was balanced between two work horses, his feet dangling off the ground, he pried a stubby strip of dried caulk from the hull of the *Parlando* and tossed it on the floor with the rest of the droppings from his morning's labor.

"This is a pleasant surprise. Playing hooky?" Bathard said as Cubiak lowered the volume on *Aida*.

"It's a working lunch." The sheriff held up the white paper bag and circled the boat, peering at the gaps between the curved planks.

Bathard dropped off the scaffolding and rapped on the hull. "Hear that? Sounds hollow. When I'm done, it'll have the fine timbre of a taut drumhead." He pulled off his gloves. "You want to go to the house?"

"This is fine." Cubiak handed a sandwich to his friend. "I don't have a lot of time."

"Something wrong?"

"Not necessarily wrong. But complicated."

They stood at the counter and, as they ate, Cubiak told Bathard what he'd learned about Joe and the three dead friends from the widows and Agnes.

At one point, Bathard put down his lunch, inclined his head, and listened until Cubiak finished.

"Well." The physician folded his arms to his chest and sighed. "I had no idea. But that was the whole point, wasn't it? If they hadn't conformed to societal norms, they'd have been ostracized and condemned. Now they'll be condemned for a lifetime of deceit." Bathard looked up. "This certainly casts a different light on their deaths."

"Yes, but it doesn't help clarify the circumstances. I still don't know if Big Guy and the other two were murdered of if they died accidentally."

"Agnes?"

"She killed Joe, but I believe her when she says she had nothing to do with the other three dying."

"Assuming they were killed, you still think their deaths are connected with gambling?"

"I can't rule it out yet. And it's certainly one way of explaining why their incomes were so over the top."

"You said Stella attributed their success, at least hers and Jasper's, to hard work and luck. You have to allow for that possibility."

"Lots of people work hard." Cubiak crumpled the empty chip bag and tossed it into the trash.

"But not everyone in this world enjoys good luck." Bathard brushed an invisible crumb off the counter. "Of course, there may be more to it than good fortune. Why is it, I wonder, that I see Huntsman's trucks all over the peninsula? There are scores of plumbing firms around, good ones, too. You have to ask yourself why someone at the south end of the county would bypass local businesses and hire someone from forty miles away."

"Longstanding friendship or even loyalty that stems from their service days might account for some of it. Maybe he charged less than the others."

"Perhaps. But what about Swenson and Wilkins? They seem to have been fairly adept at empire building as well."

Cubiak leaned back and looked up at the boat. Once in the water, more than half of it would be submerged and hidden from view. Like much of what went on at Huntsman's Rec Room. "Besides the weekly card games, the men hosted parties as well. A little too much alcohol during one of the gatherings or on a charter run, a compromising situation, a convenient photograph, and a gentleman's agreement: silence exchanged for business."

"Blackmail?"

"Of a sort, maybe."

"Up here a photograph wouldn't be necessary. A rumor would be sufficient to ruin a man's reputation."

"You think?"

"No question. But something about this isn't sitting right. If what you're suggesting is true, think of the risk those three took with their own reputations. They couldn't guarantee that someone wouldn't talk. Why would they take that chance?"

Cubiak showed Bathard the lists of clients that he'd gotten from Ida and Olive. "These are people who either did business directly with Huntsman or, in the case of Swenson, recommended his charter service."

Bathard didn't respond immediately. He picked up several chisels and hung them on the wall in ascending order. When he finished, he turned back to Cubiak. "These are some very prominent people. I know one of the men quite well. I won't tell you which, but I will talk to him in confidence and see what if anything I can learn."

"Thanks. That would be helpful. In the meantime, I'll question Bruno Loggerstone. He's not on the list but he stormed out of the sawmill social club when the men started collecting money for funeral flowers, and Fielding said he's got a long-term grudge against Huntsman."

WEEK TWO: SATURDAY

12

The puppies were four weeks old and ready to start moving. Natalie had designated the kitchen as their playpen, and Cubiak had just returned from buying a child's safety gate. "You sure this is going to work?" he said as he secured the gate across the doorway, blocking the path to the rest of the house.

The vet peeked past his shoulder. "It's fine. But just to be safe, you probably should cover the bottom half so they don't try to crawl through and end up choking themselves."

"Damn dogs are more work . . ." Cubiak took the piece of cardboard Natalie handed him and taped it in place.

"You can't smile and complain at the same time. It's not allowed." The vet checked his handiwork and then rolled up the rug at the sink. "No rugs for a while. You'll have to wash the floor every day, at least once."

He groaned.

"I assume you own a mop."

"I even know how to use it."

On the porch, the puppies yipped. Buddy, Nico, and Scout sniffed the back door as Kipper hung over the edge of the basket, ready to tumble out head first. Cubiak scooped her up and carried her inside. "She looks so small!" he said as he set her on the floor. Kipper pushed her nose into the soft leather of his boot and then backed away, slipping on the linoleum. Cubiak bent down for her.

"Don't. Let her be. She'll learn," Natalie said.

It almost feels like home, Cubiak thought as he fried a pan full of bacon and the litter mates explored the room. By the time Natalie spread newspaper and set up the dogs' food and water dishes, the meat was nearly crisp, the way he liked it. He popped an English muffin into the toaster, pulled plates from the cupboard, and poured coffee. Lauren had made breakfasts like this on Saturdays when he wasn't working. The bittersweet memory lifted him away to another time and place, releasing an avalanche of pain so fierce it stopped his breath. Cubiak braced against the counter and turned on the radio. This was his new life.

"Do you think they'll like classical music?" he said, finding it hard to talk.

"They'll love it." Natalie smiled at him.

As they ate, she told Cubiak about the animals she'd treated that week. Listening to her easy chatter, he felt his equilibrium return and he shifted his attention to the pups. "Scout's missing," he said.

Natalie pointed under the table where the puppy lay draped across his foot.

"Too bad, I can't get up."

"A poor excuse for not having to wash dishes."

"That's what dishwashers are for."

"But you don't have one." Natalie began to clear the table. "You'll have to have someone check on the pups next Saturday," she said, talking over the running faucet.

"I was going to duck out and . . ."

"You're the best man. You can't leave. You have to find someone else to take care of the dogs for the day." She paused. "I can pick you up, if you like. We can go together."

"I have to be there early." It was a poor excuse and Cubiak knew it. He stood, forgetting the sleeping dog. He was being unfair. The only reason not to attend the wedding with Natalie was his vague awareness that Cate might be there.

"Fine," Natalie said and turned back to the dishes.

A phone rang, breaking the silence. Natalie pulled out her cell, and after a short, clipped conversation, she reached for her jacket. "There's been an emergency. I have to get back." She gave each of the pups a pat on the head and Cubiak a peck on the cheek.

When her car had cleared the driveway, he walked to the mailbox. As usual, it was empty save for a bill from the local utility and a flyer from a lawn care service. Across the road, Lewis Nagel rolled a vintage lawn mower over a stubby patch of grass.

He waved to the sheriff. "How're the little ones doing?"

"Good."

Butch had emerged from the woods and materialized at Cubiak's side. When the neighbor reached into his pocket, the dog trotted over the blacktop and Cubiak followed. Nagel fed the treat to the dog and then scratched her head. "Popular fella," he said finally.

"What do you mean?"

"Well, you got one lady with a red SUV visiting and another one in a fancy black sports car looking like she wants to visit."

Cate? But her car was red. The one he remembered.

"Yep, she pulled into the driveway but she must have seen the other car because she backed out and drove away. Real fast-like. Heading that way." Nagel pointed north.

Cubiak rubbed Butch behind the ears. Had someone told Cate where he lived? "Could have been someone just needed to turn around," he said.

Nagel shrugged. "Could be. 'Cept that's the way she came from."

Had Cate come back for the wedding? Was she here to stay? Maybe it wasn't Cate. Cubiak quieted the urge to get in the jeep and drive to the tip of the peninsula. What would he do if he found her?

Despite the puppies scattered around the floor, the kitchen seemed empty. Cubiak pictured Natalie sitting at the table, talking in her easy, friendly way. He missed her, and then Natalie became Cate and he found himself thinking about her. What did he know about Cate anyway? Were his memories of her real or a fantasy he'd created from the little time they'd spent together? Did she even like dogs? He dropped his dish and spoon into the sink and stared at the back door, wishing Lauren would walk in, wanting his old life back. Too restless to stay indoors, he put on his jacket again and searched the pocket for the crude map Ida had drawn for him. He had nothing else planned for the afternoon; he may as well check it out.

Nagel's yard was empty but Cubiak suspected the retired machinist was watching from a window. At the end of the driveway, he turned south.

Visitors generally thought of Door County as the peninsula that jutted northeast from Sturgeon Bay. In fact, the region extended south of the town as well, like the foot of a sea anemone that attached the fingerling of land to the rest of the state. Cubiak wound down a series of county roads to that little-heralded area. Halfway between two roads named for early homesteaders and nearly a mile from the nearest house, he found the unmarked dirt strip that Ida had directed him to. The lane was little more than a narrow slit in a forest of old cedars and pines and looked like an access road to a hidden field or an unmarked shortcut known only to locals. There was no mailbox at the entrance and no utility lines running alongside, nothing to indicate that anyone lived at the end of the track.

A canopy of tree branches blocked much of the light and shadowed the passage. On either side, dense undergrowth added to the gloom and sense of claustrophobia. Branches and brambles brushed the windshield and sides of the jeep as Cubiak crept forward. The silent, encroaching forest made him uneasy. He'd gone about a quarter mile and was ready to give up when the woods thinned and opened to a fenced compound, a dismal patch of rural poverty that he didn't associate with either the Midwest or Wisconsin.

Cubiak rolled up to a hand-painted No Trespassing sign nailed to a lopsided log gate and shifted into neutral. Three tarpaper shacks sat in the middle of the half-acre yard. There was a large garden on one side of the houses; on the other, a half-dozen scrawny chickens pecked at the ground between a pen that held a mud-caked sleeping pig and a large doghouse. A rusted-out Chevy stood behind the doghouse. The car had been stripped of its wheels and a metal chain was looped around the car bumper but there was no dog on the end of it. The rest of the home-stead was little more than dust and dirt piled with discarded appliances and old farm equipment. This was life from another era: a well and hand pump for water, an outhouse for sanitation, firewood for warmth. The thin ribbon of smoke from the chimney of the middle house was the only sign of comfort in the sad habitat.

Who are these folks? Cubiak wondered. What kind of mindset allowed people to live like this?

Inside the house with the smoking chimney, a curtain fluttered and a dog began to bark. Cubiak had seen enough. He put the jeep in reverse and backed out through the trees. The first time he'd met Ida, she'd been sitting on a peach-colored sofa, her feet firmly planted on a pure white carpet looking out onto a picturesque bay. Even in mourning, she'd expressed an air of quiet reserve and dignity. He tried to imagine her decades earlier as a frightened, pregnant teenager desperate to escape a life defined by squalor and hopelessness. Rescued first by Christian Nils and then by Terrence Huntsman.

With Nils, she would probably have been happy and enjoyed a modest lifestyle. With Big Guy, she'd compromised but prospered. Just how well had they done? he wondered. Earlier that week Cubiak had asked Rowe to secure Huntsman's business and personal banking records, going back as far as possible. He stopped on the side of the road and called his deputy.

"Sorry to interrupt your day off. Did you get the bank records?"

"They'll be on your desk Monday morning, Chief."

"Good. Thanks. I'll need the same for Swenson and Wilkins. Enjoy the weekend."

Bruno Loggerstone lived on a farmette between Egg Harbor and Fish Creek, half a mile from the Meadow Blossom Orchard and Craft Market. Some fifty years earlier, he'd started the business as a simple fruit and vegetable stand. Now retired, he split his time between his home in Door County and a condo in New Mexico.

Cubiak found him in the backyard, coatless despite the chill and still tan from his southern sojourn, walking a frisky black Lab pup on a leash.

"Name's Daisy. Cute but not mine to keep," Loggerstone said. As he led the animal up and down the driveway, he gave Cubiak a quick lecture on the process of socializing young dogs to be trained as guide dogs for the blind.

"You got a dog, Sheriff?"

"Yeah. A mutt. Just had pups."

Loggerstone brought his charge into the house. In a tidy kitchen decorated with baskets and Americana, he gave the pup a treat and then led her to a metal crate in the den. "Them's the rules: leash or kennel," he said and leaned against the desk, his arms folded across his thick chest. Behind him, three photos hung on the wall. One showed Loggerstone as a groom with his bride, one as a fruit picker perched on a ladder under a cherry tree, and one as a gangly young man standing awkwardly in front of the original produce market.

Cubiak took up a position near the window. "I'll get right to the point. I'm investigating the deaths of Terrence Huntsman, Jasper Wilkins, and Eric Swenson."

"Investigating? Why? They died accidentally, didn't they?"

"Maybe."

Loggerstone frowned. "Maybe? What the hell does that mean?" He pulled at his sleeve. "You think someone did them in, and that I had something to do with it?"

"No." Not yet, Cubiak thought.

"Then why you here?"

"I'm trying to get a clearer picture of who the men were and who might want to see them come to harm. Seems to me you might have something useful to contribute."

"I hardly knew them."

"You were in business and so were they. Your paths had to cross. That day at the sawmill you refused to contribute to the fund for the funeral flowers. Which indicates that you didn't care for these three men who were being lauded as pillars of the community. I wonder why."

Loggerstone didn't blink.

"There has to be a reason."

"There is."

Daisy whimpered. Loggerstone ignored her.

"Off the record. I give you my word that your name will not be linked to anything you tell me."

"Like going to confession."

"If you like."

Loggerstone's eyes narrowed. "Except I don't have anything to confess. They're the ones who needed to seek forgiveness."

"From you?"

"Me and plenty of others as far as I know." He took a quick, deep breath and stepped toward the sheriff. "You know about the Rec Room?"

"The poker games, the card tournaments, yes."

"Oh, there was much more than that going on. There and on the boat and out in the woods, weather permitting. Parties. Invite a couple friends over, one or two of the big resort managers, or the owners of prominent enterprises, men in a position to steer business your way. Then bring in the broads."

"Women?"

"Yeah. What we used to call floozies. Not locals, probably from Green Bay and gawd knows where else. One or two for every guest. Some of 'em just kids. Turned my stomach to think what they were expected to do."

"A honey trap with plenty of liquor and gambling."

"Something like that."

"For purposes of blackmail?"

Loggerstone jeered. "Friendly persuasion at its worst. We give you a good time, the kind you might covet but not pursue on your own, the kind your wife or steady girl might not take kindly to, and in return you give us your business."

"You didn't buy in?"

"I got three daughters, Sheriff. I had a wife, too, then. I don't use women as sex toys."

"When was this?"

"Thirty years ago at least."

"And what'd you do?"

"Walked out. Told them never to ask me back. Stayed clear since then."

"How many guests were there that evening?"

"Just two. Me and another fellow."

"Someone you knew."

"Sure. Up here everybody knows everyone else, especially if you're in business."

"You ever talk to him about it afterward?"

"Nope. No good comes from judging your neighbor. I kept my thoughts to myself and looked the other way just like everyone else did."

"Then how do you know how this all panned out?"

A dog barked in the distance. Loggerstone looked past Cubiak and didn't start talking again until the yapping ceased. "I don't know anything, Sheriff, but I can surmise from seeing how the dominoes fell into place. Huntsman started doing an awful lot of plumbing work, Wilkins started delivering milk and cheese to resorts and restaurants up and down the peninsula, and Swenson started buying new boats to keep up with the business that began coming his way."

"And all three got rich."

"They did very well for themselves. Never cut corners on anyone, I gotta give 'em that. But there are plenty of others around here who could have used some of that business."

"How long did this go on for?"

"No idea. 'Course once their reputations were established as the go-to guys, the best, the ones to call, it didn't matter. People followed the herd."

"The other man who was there that night, will you tell me who he was?"

"No, sir. That I will not do."

"I don't suppose it would be worthwhile showing you a list of names hoping you'd point him out."

Loggerstone moved toward the door. "Wouldn't want to waste your time, Sheriff."

One good man, Cubiak mused as he headed to Fish Creek. One man strong enough to stand on principle. A Diogenes. If his story was true.

Despite sparse crowds, most of the Founders Square shops were open. A couple in knee-length suede coats studied the window display at the new gallery; three children danced from the candy store, clutching red-and-white-striped bags, their thin jackets unzipped and the west wind blowing their hair. Cubiak had the heater cranked up in the jeep. Kids, he thought.

Nearby, Timothy and his girlfriend sprawled on the stone wall. An open pizza box sat next to Tim and another lay on the ground along with empty soft drink cups. Three more of the posse hovered behind, Roger Nils among them.

The sheriff eased out of the jeep. "Little chilly for a picnic," he said.

"For pussies, maybe," Tim said.

The sheriff kicked a paper cup across the walkway.

"Anything wrong, Sheriff?" Roger said.

Cubiak held up a hand and counted on his fingers. "One, loitering. Two, littering. Three, creating a nuisance." He looked past them into the dim interior of the Woolly Sheep. Kathy O'Toole had closed shop early. "I'm sure I can find something else if I stay here long enough." He paused. "But I don't think you're going to make me do that. Instead, you're going to pick up your garbage and pack up the rest of the goodies and disappear somewhere."

The five glared at him.

"I'm waiting," he said.

The girlfriend reached over and slammed the lid on the box.

"Hey!" Tim grabbed her wrist.

"I'm cold," she said, as she slid off the low wall.

"Fucking cunt," Tim said.

The girl stumbled.

"You don't talk to a lady like that," Cubiak said.

"Lady? She ain't no fucking lady," Tim said. The girl turned her face away quickly but not before Cubiak saw the tears welling in her eyes. How much would it take for her to become one of the floozies Loggerstone had described? he wondered.

Tim lumbered up off the wall. At a nod from him, the others gathered the trash and tossed it into the basket ten feet away.

As they dispersed, Cubiak corralled Roger. "I'm headed to the high school for the wrestling match. You want to come?"

"Get your own fucking date. I'm through with that shit."

"You're a real smart ass, you know."

Roger snickered. Then he spun on his heel and hustled after his friends.

The gym was hot and bright and the tournament underway when Cubiak arrived. He stripped off his jacket and climbed to a spot five rows up behind the home team.

The crowd cheered as young men stepped up to the mat in pairs and took turns flinging one another to the rubber. Cubiak didn't understand the sport and amused himself surveying the audience: school friends mostly but quite a few parents and grandparents as well.

At the break, he bought a donut and cup of coffee from the 4-H stand in the lobby. He was looking over the display cases filled with trophies for football, baseball, basketball, and wrestling when the reporter Justin St. James came up, scribbling in a notebook.

"I didn't know you were a sportswriter," Cubiak said.

"Just filling in. Actually that's something I do a lot of at the paper. Comes with the territory. I even take some of the official photos." He moved toward the wall where Roger Nils's picture hung with those of other student athletes.

"Who's that?" Cubiak said, pointing to a photo of a distinguished-looking man with salt-and-pepper hair, a square jaw, and a thick neck.

"Bill Vinter. The former coach. I did a piece on him a couple of years ago. He's the guy who transformed Roger Nils from a pretty good athlete into a star. Made sure he got plenty of action when the scouts were around, too. From what I heard, he even tutored Roger to make him scholarship eligible. And what does that stupid kid do with that golden opportunity? Throws it all away."

"What do you think happened?"

St. James shrugged. "Who knows? Drugs. Booze. Lot of beer flowing on college campuses. But it could have been anything. Maybe Roger couldn't handle the transition from big fish, small pond to small fish, big pond. I wouldn't lose any sleep over Roger. He's not the first kid to flame out."

SUNDAY

13

When the first alarm rang at 5 a.m., Cubiak groped for the clock in the nightstand drawer and silenced the noise. At 5:10, a second alarm buzzed from the top of the dresser. He ignored the racket for nearly five minutes before he rolled out of bed. Sunrise was still half an hour away but predawn light filtered along the edge of the window frame and cast dim shadows in the room. Somewhere in the woods behind the house a family of crows made ugly sounds, their way of heralding the coming day. In the kitchen, Butch barked, hungry as always.

Cubiak tended to the dogs and rinsed his mouth at the sink. By the time he stepped outside, the sun had crested the horizon and started to burn off the mist over the water, revealing the cold, rippling surface of the lake. Cubiak slouched down the driveway. At the road he turned south and began running toward the coast guard station, pulled along by the melancholy dirge of the foghorn that warned boaters away from the rocky shoals at the entrance to the Sturgeon Bay canal. He saw no one and no signs of life at the neighboring houses tucked back among the trees. The crows had gone off to seek their morning meal, leaving him alone with the fog that the sun had yet to reach.

The sheriff had not slept well and it took him several minutes to hit his stride. Even then, he felt lightheaded. Pausing at the end of a driveway, he locked eyes with a deer. For a moment, both man and beast held still. Then the deer flared its nostrils, flicked its white tail, and leapt into the woods.

Cubiak started off again. Moving through a strip of tall weeds, he watched for loose gravel. No doubt he'd surprised the doe, but in Door County, deer were generally accustomed to people and unperturbed by their presence. He'd frightened the animal. The panic he saw in her eyes was the same kind of fear he'd sensed the previous evening in Timothy's girlfriend and had seen in Roger Nils's hard stare. The other punks were defiant, but the girl and Roger were scared. He was sure the girl was intimidated by Tim, but what about Roger? Something had turned that boy on his granddad and soured him on life. What was it? Cubiak wondered. He had his own theory about Big Guy's gambling activities, and Loggerstone had hinted that Huntsman had been behind a carefully orchestrated blackmailing scheme. But those events had been kept under wraps for decades. Even if Roger had learned of them, would he care?

Cubiak's foot came down along the edge of a rock and he pitched forward onto his knees. Cursing his clumsiness, he stood and brushed off.

The foghorn moaned as Cubiak limped home.

While coffee brewed, he filled a plastic bag with ice and duct-taped it to his knee. Breakfast was toast with peanut butter consumed while sitting on the floor with the puppies as Butch watched from her station by the door. "Don't be jealous," Cubiak said, and held out his hand. The dog hesitated. "Come on." Pacified, she trotted over and pushed her snout into his palm. Cubiak scratched behind her ears.

It was late afternoon when he got to Bathard's. The door to the boat barn was rolled back, and once again Bathard was on the scaffolding alongside the *Parlando*. A mallet in one hand and a black chisel-like tool in the other, he stared at the skylights and listened to Pavarotti.

"Ah, here you are," he said as the tenor's voice faded. "You know that one, of course."

"'Nessun Dorma.'"

"Correct." Bathard pressed a strip of white caulking cloth into a seam and tapped the head of the chisel to wedge the caulking in farther. "I'm 'paying the cotton' in case you're wondering," he said as he continued working the ropelike fabric into the narrow space between the planks. "Have to be careful not to hammer it in too hard. To seal the gap, it needs room to expand once it goes into the water."

"There must be an easier way to do this."

"There is. But I prefer the old-fashioned method."

After Bathard finished with the length of caulking, he mixed red lead powder into linseed putty. "You want it the consistency of modeling clay so you can roll it into thin strips. Like this"—he rubbed the glop between his palms—"like when you were a kid with a new can of Play-Doh. Then you press it into the seam over the caulking rope and smooth it out with a putty knife so it's flush with the planks." Again he demonstrated. "Here," he said, handing the mixture to Cubiak, "you can start where I finished with the caulk."

The CD player had stopped, and slowly the sound of opera was replaced by a different kind of music as the tapping and scraping of the mallet and putty knife took on a rhythm of their own. Finally, the coroner laid down his hammer and motioned his assistant toward the open doorway. "Go on, you can use the air," he said.

Bathard followed with coffee for them both. Angling his tall frame against the door jamb, he sighed and closed his eyes to the warm sun. "About our discussion yesterday," the coroner said after a while. "I contacted my friend and had quite the interesting chat." He straightened and looked at Cubiak. "Your theory was correct, but only half so. Huntsman et al. were guilty of systematically luring prominent male citizens into compromising situations. But the indiscretions did not involve other men as you surmised, but women."

The sheriff nodded and tossed the dregs from his cup at the base of a fir tree.

"You don't seem surprised."

"Only because I heard essentially the same story from Bruno Loggerstone. Oldest trick in the book. Stag parties with scantily clad females. Not local women, certainly, but a friskier variety imported from Green Bay. And no photos, as you had suggested. The three of them were far more clever than that. It was very subtly done, something akin to a gentleman's agreement to become business clients."

"So their income came from legitimate transactions."

"Precisely. Furthermore, there were never any complaints about the services provided."

The wind came up and Bathard lifted his collar. "When you think about it, they were damn clever to fall back on the old conceit of plying men with alcohol and women. They'd already concealed their sexual identities behind the façade of marriage. By creating and welcoming others into this kind of bawdy milieu, they projected a macho image that added another layer of obfuscation."

"That's true. But why wasn't the macho conceit by itself sufficient for their purpose? Why the indirect blackmail?"

"They wanted money and saw an easy way to get it."

Cubiak glanced back toward the *Parlando*. "Or they needed it for some reason."

Inside the barn, Bathard's phone vibrated on the counter, raising a small cloud of dust. He checked the screen. "Time for tea. Sonja and her granddaughters have been fussing in the kitchen all afternoon."

"I can't . . ."

"You must. You're the guest of honor."

Bathard's fiancée greeted them at the back door. Sonja was tall and willowy and, despite the striped apron snugged around her waist and the dusting of flour on her hands, there was something regal in her appearance. Cubiak had met her shortly after Bathard had started seeing her and was struck by the contrast between her and his friend's late wife. Cornelia had been subdued and introspective, though how much of that stemmed naturally from her personality and how much had been dictated by the cancer that took her life he didn't know. Sonja, on the other hand, was robust and outgoing. Through a stream of chatter, she kissed Bathard on the cheek, hugged Cubiak, and introduced her twin granddaughters, Madeline and Sofia.

The girls immediately took charge of the sheriff and led him off to the dining room, talking about the cookies they'd made that afternoon. The twins were nine, coltish, blonde, and blue-eyed. Even though they looked nothing like Alexis, everything about them reminded Cubiak of his daughter. The girls gave him the water view and then, oblivious to his discomfort, they sat opposite and peppered him with questions about the puppies.

"Can we come see them, please, Mr. Dave?" Sofia said, her freckled face eager, her hands clasped in supplication beneath her chin.

"If your parents say it's okay," he said, terrified at the thought.

"Isn't a kipper a fish?" Madeleine said, or was it Sofia, after he'd told them the puppies' names.

"It is, but I . . . my . . ."

Bathard entered with a soup tureen, sparing him from further explaining. The rest of the meal was already laid out on the sideboard: intricate open-faced sandwiches, a selection of fruit and cheese, and a platter heaped with homemade cookies.

They served themselves. There was lemonade for the girls and white wine for the adults. Cubiak drank more than he meant to as he listened to the girls' tales of school and scouts and surreptitiously watched the interaction between Bathard and Sonja. The tenderness between them was unsettling and resurrected the gnawing emptiness of his own existence.

After Sonja took the girls home, he joined Bathard in the living room, drinking dry sherry and watching another spectacular Door County sunset. In the cozy setting, Cubiak's despondency deepened. Wrapped in the warmth of Bathard's revived life, he felt overwhelmingly lonely. Silent, he poured another drink, tossed it down, and refilled his glass a third time before sinking back into the sofa.

"I wish I had your life," he said, embarrassed by the bitterness in his voice. He'd never before been angry with Bathard but didn't know how to stop himself. "You've got it all figured out, don't you?"

"What do you mean?"

"Your wife dies, you marry another woman, just like that," he said, with a clumsy snap of the fingers.

"I think you've had too much to drink, Dave."

"I don't think I've had enough." Cubiak started to get up but fell back into the cushions. "Doesn't matter." The world beyond the window had gone a bluish-black, matching his bleak mood. "You know what I want to know?"

"What?"

"What the hell Cornelia would say about her replacement."

Bathard shrank back as if struck. When he finally spoke, he was defensive and curt. "No one can replace Cornelia. No one is trying to. Certainly not Sonja, just as I am not trying to replace her late husband."

Cubiak grunted. He wished he could take back what he'd said, but it was too late.

"We're two individuals who've been given a second chance at happiness. Some people don't get even one." The coroner rested his elbows on his knees, his hands clasped in front of him, his face in shadows softened. "Cornelia was ill for two years. The long duration of the disease was both a curse because of her suffering and a blessing because it gave us time to talk, difficult as it was. She liked to reminisce about the past, all the good times." As if lost in memory, Bathard fell silent. "She talked about the future, too. My future. 'Find someone, Evie,' she said."

The doctor's voice cracked with pain. Cubiak looked away, embarrassed to have stirred such painful memories.

After a moment, Bathard went on. "I argued with her. I said I couldn't imagine such an eventuality. And I meant it. Truth is, I still can't imagine it even as it's happening, but I know that Cornelia would understand and be pleased."

The coroner looked at Cubiak. "You must have had the same conversation with Lauren, only the other way around. You were a cop, for god's sake. Every time you walked out the door, she didn't know if you'd come back alive."

Cubiak steeled himself, knowing what was coming.

"What did you tell her you wanted for her?"

"You know damn well what I told her." His anger melted as he spoke.

Bathard rested a hand on Cubiak's arm. "I do. I know, son. And I'm not going to tell you any of this is easy, because it's not. And I'm not going to advise you on what to do, because you have to find your own way in life. And only you can decide what that means."

Bathard fixed a pot of strong coffee for Cubiak and then insisted he lie down in the study before venturing home. Cubiak hadn't meant to fall sleep but he did. The house was dark and quiet when he woke and let himself out. Bathard's message, imbued with both sorrow and hope, followed him across the peninsula. Intellectually Cubiak knew that his friend was right. But the heart often struggles to embrace what the mind knows is true.

Cubiak came home to a hungry dog, ravenous puppies, and a floor that needed washing. He sat on the damp linoleum and leaned back against the wall. Scout and Nico shimmied into his lap and then clawed up his chest and licked his chin. Cubiak stared at the kitchen phone. His life had been altered forever but he still had a life. He would take things one step at a time, he decided. He would start by calling Natalie and asking her to attend Bathard and Sonja's wedding with him.

After only two rings, Cubiak faltered. His courage gone, he hung up. And only then did he realize that he hadn't called Natalie. He'd dialed Cate's old number.

MONDAY

14

Justin St. James was chatting up Lisa when the sheriff arrived at headquarters.

"I brought that article I did on Bill Vinter, in case you're still interested," he said, pulling a manila envelope from a battered canvas briefcase. "The former wrestling coach?"

"Oh, right. Thanks," Cubiak said, recalling their conversation from the tournament on Saturday. "You got a minute, come on in."

Lisa followed the men with two coffees.

"You know it's my cousin she's marrying," St. James said as the assistant walked to the door. "Nothing against you but she's being nice because she wants me to photograph the wedding."

Lisa glanced back and rolled her eyes.

"You're that good?"

"The best." St. James had to be about thirty-five, but his shoulder-length blond hair and the slim physique of a long-distance runner made him look younger. He grinned and spread the article on the sheriff's desk. "You weren't here five years ago, were you?"

"No, something happen?"

"Fireworks like you wouldn't believe. Door County High won the state wrestling championship for the fourth year running. I did this sidebar"—he put a finger on the article—"as background about the program. Actually the photo pretty well sums up the history of the whole program. Here's Huntsman, Walter Nils, Vinter, and Roger Nils. That season Roger wrestled at one-fifty-two and was on the frosh squad." The three men and the boy were relaxed and smiling. The coach stood between Walter and Roger with his arms around their shoulders. Big Guy was looking at the trio.

"How come Big Guy and Walter are in the picture?"

St. James swallowed a mouthful of coffee and coughed. "Sorry. Hot." He took a quick breath. "Huntsman was pretty much the father of the program. Hell, he'd been funding it for years, started when Walter was a kid. There's not a whole lot to do up here in the winter and he thought the boys needed something to keep busy when the snow started." The reporter grinned. "Remember, we're talking Ice Age here, way before the Internet. At first it was just an informal after-school activity. Eventually Big Guy convinced the district school board for Gills Rock and the other towns up there to take it on as an official school sport.

"Vinter was the coach when it was started and the first hired by the school district. Naturally, Walter was on the first team. Eventually, Door County High started a squad and lured Vinter down here. Then Roger made the team and won the individual state championship."

"One big happy family," Cubiak said.

"Some folks are lucky that way." St. James launched his cup into the trash. "Two points. I've got to run. Interviewing the mayor about the new street signs. Call me if you need anything."

"I will. By the way, good article today, about the funeral and everything."

"Yeah, well, it's the kind of story that pretty well writes itself." He stopped in the doorway. "There'll be more about them later. I'm working on a special feature to run the weekend the new cutter is commissioned."

The door closed. Cubiak put aside the clipping St. James had brought and turned to the envelope Rowe had left for him. Inside were two folders. The first held copies of the bank statements for the Huntsmans' joint savings and checking accounts and an individual money market account in Big Guy's name. The couple had a bucket of money to play with and weren't shy about spending it, but Cubiak found nothing irregular.

Material in the second folder indicated that Huntsman's business did very well. Deposits were substantial and steady. Besides payroll checks and routine expenses, Big Guy had authorized a monthly electronic transfer of two thousand dollars to Great Lakes Office Support and another for thirty-five hundred to Pepper Ridge Associates. Huntsman had six employees and a company headquartered in a metal barn. What kind of office support did he need that ran to twenty-four thousand dollars a year? And what did Pepper Ridge do to earn nearly double that? Big Guy could afford the expense, but what was he getting in return? Or were the payments part of a scheme to launder dirty money?

Cubiak was operating on four hours' sleep. As his attention drifted, he propped his elbows on the desk and rested his head in his hands. If he could close his eyes for just ten minutes, he'd be okay.

A thud on the door ended the reprieve. Cubiak jolted to attention. The wall clock had jumped forward twenty minutes. "Yeah, come in," he said, trying to look busy.

The door banged open. The man who walked in was tall and wide, the opposite of his earlier visitor. "Marty Wilkins, prodigal son," he said. He spoke like a man accustomed to making himself heard over the roar of an angry ocean.

"Marty, thanks for coming in. Sorry about your father." Cubiak stood and motioned toward a chair.

Marty snared the sheriff's hand in a crushing grip. "Appreciate it," he said, ignoring the invitation to sit. "I'm heading out tonight. Don't have a lot of time, and what I do have I ain't spending in here. You like, we can talk on my boat." He juggled a handful of keys and eyed the four walls as if expecting them to close in.

"Give me ten, and I'll meet you in the lot," Cubiak said.

Marty filled the front seat of a moss-green Hummer. Despite the chill, he had the windows down, listening to Dylan at full volume. The man's got a soul, thought Cubiak, trailing him to the highway. After a short, swift drive, the Hummer pivoted onto an unmarked dirt road and kicked up dust for a mile before it roared up to the Sunset Marina. Unlike so many Door County harbors, this one was filled with workhorse vessels, not a pretty boat in sight. Before Cubiak was out of the jeep, Marty was halfway down the last pier, where the smallest and meanest looking of the lot was docked. At the end of the wharf he high-stepped over the side of the *Can-Do* and started freeing the mooring lines. "Welcome aboard, Sheriff," he said, kicking a patched vinyl cooler out of the way.

"Where we headed?" Less than graceful, Cubiak negotiated the divide between dock and boat.

Wilkins waited until the sheriff was steady on his feet before he started the engine and eased away from the pier. "Out there," he said, lifting his chin in a forward motion as he steered the boat into a narrow channel. "You ever been out on the bay?"

"No."

"It's nice."

As they came around the low breakwater that protected the opening to the channel, Marty opened the throttle and pointed the power boat into the chop. "This baby'll handle anything," he said. He spoke with the swagger of a man who liked things to move fast.

The sheriff lurched across the cockpit. "How come you got a boat here? I thought you were never around?"

"Oh, I get back every now and then. Not too often, though. When I'm gone I got a friend who uses it."

Cubiak regained his balance. "Walter Nils?"

"Yeah. How'd you guess?"

The sheriff shrugged.

After that the men fell silent. Facing into the breeze, Wilkins steered with one hand on the wheel and one on the throttle. Cubiak gave up trying to stand and lowered himself onto a bench. He was colder than he'd been in a long time and eyed the cabin, but figuring that the ride might be even rougher inside he lifted his collar, lowered his head against the wind, and fought the urge to cross himself. Despite the bad conditions, he was relieved that they never lost sight of shore. Past a trio of white barns, Wilkins steered toward the open water. "That's where the *Lindy Lou* went down. A thirty-five-footer, made for the ocean. I was just a kid. Sudden storm came up and swamped the boat out from under the crew. Good sailors, the whole bunch, and one an Olympic swimmer. Two made it to shore; two didn't. Bodies washed up there." He swiveled back toward the three buildings that suddenly looked inconsequential compared to the vast expanse of Green Bay.

"Did the swimmer make it?"

"Nope. Gave her lifejacket to her friend. Silver medalist died. Friend lived." Marty looked at the sheriff. "You a good swimmer?"

"No."

"Then you get the jacket," he said and grinned.

A few minutes later, Marty slowed and pivoted the boat toward a long, curved finger of land. A wave hit broadside and sprayed icy water over the cockpit. As they entered a narrow inlet, he nodded toward the hatch. "You go on in. I'll be right after."

Cubiak didn't argue. The cramped cabin was dim and musty but the lack of wind made it feel warm. He dried his face on paper toweling and perched on the edge of a red plaid berth, arms crossed and tight to his chest. What the hell was he doing out here? he wondered. He couldn't see what Marty was up to but he felt the boat settle. The engine faded and he heard the splash of an anchor thrown overboard.

Marty clambered down and tossed the small cooler onto the square of counter alongside the miniature sink. Shivering like a large wet dog, he unzipped the cooler and took out a beer. "Want one?"

Cubiak shook his head. "I'm on duty."

"Yeah, and probably freezing your balls off, too." Marty raised the beer in a mock salute and drank. "Working the North Atlantic you learn how not to be cold if you wanna drink. But you didn't come out here to listen to tales of adventure on the high seas, did you? I'm guessing you wanna know about my old man and those other two, and why someone might have wanted them dead."

Cubiak forgot about being cold. "Officially, their deaths were an accident."

Ducking under the low ceiling, Marty slid past the sheriff and dropped onto the couch opposite. Elbows to his knees, he stared at the floor. "Yeah, right. I got that. But three men can make a lot of enemies," he said at last.

Was Marty referring to Bruno Loggerstone's charge of soft blackmail or was there something else? Cubiak figured the best way to find out was to play dumb. "Hardly seems likely for such highly respected members of the community."

Marty laughed, but the sound was dry and mirthless. "Yeah, they did a good job polishing their public image, didn't they? The three small-town heroes. Decorated war veterans, respected family men, successful business leaders whose money supported the local volunteer fire department and a whole rainbow of amateur athletic programs for kids. You know about the county's wrestling program? Huntsman started it when I was in sixth grade, but my old man and Swenson were on board from the get-go."

"You wrestled, I understand."

"Yeah, sure, almost all the boys did. I liked everything about wrestling, but mostly the chance to make friends my own age. Farm life is pretty isolated. And my mother was a real hard-ass most of the time. My dad tried to make up for her, but she got down on him for being too soft with me. That's what she called it, being soft. He was always good to me, I gotta give him that. When he wasn't working, he took me fishing and camping. Showed me how to fix stuff around the farm, too." Marty held up his hands. "Guess I owe my mechanical know-how to him. After I started wrestling, he came to every match. He didn't really know the rules and didn't pay much attention but I didn't care. It was just nice that he was there. He and Eric Swenson would sit together behind the bench and shoot the breeze with Huntsman."

"Sounds like he was a good father."

"Yep."

"Like Huntsman."

Marty scraped his hands through his tangled hair. "You gotta be kidding. Big Guy put on quite a show, that's for sure. Fooled me when I was a little kid. Couple of times when I was younger, we were invited to their house for a cookout or something, like on the Fourth of July. Man, what a difference from things at my house! Big Guy and Ida being sweet to each other and joshing around with Walter. Like Ozzie and Harriet on TV. That was the family I wanted to be part of. That's what I thought until Walter eventually owned up to Huntsman being a mean son-of-a-bitch. He used to talk about how if his real father hadn't been killed in the war, things would have been different for him and his mom. Walter liked my dad. I think one of the reasons he wanted to be friends with me was so he could hang out at my house and hear a kind word from my father every once in a while."

Marty lobbed the empty can into the sink. "Get me another one of those, you don't mind," he said over the echoing ping of the tin cylinder rattling against the metal bowl.

"Wrestling was the thing that brought us together. Walter was older than me, and since we didn't go to the same grammar school there wasn't that much chance for us to meet up before that. I was in the public school, just one room for all of us. Walter went to the Catholic school in town. And I had all my farm chores. So we didn't see much of each other until we signed up for the after-school program.

"By my senior year in high school I'd been wrestling for"—he held up a thick hand and counted off the years—"one, two, three, four . . . six and a half years. And, man, I loved it. Everything about it. All the crazy shit we had to do to come in at weight. I'd swear, I think every week I had to put on that plastic suit and run laps around the gym to sweat out a pound or two. When I couldn't run anymore, I'd have the guys stack a bunch of mats on me, so I'd keep sweating. You know, we'd even go into the bathroom before a weigh-in and spit out saliva to get rid of an extra few ounces. That's how strict things were. Afterward, we'd pig out on burgers and fries, all the greasy shit."

As he talked, Marty grew increasingly agitated. "It was nuts, but we were in it together and that made it all right. And the coach? He was right there with us. Pumping us up, telling us how special we were. Making us feel like we could take on the world."

Suddenly, Marty hunched over, silent again. "Right," he said. He sat up and swiped at his mouth. "I turned eighteen that first semester senior year, beginning of November." He gave Cubiak a meaningful look. "You know what that means?"

"You were of legal age."

"Right. Old enough to buy a beer. Old enough to be drafted."

"And old enough to be a consenting adult." The comment came out before Cubiak had a chance to consider the implications.

"Yeah. That, too."

The cabin filled with a heavy, sad silence.

"Who was it?" Cubiak said finally.

Several minutes passed. Marty squirmed as if both the cold and the truth were penetrating through the layers of clothing and emotional denial he wore. "The coach. Bill Vinter."

Marty's right heel began to thump against the floor. He clamped his hand on his knee, holding it down, and worked his mouth as if rehearsing what to say next. "You have to understand that Vinter *was* the program. He'd shaped it from nothing and then moved up to the school with it. Sure, we all worked hard for the individual glory and the team, but really, we worked for him. For that word of praise, that pat on the back. His approval meant everything, and suddenly it all turned to shit."

His face etched with misery, Marty glanced at Cubiak and then trained his eyes on the floor. "I never saw it coming. Once a month or so Vinter would have the team over to his house for pizza and movies. His wife was always around, his kids, too. Senior year, the Saturday after Thanksgiving, he invited me over to talk about new strategies for the team, and I didn't think anything of it. No one else was home, but that didn't bother me. It was late afternoon and he had all this food laid out. Not just leftovers, fancy stuff I didn't even know the name of. We talked wrestling and he started pouring me beers, one after the other. I was no stranger to drinking but it was a six-pack, maybe more. I don't know how much."

Marty pressed his fist to his mouth, as if trying to keep from saying more. After a moment, he gave up and went on. "I must have blacked out because when I woke up, it was light again. I was undressed and lying next to Vinter in his king-size bed. Funny how at first the bed was the only thing that registered. I'd never even seen one like that. Then it hit me. The coach was naked, too. I didn't know what he'd done. What I'd done! He must have put something in the beer. I crawled out of the bed and started to get dressed. Vinter woke up and started clapping. Thanked me for a real good time. I felt all crazy. I wanted to kill him but I couldn't move. I started yelling at him. He got up and shoved me into a chair. Said if I had any funny ideas about telling anyone what we'd done—not what he'd done to me, but what *we'd* done—that he'd blow the whistle on my father and Big Guy and Eric and tell everyone how'd I'd been coming on to him all year.

"I didn't understand half of what he was saying. Later, it hit me, what he'd meant. He'd ruin me; he'd ruin everyone."

Marty fell back against the bulwark and looked at Cubiak. "I'd no idea about my dad and his friends. The three of them grew up together, you know. I always thought that was why they spent so much time hanging out with each other. Childhood friends who'd never outgrown their childhoods. I didn't know what to do, Sheriff. I loved my father, and all of a sudden I couldn't look him in eye. I didn't know who the fuck he was! I was so confused, but I knew I couldn't hurt him. I couldn't let Vinter say those things, even if they were true.

"On Monday, I quit the team. But it was hard even to walk into the building. I kept replaying all those years when the bastard had his hands on me—that's what a wrestling coach does, isn't it?—and then I started imagining what had been going through his mind, what he'd really been after. Freaked me out. I couldn't focus on school. Started cutting classes. Drinking, a lot. All that shit people say happens is true. I kept wondering *Why me?* What was wrong with me? What had I done? Like being a kid all over again thinking everything's your fault.

"After Christmas break, I dropped out and enlisted in the navy. Did one tour in Hawaii then re-upped and was sent to Nam. Fucking nightmare but it finally made me forget. After that I joined the merchant marine and went as far away as I could. Stayed away, too."

"If you were drugged and coerced, it was a criminal offense."

"Yeah, but his word against mine."

"You never told anyone?"

Marty reared to his full height. "I couldn't take that chance. And who would have believed me? Coach Bill was like some kind of god to people on the peninsula. Like I said, his word against mine, and I'd had a couple run-ins with him earlier in the season. No, I didn't tell anyone."

"Not even Walter?"

"Not then. I hadn't seen Walter in a while. He'd gotten married and moved to Sturgeon Bay. I'd heard things weren't going really well and didn't want to bother him with my problems. My first time back, maybe ten years later, I tried telling him but he wouldn't listen. Said I was nuts."

The boat rocked beneath them.

"Wind's shifting," Marty said.

Cubiak pictured monster waves forming on the bay. "Maybe we should go back."

Marty muttered something but didn't move, and Cubiak knew the man had more to say. His only option was to wait, bad weather or not.

The sheriff managed to get the last two beers from the cooler. He handed one to Marty and cracked the other for himself.

"Off duty, Chief?"

"Thirsty." The beer was icy cold and nearly tasteless. "Too bad you didn't get back to town for the funeral," Cubiak said, fishing for something that would get Marty going again.

"Oh, I was here. I just didn't go in for the service."

"You got the message in time?"

"Yeah. I was working a rig off the Texas coast."

"Your mother thought you were halfway around the world."

Marty took a swallow of beer and set the can between his boots.

"I didn't see you anywhere around."

"Nobody did. I didn't want to be seen. Camped out on the boat. The morning of the funeral, I took it up the bay side and beached it on the stretch of rocks near the park."

The cove with the black rocks, near the path to the cabin, Cubiak thought. "Why not go to the funeral if you were there in time? At least for your mother's sake. Or Walter's."

"I don't know. Just couldn't bring myself to, I guess. All that pomp and circumstance."

Marty pulled at the corners of his mouth and then settled his gaze on Cubiak.

"There's something else. Something from when I was a kid. I'd pretty much forgotten about it, but just being here again . . . well, there it was staring me in the face."

Cubiak stayed silent. Too many words from him might derail Marty.

"May not mean anything. It was all a long time ago. But during the funeral, I went into town. Figured what the hell, why not, I was there and anyone who knew me well enough to recognize me after all this time would be at the church. Anyone else would think me a stranger. Place's changed a lot, especially with the ferry dock being moved. I didn't know about that. More new houses than I would have thought.

And a war memorial down by the marina. Nothing fancy, a pillar with names of the guys from Gills Rock that had been killed in all the wars up till now."

Cubiak nodded. He'd seen the obelisk.

"You heard of Christian Nils? His name's there, too. Nils, they called him. Walter's real dad. You know, he died before Walter was even born."

"I know."

Marty snagged his beer and guzzled. "Like I said, all this happened a long time ago. I was seven, maybe eight, when I sent off a stack of cereal box tops for membership in a national adventure club. There was a form that had to be sent in; it looked real official so when I filled it out I used my real name, Jasper Martin Wilkins. In a couple weeks, a big manila envelope came in the mail, addressed to Jasper Wilkins. I thought it was for me and ripped it open.

"There was an old photo inside. The picture was pretty grainy but I knew it was my father and the other two, Huntsman and Swenson. They were in uniform so it had to be during the war and they were standing in this boat, looking up at whoever was holding the camera. There were half a dozen soldiers behind them, too, huddled on benches. There was a note with the photo: 'Where is he?' it said.

"I was in the kitchen looking at the picture when my dad walked in. 'What's that?' he said, and I suddenly realized that it was his mail, not mine. When I gave it to him he went all white, like he'd seen a ghost. Scared me to see him like that. Then, like remembering I was there, he tried to act real casual. 'Just a joke from an old service buddy. Don't mean nothing.' He shoved the picture and the note back into the envelope and threw it in the trash. Told me go out and do my chores. When I finished, I came back inside and looked—I was curious. But the envelope was gone.

"My prize came a couple days later, a cheap piece of junk, not at all what I expected. I threw it away and forgot all about it and the photo until the other day. Seeing Nils's name again triggered something in my head. Brain's funny that way, letting things get away on you, stuff you don't understand or want to think about."

The wind rose and something banged on the foredeck.

"You see a lot moving around the world the way I do. After a while, things I didn't understand as a kid started to make sense. The Rec Room, for one, the fact that there was often a fourth man hanging out with my father and the other two. Sometimes it was Vinter.

"So when did this start? I wondered. What if there'd been a fourth man before the coach? And what if that man had been Christian Nils, and something went wrong between them? You know the unofficial coast guard slogan?" Marty sat up and intoned solemnly: "'You've got to go out but you don't have to come back.' You know what that means: you answer the call no matter what, with no regard for your own safety."

"Like when they tried to save Nils."

Marty tried to cross one leg over the other but gave up and planted both feet back on the floorboards. "That was the story after the war when they came home. They were the local heroes who risked their lives trying to save their friend. And I liked that. I liked that my dad was a war hero. And Big Guy? He married Nils's widow, making himself even more of a hero. Everyone here bought into their version of what happened. Claimed they couldn't bring him back because there wasn't room in the boat. But that's just it—the boat wasn't full. Not in that photo. What if the *he* in the note was Nils? What if they decided he didn't have to come back?"

Cold as he was, Cubiak felt a deeper chill. "You don't know that the note was about Nils."

"I don't know that it wasn't."

"You don't even know when the picture was taken."

Marty cracked his knuckles. "Sure I do. The army had a reporter named Charles Tweet from *Stars and Stripes* documenting the campaign. It was in the *Herald* toward the end of that story about the three of them. He was probably the one who took the picture. Who else would be out there with a camera?"

Cubiak swore to himself. How could he have missed that?

"That's why I didn't go into the church for the funeral. I couldn't stand the phoniness of it all."

"If you're right."

"Even if I'm wrong about Nils, they're still phonies. My father included, God rest his soul." Marty stood and stretched as much as a big man could in the cramped quarters. "And if I'm right, they're a lot worse than that."

The wind at their back, the two men reached the marina quickly. As Marty tied up the boat, Cubiak tossed the cushions into the hold. "Anyone else know about the photo?" he said.

"No one."

"You didn't tell Walter?"

"I never told anyone. Who knows? I was just a kid, maybe I imagined the whole thing."

Or maybe not, Cubiak thought. If the photo did exist and it proved that the three friends had left Nils to die, then the *Stars and Stripes* reporter who took it had a powerful hold over them. Bank records showed that for years Huntsman had been paying fifty-five hundred dollars a month to Great Lakes Office Support and Pepper Ridge Associates. Earlier Cubiak thought these could be fronts for laundering money but maybe they were covers for blackmail payments to the army journalist.

On the dock, Marty handed the key to Cubiak. "I ain't gonna be around for a long time. No use it just sitting here. You can share it with Walter."

"I can't . . ."

"Sure you can," Marty said and began walking away. When he reached the end of the pier, he gave a backward wave. "Whatever you find out, you'll let me know?"

In the waning light, Cubiak nodded, but Marty was gone.

TUESDAY

15

Death was rarely simple. The fatal carbon monoxide poisoning of three old friends who died playing poker on a chilly Friday night should have been an open and shut case. It should not have been a case at all. When the unfortunate and presumably accidental deaths were quickly followed by the brutal murder of one of their associates, Cubiak was sucked into a miasma of secrets that hinted at illegal gambling, possible blackmail, and sexual behavior long considered not just scandalous but sinful. Then Marty Wilkins, the son of one of the first three victims, alluded to an old photo that complicated the situation further. How to factor in Christian Nils, a soldier dead more than half a century? What to make of Charles Tweet, a contemporary of the Three of a Kind, perhaps the man who shot the potentially damning photo, and, according to the *Herald*, a successful player in the booming marketplace of World War II memorabilia?

Driving to headquarters, Cubiak mulled over the circumstances. He was still distracted when he walked in. Lisa coughed twice before she had his attention.

"Someone to see you," she said, handing him a message and nodding toward a lanky man curled in a chair along the far wall. The visitor looked familiar but his head was lowered to his chest and his face hidden by the brim of a faded black cowboy hat.

Cubiak mouthed the word *who*.

"Walter Nils."

Now what? Cubiak thought. "Give me a few minutes to take care of this" — he held up the note she'd given him — "then send him in."

The message was from Natalie. He called her, hoping she wouldn't mention the wedding and was relieved when she asked about the puppies and reminded him to start them on gruel the next day. "I left the instructions on the counter, remember?"

"I remember." There was a knock on the door. "Sorry, have to go," he said and hung up, then, louder, "Come on in."

Walter Nils pushed the door in a few inches and slipped through the narrow opening like he was trying to fold into himself. His jean jacket was stained. Thick stubble covered his jaw. "Sheriff," he said, blinking hard and clutching the worn Stetson in both hands.

Less than twenty-four hours earlier the sheriff had spent several hours in close quarters with Walter's childhood friend Marty Wilkins. Despite their common backgrounds, they seemed marked more by differences than by similarities. Marty had blown into his office with a swagger that conveyed self-confidence and bravado, even if it was contrived. Walter was unsteady and tentative.

As a show of courtesy, Cubiak stood. "Here, have a seat. I understand you wanted to see me about something?"

Walter elbowed the door shut, crossed to the desk, and sat down heavily in the chair that Marty had eschewed.

"Coffee?"

"No. No, thanks." Walter rubbed a rough hand over his mouth.

"Something wrong?"

Walter made a sharp sound, like a bark. After more fidgeting, he squared his shoulders and looked at Cubiak. "I did it," he said.

"Did what?"

"Killed Big Guy and the other two." Walter dropped the hat between his feet and held out his hands.

Cubiak didn't move.

"Well, ain't you gonna arrest me?"

The sheriff leaned back. He didn't believe Walter. "You put the leaves in the vent?" he said, stalling.

"Yeah. You saw it yourself. I know I said it was squirrels but it was me."

"Why?"

"I got my reasons."

The same answer Agnes had given when Cubiak asked her why she'd blasted a hole in her husband's chest.

"You're going to have to tell me, you know that? Sooner or later."

"No, I don't. All's I gotta do is confess."

"You need a motive."

"I got one."

Cubiak tapped the intercom button on the phone console. "Lisa, when you get a minute, would you mind bringing us a couple of coffees?" *When you get a minute*—their agreed upon code for ASAP. The sheriff remembered Walter at Ida's kitchen table. "Sugar. Extra cream. And cookies, if there are any." To Walter, he added, "The ladies bake but they're always dieting, too. Mostly they bring the stuff to work and I eat more than I should." Walter said nothing and while they waited, the sheriff scanned a stack of traffic reports. The silence held until Lisa set down the tray.

"Go on, the coffee'll do you good," Cubiak said, reaching for an oatmeal cookie as well. He knew he should march Walter to an interrogation room, read him his rights, and record their conversation but he figured that was step two if things went that far. This was step one. An informal chat.

"I've learned a few things the last week or so," Cubiak said as Walter ripped open a sugar packet and dumped the crystals into his cup.

"To begin, Huntsman wasn't the model father you said he was. Your old buddy Marty put me straight on that."

Walter stopped stirring his coffee. "You talked to Marty?"

"I did."

Walter frowned and worked his mouth as if he were trying to figure out just what Marty had told the sheriff. Letting him stew over the possibilities, Cubiak picked up a pen and drew a small circle on a sheet of paper, then another interlocking with the first. When the row of circles stretched across the page, he looked at Walter. "So, the question remains: if you murdered Big Guy and the other two, why did you do it?"

"I told you." Walter had grown increasingly pale. Against his alabaster complexion, his ebony eyes looked like bottomless pits.

"I know, 'You got your reason.'" Cubiak started the circles down the right margin. As he doodled the sheriff rehashed the mangled chain of recent events, searching for a pattern amid the confusion. There was something missing, something that linked the past with the present and connected one person with another. Something that propelled an innocent man to confess to murder.

Suddenly, he put the pen down. Looking at his visitor, he realized that the sorry, sad answer had started taking shape the day before when he'd been listening to Marty. "It has to do with Roger, doesn't it? This is all about him," he said quietly.

Walter blanched. Tears rimmed his eyes. "Yeah. It's about Roger," he said after a minute. "Marty claimed he left Door County because of Coach Vinter, 'cause of what he said the coach did. Once when he was back, he told me what happened, but I didn't believe him. I'd never heard anything like that, not even a hint of it and I'd been on the team for years, knew all the other guys. The coach seemed like a stand-up guy. Hell, he was married and had a couple of kids. I'd worshipped Vinter when I was young. We all did!

"And Marty? He was a bum that time when he came to see me. Bloodshot eyes, drunk all hours. He was always a big guy, wrestled at one-seventy junior year, and here he was skinny as a post and jittery, like he was shooting up dope or something. Hell, half the stuff he said made no sense. I figured he was making it up, about the coach and all that shit about his father and the others. I punched him out, told him he was off his rocker."

Walter rearranged his feet on the floor. "I knew about the parties with the women and had these men pegged for studs. You know that's how they finagled their great success as businessmen, right?"

"I do."

"You do?" Walter's face brightened. Then he snorted. "Well, I believe you do. Funny nobody else figured it out."

"No one had reason to question it."

"That's just what they wanted, wasn't it? To fool everyone." Walter scrubbed his face with his hands. "They were smart. Had everything figured out. And here I am, the biggest fool. I didn't see Marty for years after that. After a while, he started coming back regular-like every few years. Even bought a boat to have handy when he wanted to go out on the water. Eventually we got to talking again, but not about that. *That* was never mentioned again. All the more reason I thought it was just some crazy story he'd concocted when he was drunk or drugged up or something. After my wife left—the second one, Roger's mother—I had my hands full raising the boy and running my business. Didn't do a very good job with either. But I tried. Sent him to scouts and to church. Made sure he did his schoolwork. Every sport he wanted to try, I was okay with it. And when he made the wrestling team freshman year, I was proud. I didn't think twice about Vinter." Walter rubbed the back of his neck.

"Look at me, Sheriff. Compared to Huntsman, I'm a bust-out. A lousy husband. A half-bad mechanic. Bit of a boozer. A man with no ambition, nothing much up here." He tapped his head. "Big Guy always used to tell me I was an embarrassment. But I felt proud of what I'd done for Roger. And when he got that scholarship and won that medal, I felt like I could stand up next to anyone. Then it all started falling apart. Roger changed. I saw what happened to him over the summer and at first wrote it off to nerves. Figured once he got to that school, things would settle into place. But everything got worse. After he dropped out, I remembered Marty's story, and started wondering if maybe Marty had been telling the truth. It made me sick to think that my son had been through the same. I finally made Roger tell me what happened. It was the same fucking story as with Marty. The same goddamn thing," Walter said, flushed with rage.

"Why not take your revenge on Coach Vinter?"

"He wasn't here anymore. Moved away to Florida or Arizona. And anyway, it didn't start with him; it started with *them*, Big Guy and his pals. They were behind the wrestling program. They brought Bill Vinter here and then gave him a supply of young men to prey on."

"From what I know, Vinter never touched any of them when they were still boys."

"Yeah, well, maybe that's something to the law but what he did to Marty and Roger was bad enough." Walter looked at Cubiak. "I couldn't protect one of my own. What kind of man is that?"

Cubiak flinched. The same kind of man who couldn't save his own wife and daughter from a drunk driver, a man like him who must learn to live with things he cannot change. "You didn't know," he said.

"I didn't want to know. Marty tried to tell me but I wouldn't listen. Went around with my head in the sand and my gut full of booze. What could I have done anyways? Marty was gone. There was no proof of anything. Big Guy would have run me off the peninsula if I started shooting my mouth off.

"I was up there Friday afternoon when that St. James fellow brought copies of the *Herald* to the house. Said he was thinking of writing a book about the coast guard in the war and they'd be in it. Said he'd heard the governor was coming to the ceremony honoring them. Even the senator would be there. You should have seen Big Guy all puffed up. Him and the other two bragging and joshing around. I couldn't stand it. And then after Roger told me what happened, I swear to god, if I'd had a gun, I would have gone back up there and shot them all. But I was never any good with a gun, so I had to come up with a different way of dealing with them."

"The leaves in the vent."

Walter nodded. "Once that article came out, they'd be praised all up and down the peninsula. Then the ceremony! Christ! I grew up on stories about what a fantastic guy Huntsman was. All of them. But they were hypocrites. Phony husbands and phony fathers. Phony war heroes, too!" He kicked the desk. "They didn't fight any Japs up there in the Aleutians. They ferried the boys like my father who did. Christian Nils faced the enemy. He died protecting this country. He was one of the genuine heroes. He should be the one honored at the ceremony."

"I'm sure he will be mentioned," Cubiak said.

"Maybe. But he won't be there to hear his name called, will he?"

"Neither will they."

"That's right. I made sure of that, didn't I?" Walter said with smug satisfaction. "Unless they're listening from down there." He made a face and pointed toward the floor.

WEDNESDAY  16

As he prepared a batch of gruel for the puppies, Cubiak went over the previous day's conversation with Walter. If what he'd said about his son was true, then everything Roger had done made sense. Poor kid, Cubiak thought. Violated by someone he admired and trusted: the worse type of abuse. And it may have been felony criminal behavior. He'd have to confront Roger and get him to tell his side of the story.

Cubiak stirred the baby food beef, oatmeal, and milk that he'd spooned into a small bowl. Nasty stuff. He felt a pressure on his right foot and looked down. Kipper had climbed onto his instep and was trying to scale his ankle. "Now what?" he said as she slid off his boot and made a soft landing with her bottom. Scout was right behind, eager for his turn. The other two pups chewed the laces on his other boot. Across the room, Butch lay with her head on her paws and watched the circus. Normally, she'd be on her haunches begging for her share of the food, but even she seemed put off by the puppy pudding. Cubiak glanced at Natalie's handwritten recipe to make sure he'd followed her instructions.

"Okay, guys, breakfast," he said.

Cubiak lowered himself to the floor and set the bowl amid the quartet of pups.

They would need his help learning to eat solid foods, Natalie had said. The dogs didn't know how to consume anything other than milk and weren't strong enough to stand at the dish.

Cubiak picked up Kipper first. She'd caught up with the others and he wanted to make sure she maintained her weight. Slipping a hand under her belly, he guided her head toward the mush. She wiggled and pulled back until he dipped the tip of his finger into the gruel and held it to her mouth. She gave a tentative lick and then began to nip eagerly at his finger. As she ate, Cubiak thought about Walter. He wasn't someone he'd peg as a murderer, but Cubiak knew that paternal instinct could overrule a sense of right and wrong, and that anger fueled by alcohol could make a man do things he wouldn't normally consider.

Kipper was halfway through her second helping of mush when a car rolled up the driveway. A door slammed. It was probably Natalie, he thought, coming to make sure he was doing things right.

The abrupt knock on the back window meant the visitor was someone other than the vet.

"It's open," Cubiak said.

Solid footsteps dragged across the porch and then the kitchen door opened to Roger Nils. The sheriff wasn't entirely surprised to see him.

Roger was pale and wild-eyed. His clothes had that slept-in look and his hands twitched at his sides. He seemed confused by the sight of Cubiak on the floor with the puppies and swayed uncertainly as if preparing to turn and flee back into the yard.

"Roger, have a seat. What brings you out here?" Cubiak said, pushing up from the floor.

The boy remained standing. Had young Nils heard about Walter and come to plead his case? To help put him at ease, Cubiak handed the boy the squirming pup. "You mind holding her for a minute while I set the food on the counter? I'll feed the rest of them later."

Reaching behind his visitor, the sheriff closed the door. "Coffee?"

Roger held Kipper at an awkward distance and shook his head.

"You had breakfast?" Cubiak said as he poured a steaming cupful for himself.

"I ain't hungry." Roger pulled the pup to his chest and began to tremble.

"Why don't you sit down, relax a minute," Cubiak said as he guided the boy to a chair and pried the startled puppy free.

Roger swallowed a sob. After a minute he straightened to his full height, just as Walter had done the day before. "I came here to confess," he said.

"Confess to what?"

"Murdering those men. Big Guy, Swenson, and Wilkins."

The sheriff was startled but reacted with studied calm. "You killed your grandfather and his friends?"

"Yes. I didn't mean to. I mean, I did, but . . . then I didn't."

Cubiak put a mug of coffee in front of Roger and took a seat across from him. Nearby the pups frolicked, oblivious to the weighted silence in the room. "Tell me what happened," he said.

Roger traced a finger along the grain in the top of the table. "I knew they'd be in there that night," he said finally, his hand gliding across the oak. "And that they'd have the heater on. So I went up there and blocked the vent."

"How'd you know to do that?"

"Basic safety stuff. My dad's got a space heater in the garage. Used to lecture me all the time about making sure the vent wasn't plugged up."

"What'd you use?"

"Insulation pellets. There's a box of it at the garage."

"Why?"

Roger hung his head.

"When you confess to a crime as heinous as this, I need to know the reason." Cubiak reached down and stroked Nico's soft belly. "If you don't tell me, I might think you're lying to protect someone else."

The boy looked up. "Who?"

"Your father."

Roger blanched. "My dad?"

"Same MO, except he used dry leaves. He's been in jail since yesterday. I thought word would have gotten around town by now."

"I wasn't in town. You can't hold him. I don't know why he confessed but he didn't kill them. I did. I must have."

"What do you mean, you 'must have'? What'd you do?"

"I already told you, I stuffed the vent with insulation pellets."

"What time was this?"

"Just after midnight."

"You said you knew they'd be in there that night."

"Yeah. My father showed me a copy of the *Herald* with that article about them. Said the three of them were at the house, celebrating and getting ready for their Friday night game."

Roger wrapped his hands around the blue cup and frowned. When he picked up the story again, his voice was thin and tight. "I should've just left when I got done but I hung around a bit, to see what would happen. The front curtain was open and I could see them sitting around the table. I watched Big Guy play his cards. Like this"—he whipped his hand through the air and with a flourish threw his imaginary cards at an invisible table—"and the other two moaned and complained. Jesus, they were pathetic. Three old men. Three drunk old men." Roger hunched over and pulled into himself. "I couldn't do it. I wanted to, but I couldn't. I went around back and pulled the shit out of the vent and left before I changed my mind again. Next morning when my dad called and told me they were dead, I freaked. Figured I must not have cleaned everything out. I killed them, Sheriff."

"If you say." Cubiak sipped his coffee. "Nobody saw you going there or back?"

"No. It's easy enough to get around without being seen."

"Is it? I suppose you used Marty Wilkins's boat and came up around the bay side to that little cove with the black rocks?"

Roger started. "How . . . ?"

"Marty took me for a ride before he left town and explained how he left the key for the boat with Walter. Figured you just borrowed it for your own little escapade."

Butch nudged the sheriff's knee. "Excuse me, gotta let her out," he said.

When he came back, Roger's cup was empty.

The sheriff refilled it. "Now. Let's start this all over," he said as he sat down. "Why'd you do it?"

"It's personal."

"Murder usually is, unless it's part of a larger crime like robbery. Murdering a family member, someone you've known a long time, now that's usually a crime with roots that go way back. Personal stuff, like you said."

Roger squirmed.

"I don't know much about those three gentlemen, but I'm starting to get a sense of the real story behind the public image. Sorry to say I wouldn't be overly surprised if your involvement—whatever it may be—is connected to whatever turned you from a high school wrestling champ into the bust-out you're trying to become." Cubiak watched the boy carefully. When Roger tensed, the sheriff knew to keep going. "Something happened between the time you graduated last June and now. I think I've got a pretty good idea what."

"You don't know shit."

"Possibly." Cubiak paused. "But if I had to guess, I'd say it had something to do with Coach Vinter."

Roger squeezed his hands until his knuckles were white. "How . . . ?"

"That's not important right now. Nothing happened while you were in high school, correct?"

The young man nodded, still on high alert.

"What changed?"

"I don't know."

"You graduated and were no longer a student. You also turned eighteen."

"So?" Roger looked blank.

"You became an adult. Legally at least. If something happened the summer after your birthday and with your consent, then there's no problem," Cubiak said, laying out the best case scenario he could imagine. "Vinter did not prey on you, didn't force himself on you. He waited until you were of age and he approached you, came on to you as it were. You were free to say yes or no. Correct?"

"No." The response was terse, strangled.

"I see." Then it was like with Marty, Cubiak thought. "He fed you booze, maybe drugs, too. You blacked out and woke up naked next to him."

The color vanished from Roger's face. His mouth was set, his eyes wide.

"You have no memory of what happened."

The boy rocked back and forth. "How . . . ?" The word was a whisper.

"He did the same thing to Marty Wilkins. Years ago."

Roger doubled over and began to sob.

Cubiak waited. He'd lost count of the times he'd sat with someone in their kitchen or living room and walked them through circumstances no one should have to deal with. It was never easy to do and hard to comprehend how one human being could brutalize another. For the pleasure of it? No, it was always for the power.

The room quieted. "You did nothing wrong, but what Vinter did was criminal. You could have pressed charges," Cubiak said.

Roger was still alabaster but the fear in his eyes had softened. "He said that if I told anyone, he'd turn the tables and say it was me, that I'd been after him all year. He said he would see that I lost my scholarship and place on the UW roster. He actually bragged about it. 'I can do that and you know it.'"

The boy's voice wavered. Cubiak poured more coffee and set Buddy down in front of him.

As he talked, Roger cuddled the puppy. "I was scared. Why are you doing this, I asked him, and he snickered and said he thought it ran in the family. When I asked him what he meant by that, he laughed again and said I should go ask Big Guy."

"Did you?"

Roger took a deep breath and nodded. "I drove up to see him the next day. Big Guy was in the Rec Room. Talking, like he always did. Telling me about the new boat he was gonna buy. About his plans for another van. There were chips at four of the spots at the table. It was gonna be him, Swenson, Wilkins, and that Joe Millard guy playing that night. I'm standing there not knowing what to say and suddenly I see everything clear as day. And I tell him about Vinter and what I'm thinking when I see this setup. He said that was too bad about the coach but I shouldn't worry 'cause Vinter was moving and I'd probably never see him again. 'What about you?' I said, and he told me that how he lived his life was none of my business."

Roger studied the floor. "Maybe he was right, except that I'd idolized him my whole life. We weren't close but that didn't matter. I grew up on the stories of what a terrific guy he was. I had this big chance because of him, because of wrestling, because I'd lived by that fucking pledge."

"The pledge?"

"Yeah. From the very beginning, if you wanted to be on the team, you had to promise to fight clean. To be honest in the way you approached both the sport and your life. To be a gentleman." Roger almost choked on the word. "A gentleman! Me? The idea went to my head, thinking that maybe I could make something of myself, be somebody, not just some grease monkey fixing flat tires for rich tourists. What a bunch of horseshit, huh? You know who wrote the pledge? Big Guy!"

Roger shot to his feet, startling Buddy and the other pups. Butch lifted her ears and made a deep, throaty sound. "To be honest about the way you lived your life! Like Big Guy? What a joke. He wasn't up there playing with himself, you know. Eric and Jasper and god knows who else were in on it, too. They weren't honest about anything." The boy slumped against the counter, the piss and vinegar gone.

"You think they could have been back then?" Cubiak said after a moment.

"I don't know. Maybe. No. I guess not." Roger kicked the door. "Shit."

"What happened then?"

"Nothing. I told my grandfather I was through with him, and I left." Roger paced between the door and the sink. "Hung around town until it was time to go to Eau Claire. I was on the team but I couldn't wrestle. Hated it. Couldn't put my hands on the other guys without thinking about Coach Bill."

"You had no one to talk to?"

Roger grabbed a chair, swung it around, and dropped down. "I didn't know anyone except the other guys on the team, and I sure as hell wasn't gonna say anything to them. Then I came back home one weekend and heard about the cutter launch and the big ceremony being planned. I couldn't believe it. My life was falling apart and Big Guy and those other two were gonna be held up like heroes. I couldn't stand the thought and knew I had to do something to try and stop it."

"Chief Dotson got a half-dozen threatening messages last fall. You sent those, didn't you?"

Roger looked surprised. "Yeah. The team had a heavy traveling schedule and every time we were in a different town, I mailed a letter to the station chief. I wanted him to think there were people around the state who were unhappy about this, hoping he'd change his mind."

"But he didn't, and in the meantime, you dropped out of school."

Roger gripped the chair and leaned back. "I had to. I'd flunked all my classes and lost the scholarship. There wasn't anything else to do but leave, and I had nowhere to go except to come back here."

"Did you tell Walter what happened?"

"Hell, no! Not then. I knew he was disappointed, so I tried to make it up somehow. Got a job delivering pizzas and then working at the coast guard station. Pretty crazy, huh? I blame Big Guy for ruining my life and then find myself fixing up things for this big event where he'll be one of the stars. What the fuck, I thought. One day I found these cartons in the storage room. I'd heard that some of the stuff was gonna be put on display and figured if I couldn't stop the event, I could try and sabotage it. So I took a couple of the boxes."

"Where'd you put them?

"In the loft at the garage. I didn't want my roommates to find them."

"What's in the boxes?"

"A lot of papers. Old pictures and shit. I didn't really pay that much attention at first."

"Your dad found the stuff?"

"Yeah. He was really pissed at me, too. Kept bugging me about walking off with the archives. I told him I just borrowed some stuff 'cause I wanted to know more about the coast guard and local history. He knew I always liked history in school and at first he bought it. Then he got on me about taking it back, but by that time I'd stopped working at the station. He couldn't understand any of it. He was really disappointed that I quit school, kept saying he didn't want me to be a bust-out like him. He was on my back about it all winter, telling me to talk to someone and reapply.

"That Friday evening, I was at the garage going through all those records and shit, getting really pissed off. Every time I saw a picture of Big Guy, the other two were with him. Jesus, it was so fucking obvious. Then my dad came in with the *Herald*. He was already half in the bag and mad, too. When he saw what I was looking at, he grabbed a couple of the photos and tore them in half. 'Fucking hypocrites,' he said. I'd been drinking some myself and wasn't exactly sure what he meant but somehow we both started going on about Big Guy. Suddenly my father got real quiet and looked at me kind of funny. 'You gonna tell me what the hell's been going on or do I have to guess?' he said."

"You told him?"

"Yeah. Everything." Roger played with his thumbnail. "I don't know why. Should have just kept quiet about it but I guess I finally had to tell someone, so I told him."

Just as Marty had so many years before. "How did he take it?"

"I never saw him so out of control. He started throwing things and yelling. Cursing the coach and Big Guy, blaming himself. Said he'd failed me and begged me to forgive him. I kept pouring him shots just to calm him down. Finally he passed out."

"And you?"

"I filled my pocket with Styrofoam and took the boat up to Gills Rock."

Cubiak dropped two slices of bread into the toaster. When they popped up, he put the toast on the table with jars of peanut butter and cherry jam. "Here, I already ate," he said.

Roger forgot that he wasn't hungry.

"Then on Sunday night you came back and vandalized the shed, just to muck things up a bit," Cubiak said.

Roger grimaced, his mouth full of food.

"And the boat?"

"I didn't go near the *Ida Mae*. I wouldn't do that, not to something with my grandma's name on it."

"Did you write the note?"

The last of the food disappeared off the plate. "What note?"

"There was a message left in Ida's mailbox," Cubiak said as he cleared the table.

"What'd it say?"

Under the gush of running water, the sheriff ignored the question and thought about what he was going to do with Roger. Cubiak didn't want to lock him up with Walter where the two could compare stories. He also wanted to keep the boy—he couldn't help but think of Roger as still a kid—out of the legal system. Walter had a paltry record, several drunk and disorderly conduct charges. But Roger had a clean slate. There'd been no trace of Styrofoam pellets in the vent the morning the bodies were discovered. Cubiak was sure the boy was telling the truth but worried that according to the letter of the law it might not be enough to keep him from being prosecuted.

He held out his hand. "Give me your keys."

"My keys. What for?"

"I'm leaving you here—call it house arrest. If you give me the keys to your car, I'll feel better knowing you're not about to take off and that if you do, you won't get very far."

"You want me to stay here?"

"Yes."

Roger brightened. "Not worried I'll trash the joint or rob you blind?"

"Nothing worth stealing. Besides, the puppies will need feeding in another couple of hours and I don't have anyone scheduled to come in. The instructions and everything you need for their food are there," he said, pointing to the counter. "You just have to remember to hold them up, otherwise they'll fall face first into the bowl. They can't stand on their own yet."

"Aren't you gonna book me and let my father go?"

"There's time for that."

Roger pulled his key ring from his pocket and tossed it up and down. "You can't hold my father. He's innocent."

Cubiak snatched the keys in midair and opened the door with his foot. "Everyone's innocent until proven guilty," he said and stepped backward onto the porch.

Cubiak found Agnes curled up on her cot, her face to the wall. Was she sleeping? She had refused to make bond and seemed to enjoy the simple routine and the relative comfort of her surroundings. For the first time she could eat without slaving in the kitchen, she'd told Cubiak. In the men's wing, Walter also lay on his bed, hands behind his head and eyes open. His mouth twitched, as if he were uttering a prayer or hankering for a taste of whiskey. At the sound of the door lock releasing, he flung his feet to the floor and sat up. He looked almost cheerful as he greeted the sheriff.

"Morning . . ."

"Roger claims he did it."

The man's smile disappeared. "What the hell you talking about?"

"He's at my house now. Came out and confessed this morning."

"You ain't arrested him?"

"Not yet."

Walter wet his lips and screwed up his mouth. "He didn't do it."

"He thinks he did." Cubiak leaned against the cellblock wall. "Even told me how."

"Stupid fucking kid!"

"Why don't we start all over again? Only this time, you tell me what happened Friday night when you came to and realized that Roger was gone."

Walter rested his elbows on his knees. "It was Saturday morning."

"All right, Saturday morning. Still dark. After Roger told you what had happened last summer with Vinter and what Big Guy said to him, you drank yourself into a stupor. When you came to and saw that the key to Marty's boat was gone, you knew Roger had gone up to the cabin and figured he was up to no good."

Walter nodded.

"You went after him?"

"I couldn't. He took my keys! Probably afraid I'd get behind the wheel and kill someone."

Or yourself, Cubiak thought. "So you waited for him. And when he got back you made him tell you where'd he gone and what he'd done."

"He swore he'd cleared away all the pellets, Sheriff, and I believed him. Roger never lied to me. I was relieved he'd changed his mind. Proud of him for that."

"But you had to make sure, didn't you? Before daylight you snuck up to the cabin, using Marty's boat, just like Roger had hours before. And when you got there, Big Guy and the others were okay, still at the table playing cards."

"I don't know what they were doing. The curtains were closed and I didn't hear anything. Figured they'd fallen asleep." Walter grabbed the edge of the mattress. "The vent was clean, like Roger said, just a couple pellets inside. Not enough to do any damage."

"What time was it?"

"Four, four thirty, maybe. It was still dark."

"And no one knew you were there. If anyone saw a boat on the water they'd figure it was a fisherman heading out early. You could do anything you wanted and get away with it. You had plenty of reason to want to settle the score with Big Guy and his pals. So you brushed away the last of the foam beads and filled the vent with dried leaves, thinking you'd blame the squirrels."

"That's right. Just like I said."

Walter held the sheriff's gaze. Cubiak wanted to believe him but couldn't be sure that he was telling the truth. He might have found more bits of Styrofoam than he admitted and if so, the men might already have been dead.

Cubiak turned toward the hallway. "What about the stuff Roger took from the coast guard station?"

"Everything's still in the upstairs room at the garage."

The sheriff pivoted around. "You look through it?"

"Some."

"Take anything out?"

"No."

"I'd like to see it. Get a search warrant and go over it myself."

Walter fell against the wall. "Hell, Sheriff, you don't need no warrant. Just go on in. Front door's padlocked, but you can get in from the side. There's a door down the gangway from the alley. Key's on a nail under the eave, right side of the door."

"You don't worry about someone coming in and stealing your tools?"

Walter snorted. "I'm more worried about getting soused and locking myself out." He crushed his hands together and looked at Cubiak. "Roger's a good kid. You can't arrest him, Sheriff. I did it."

When he returned to his office, Cubiak pulled out the threatening letters that had been sent to the coast guard station chief and arranged them in chronological order across his desk while he waited for Lisa to get the number for the athletic department at the University of Wisconsin at Eau Claire.

He talked to three people before he was transferred to the school's wrestling coach, who agreed to fax a copy of the squad's away schedule from the previous fall. "I'd scan it but I can never get the damn thing to work and my secretary is out sick," he said.

"A fax is fine," Cubiak said.

The schedule confirmed that the dates and locales coincided with the letters sent to Chief Dotson. Cubiak studied the wall map behind his desk. Over four months the team had traveled to the UW campuses in Stevens Point and Platteville as well as to several other locations, allowing Roger to postmark his threats from towns around the state, inadvertently leaving a trail of evidence that would undermine any argument about a crime of passion. With this information available, a prosecutor would have little trouble arguing the state's case for premeditated murder against Roger.

Cubiak shrugged into his jacket and headed out again. "I'll be at the coroner's—sorry, Doctor Bathard's—if anyone needs me," he told Lisa.

Bathard was spreading primer over the hull when the sheriff rolled back the door to the boat barn. A Mozart piano concerto flowed from the overhead speakers.

"You finished sanding the Bondo already?" Cubiak said.

"Yesterday."

Cubiak surveyed the *Parlando*. There were still months of hard work to be done on the boat but already the vessel was taking on a regal air. "I thought you'd be getting things ready for Saturday."

The coroner gave a wry smile. "I'm getting myself ready." He stripped off his gloves and lowered the volume on the stereo. "I may have been a bit cavalier the other day, making things sound so simple and straightforward, but they're not. Truth is I question every step I've taken since Cornelia died. We don't ever know, really, the right thing to do. I can give you a dozen reasons why I shouldn't marry Sonja, and a dozen why I should. Ultimately, I simply have to decide, yea or nay."

"You mean you might not go through with it?" The wedding was three days away.

"To be honest, at this moment, I don't know."

Cubiak had never seen Bathard so indecisive and was uncertain how to respond. He needed his friend to be a rock, to show the way even if he chose not to follow. "I don't know what to say."

"There's nothing you can say."

"Does Sonja know?"

"Sonja!" Bathard chuckled. "Sonja's going through her own version of hellish self-examination."

"You've talked about this with her?"

"It's all we talk about. We'll probably be talking about it as we walk up the church steps." Bathard tamped the lid onto the can of primer. "Life is a leap of faith, son. You jump or you don't, and right now I feel the concrete hardening around my ankles." The coroner started toward the door. "Let's get out of here, go to the house. I'd like a drink."

In the library, they watched the sky fill with striations of orange and pink as the sun slipped below the horizon. Over whiskey, Cubiak told Bathard about Roger.

"It never ends, does it? And there's still this other business to sort out," the doctor said.

"Walter claims the vent was clean when he got there."

"If so, then Roger didn't kill the men. Still, in terms of intent and action, he's as guilty as his father, even though he said he changed his mind. It's also possible that Walter is lying to protect him," Bathard said.

"I'm not so sure either of them is guilty."

"Really?" The physician swirled his glass. "I don't follow. I haven't had that much yet, have I?"

"Roger arrives at the cabin around midnight. He stuffs insulation into the vent, sees the men through the open curtain, has a stab of conscience, and cleans out the pellets—or thinks he has—and then he leaves. When Walter gets there it's some four hours later. The curtains are closed so he can't see in. He doesn't hear anything, but the vent is clear and he assumes the men are sleeping and haven't suffered any ill effects from the bits of insulation Roger failed to retrieve."

"If Walter is telling the truth and not trying to protect Roger."

"Right. Walter clears out the few stray bits of insulation Roger left behind and stuffs the vent with dried leaves. But who's to say it has the effect he thinks it has?"

"There's no question the three men died from carbon monoxide poisoning."

"I understand that. I'm just not sure it unfolded the way Roger thought it had or Walter claimed it did."

"So what did happen?"

"I have an idea but nothing that's gelled yet." Cubiak stared at the darkening water and remembered how he'd done the same at Gills Rock the day the three men had been found dead. Now as then he'd hoped to find the answers to life's questions among the waves.

"What are you going to do with Roger? You can't let him stay with you."

"I thought maybe he could stay here."

Bathard slapped his knees. "Just what I need."

"You've got plenty of room. He could help in the shop. Help set up for . . ."

"The wedding."

"Yeah."

Bathard crossed to the window. A low star glittered over the bay. "I don't know why I'm doing this, but okay, send him over. I'll have dinner waiting."

THURSDAY MORNING

17

At the kitchen table, Cubiak opened his new laptop and logged on to the local marine weather website. Wind speed and direction, temperature, and wave height for the bay were the same as those from the previous Friday night. He called Rowe.

"You're a boater, aren't you?" he said.

"You kidding? I practically grew up in my dad's outboard. Got my own twenty-five-foot cruiser. Well, actually, I own it with a couple other guys. Why?"

Cubiak scanned the wide expanse of Lake Michigan visible through the window. Four miles out, blips of light flickered like neon fireflies where the sun reflected off the dozen or so fishing boats clustered along the Bank Reef. At the dropoff, the lake depth plunged from sixty to three hundred feet, and fish stacked up along the rock wall as if vying for the chance to be plucked from the water.

"I need you to take Marty Wilkins's boat up to Gills Rock. See how fast you can make it there and back."

"Marty Wilkins has a boat?"

"The *Can-Do*, moored at Sunset Marina."

"And I'm doing this 'cause . . . ?"

"I've got reason to believe that both Walter Nils and his son, Roger, were up to no good at Huntsman's cabin that Friday night the men died. If what they're telling me is true, they went up separately using Wilkins's boat, which he left in Walter's care. I need to know how long it takes to get there and back to see if their stories hold up. Whoever makes the trip has to be someone who can go at top speed, and I figure you're a good candidate."

"You got it, Chief. Around here, I can't drive my car as fast as I want but it's another story on a boat. No speed limit out there."

Unfortunately, Cubiak thought, and then explained where to find the boat and the key. "Call me when you're back," he said. "And be careful." He hung up the phone. Listen to me, he mused. I sound like I'm turning into an old fart.

Half an hour later, Cubiak unlocked the side door of Walter's garage and flipped on the wall switch. Walter was not a tidy mechanic, but the full garage indicated that he was at least a competent one. Cubiak found the box of Styrofoam in the corner where Roger said it would be. He crammed a handful of the pellets into his pocket and climbed a flight of stairs along the side wall. The door at the top opened to a loft apartment lit by a row of circular skylights, like portals on a ship.

Various bits of furniture had been dropped around the room, enough to make it livable. Three boxes of coast guard memorabilia peeked from under the bed. Each was stamped Property of Sturgeon Bay Station. Someone had written Save in black marker on the tops and sides of each box and secured the lids with duct tape.

Cubiak sat on the edge of the mattress and slid one of the boxes between his feet. He expected neatly organized file folders arranged by date or locale. Instead, the contents were a jumble. Photos, charts, weather reports, newspaper clippings, letters home, a couple of programs for religious services, as well as leaflets for mess hall dances and lectures were tossed together. No time to maintain orderly records during the war, he thought. And then, well, who wanted to remember or had time to devote to past horrors once peace had been declared? He picked up a stack of material and sifted out a handful of black-and-white prints. The photos were faded and stuck together: ships and men; boats in port and on the high seas; sailors saluting the flag, standing for inspection, playing softball behind their barracks. Nothing resembled the photo Marty Wilkins had seen as a kid.

The three dead veterans had served aboard the USS *Arthur Middleton*. Cubiak found a reference to the ship in the second box along with a stack of photos, all of them taken in a tropical setting, Hawaii perhaps or one of the other Pacific ports. The only photos linked to the Aleutian Campaign were shots of the military facilities on the islands. He unearthed no photographic documentation of the battles fought. At the bottom of the carton, in a manila envelope, he found the photos of the three friends that Roger had described, but these were pictures taken at their induction.

The contents of the third box covered the war in Europe and the Mediterranean: the D-Day invasion at Normandy, Operation Torch in North Africa, and photos and several dozen diaries and letters the sailors or their families had donated to the military. Nothing pertained to Huntsman, Swenson, and Wilkins. The three from Gills Rock had not fought in those theaters.

Cubiak took the cartons to headquarters and called the station chief.

"Roger Nils stumbled on the archives when he was working at the station. The kid's something of an amateur historian and took three of the boxes without thinking. He was curious and wanted to learn more about the war. Hard to tell if anything's missing. The items aren't organized."

"That's what I was afraid of," Dotson said. "I'll send someone over, get it off your hands."

"Actually, I'm kind of curious myself and wouldn't mind having a little more time to go through it all."

Cubiak sensed the officer's hesitation. "I was special forces. Kuwait. Hard to get a feeling for what it's like to serve aboard ship," he said. "Five days, that's all, and I'll bring everything back. That gives you time to sort out what you need for the exhibition."

Once Dotson agreed, Cubiak ended the conversation before the chief could talk about pressing charges against Roger for theft.

An hour later, Rowe called.

"That is one sweet boat Marty's got. Really souped-up. Going full throttle, I made it up and back to Gills Rock in just about one hour. Into the headwind, thirty-five minutes. With it at my back, twenty-five."

"You thought it would take longer?"

"Oh, yeah. No question. Even in my boat, which is pretty fast, I figured an hour fifteen at least."

"Would the trip take longer at night?"

"Maybe for someone who's not familiar with the bay, but if you're from around here and know the route it wouldn't make much difference. Plus the boat's got more than enough lights."

"Where are you now?"

"The marina. I called as soon as I got back, like you said."

"Do me a favor, okay? Gas up and wait for me."

"You going out?"

"Maybe."

Cubiak was going out, as Rowe had guessed. The question was whether he trusted himself to pilot Marty's power boat or wanted his deputy at the helm. The marine forecast was reassuring but Cubiak needed to check conditions for himself. At several spots on the way to the marina, he glimpsed Green Bay through the trees. No whitecaps.

By the time the sheriff reached the harbor, the sun was out and Rowe was sprawled in the cockpit of the *Can-Do*, his hat off and his face open to the rays. The boat rocked as Cubiak climbed aboard, and the deputy bolted upright, grabbing the two cups at his side.

"Chief! Here, careful it's hot. Light on the cream, just the way you like it," he said, handing one of the cups to Cubiak.

The sheriff sat across from Rowe, their knees nearly touching. Cubiak didn't want the coffee but took an obligatory sip. "Much traffic out there?"

"Just a tanker heading to Green Bay."

"No fishermen?"

Rowe slapped his cap on. "Not that I saw. The commercial boats would've come in already and it's too early in the season for the charters."

"Up at the tip, when you turned into the bay toward the cove, how much of the town did you see?"

"Nada. There's a spur that juts out near the park. It blocks everything."

Just as it had when he stood on the stone beach, Cubiak thought, shielding his eyes as he twisted and looked toward the harbor entrance. The water in the channel was flat.

"That it, then? I still got those reports to finish," Rowe said.

"The reports can wait. I need you to go back up to Huntsman's place and do one more thing."

"I was just there!"

"And what you did verified one part of the equation. There's still the question of whether stuffing the vent with Styrofoam or leaves could increase the amount of carbon monoxide in the cabin to dangerous levels."

Rowe didn't look any too happy. "I don't know, Chief. I'm not sure about wanting to be a guinea pig for some kind of experiment."

"Come on, Mike, I'm not asking you to inhale the stuff. Get a gas mask and carbon monoxide detector from the fire department and then here's what you're gonna do." Cubiak gave Rowe the pellets from his pocket and explained how Roger said he'd stuffed the vent with them and then changed his mind and what Walter had done to block it with dried leaves. "Maybe they're both telling the truth or maybe Walter is still covering for Roger. He claims the men were alive when he got there but the curtains were closed, so he couldn't know for certain," the sheriff said.

At the Rec Room, Rowe was to turn the space heater on, set the meter in the cabin, shove as many of the pellets as he could into the vent hood, and then check the meter every thirty minutes for four hours and record the readings. "Make sure the windows and door are closed and the heater is cranked up. When you're done testing the pellets, air out the room so the meter's back to zero. Then replace the pellets with dried leaves and grass and repeat the process. Just make sure you're wearing the mask whenever you go in and you'll be okay. No taking chances, got it?"

"Yeah. But, Chief, what do I say if someone sees me and asks what I'm doing?"

"Tell them you're following my orders."

"You gonna be okay out there?" Rowe said, pointing toward the bay.

"Alone? Sure I'll be fine."

"Where you headed?"

"So you know where to send the rescue team?" Cubiak put up a hand to stop Rowe's protest. "Chambers Island," he said.

THURSDAY AFTERNOON

18

He felt like Ahab.

Little matter that there was a fresh-water bay, not an ocean, beneath the hull, and that the vessel wasn't battling mountainous waves but slicing through the flat surface of a placid inland waterway. Holding tight to the wheel of the *Can-Do*, Cubiak was buoyed by a refreshing sense of mastery and freedom.

The sheriff remembered asking Ida Huntsman if she'd resented having missed the intimacy of sex during her lengthy marriage to Big Guy, and she'd said no because she had good memories and a good imagination. Cubiak had no seafaring memories but a good enough imagination to project himself into the spirit of a legendary sea captain on the hunt. Rowe had said that on the water, he could go as fast as he wanted. Piloting the boat, Cubiak understood the urge.

At the marina, he'd approached Marty's boat with trepidation and under Rowe's fretful gaze, he'd lurched away from the dock in clumsy fits and starts before crawling through the narrow channel to the bay. Once on open water, he waved to his deputy, but as soon as he was out of sight, Cubiak put the throttle in neutral and searched for a life vest. He started to slip one on, then changed his mind and dropped it at his feet within easy reach.

Giving the engine a steady stream of gas, he headed north. Land was never far from starboard, but he kept his eyes pinned on the open water and enjoyed the torrent of cool wind in his hair and the spray on his face. Would sailing be this exhilarating? he wondered.

West of Peninsula State Park, where Cubiak had briefly worked as a ranger, his target appeared: not a massive white whale breaking the surface but a dark smear of land disrupting the clear line of the horizon. As he drew near, Chambers Island transformed into a forest of pine, oak, and hemlock trees; the colorless ridge on its face turned from baleen to a rocky shoreline; and a half-dozen boathouses emerged from the afternoon shadows. A row of private docks extended into the water, and behind them narrow walkways trailed off into the woods. Besides a religious retreat center and decommissioned lighthouse, there were some four dozen cabins and houses on the island and only two were occupied year round. The modest yellow frame bungalow on the northeast corner had belonged to Ben Macklin, who had been the sole occupant for more than fifty years. After the old fisherman's unfortunate death, the landscape painter who bought the property converted the living room into a studio but left the front lawn hung with old fishing nets. A small motorboat bobbed in the water alongside his pier. No smoke rose from the chimney, but the curtains were open and Cubiak waved, in case someone was home.

A quarter mile farther, he circled toward the open waters of Green Bay and then into a narrow passage marked by two jetties. The channel led to a long metal pier. He maneuvered Marty Wilkins's boat behind a large power boat named the *Red, White, and Blue* and cut the engine.

In the heavy stillness, Cubiak surveyed the spectacle before him. Welcome to America, he thought, taking in the massive flag that fluttered at the end of the pier, the fierce American eagles painted on the sides and door of the boathouse, and the tall, spiked fence decorated with the insignias of the major armed services.

The fence surrounded a long, sloping lawn filled with restored World War II military vehicles and weapons—including an army jeep, a restored battlefield ambulance, and two howitzers—and overlooked by an impressive, two-story white colonial. The tricolored brick pathway that led to the house was flanked by a phalanx of flags. Cubiak recognized those of France, England, Poland, Canada, Greece, and Norway, all U.S. allies during the last big war.

On the colonnaded porch, the nation's motto, In God We Trust, was carved in a wooden plaque that hung above the entryway. As he reached for the bell, the front door swung open.

"Sheriff, this way, please." A short, wiry man in a brown, three-piece suit stepped back to allow him in.

The greeter stood in a vaulted foyer blanketed with articles from *Stars and Stripes* and copies of wartime declarations and newspaper headlines declaring battle victories. To the left, a wide stairway and two closed doors were roped off and marked Private. "This way," the man said again, pointing toward an arched doorway on the right.

The public portion of the house was as much museum as the yard. Glass-topped display cases crammed with regimental badges and medals lined the first two rooms. In the third, which, judging from the fireplace, had once been the parlor, dozens of handguns and rifles were displayed under the nations' flags whose armies had claimed them as their own: Walters, Lugers, Colts, Marlins, and Carbines. How many times had each been fired, Cubiak wondered, and how many were dead as a result? The fourth room, another smaller parlor, was decorated with bits and pieces of old uniforms—an Eisenhower army jacket, an American Red Cross nurse dress, a medic's helmet with the red cross painted in a white circle—hanging on racks or from hooks along the walls.

Finally they reached a long passageway at the rear of the house. The inside wall was papered with war posters—Uncle Sam Wants You, Are

You a Star-Spangled Girl?, Loose Lips Sink Ships—but the windows opposite opened to the present and Cubiak happily took in the view of the peaceful and ordinary: a wooden pergola and large stone patio, a freshly turned garden patch, a small cedar toolshed, and a metal-cage dog run where a pair of black and brown Dobermans loped back and forth.

At the end of the hallway, the suited man rapped on a wide door and rolled the panel open without waiting for a response. He motioned Cubiak in and just as quickly stepped back and pulled the door shut, leaving Cubiak inside a glass-walled annex. The oppressive heat and bright light reminded him of school field trips to the desert room at the Garfield Park Conservatory on Chicago's west side. But there were no plants in the domed room. Instead of cacti, the private greenhouse held more display cases of military medals and small firearms. In the apex stood two mannequins, one in the full dress uniform of a four-star army general, the other in the fatigues of a private.

"I like to acknowledge both extremes of the military spectrum, those burdened with issuing orders and those charged with following them." Cubiak turned toward the source of the sonorous announcement as a ghostly figure slowly emerged from the shadows. "Welcome. I must say I wondered when you'd come."

"Charles Tweet?"

"I am."

Cubiak approached. The old man held himself with military bearing despite the gray hair, parchment skin, the woolen throw covering his lap, and the wheelchair he occupied.

Tweet gave a sharp salute. "Reporting for duty, sir," he said. Then he chuckled. "Always confounds visitors. They don't know whether to take me seriously."

"Should they?"

"Depends what they want."

Cubiak held out his badge but Tweet waved it away. "I know who you are. The question is what do *you* want?"

"The truth," Cubiak said, clipping the emblem onto his belt.

Tweet patted the plaid throw on his lap as if to check on the solidity of the limbs beneath. "Whose truth?"

"Why don't we start with yours?"

Tweet dipped his head. "Permission to proceed," he said.

"The *Herald* recently published an article about the three veterans who died in Gills Rock. They had served together during World War II. You are the former *Stars and Stripes* reporter mentioned in that story."

"Guilty as charged."

"Can you explain how you were in Alaska during the Aleutian Campaign in 1943 when the Pacific edition of the paper didn't begin publication until two years later, in 1945?"

The one-time journalist cleared his throat. "You've done your homework. I was very clear with the young man who interviewed me about my assignment and rank during the campaign. At the time of the fight up north, I was an army private, working as a combat photographer. The military had guys like me in all the theaters, documenting the action. I didn't start working for *Stars and Stripes* until after the war. I'm sure the reporter got it right, probably was his editor who botched the facts. They often do, for the sake of brevity."

"You knew the three men who died—Huntsman, Swenson, and Wilkins?"

"I knew a lot of the men stationed up there."

"But those three specifically?"

"Yes, I knew them."

"Shame about them dying."

Tweet plucked at the hem of his blanket.

"You don't agree?" Cubiak said.

The former newsman looked up sharply. "I assumed it was a rhetorical statement. We all die in due course, and in my view they were old enough to die. They'd had their time and were spared the worst ravages of aging." A coughing spell interrupted him. "I have Parkinson's, Sheriff. I'm entitled to be blunt."

Cubiak waited for Tweet to settle. "There are indications that not everyone was saddened by the deaths of the three veterans," he said and explained the graffiti at Huntsman's place.

Tweet seemed surprised. "Competitors, perhaps. As I understand it they were all very successful."

"In your league, then."

Tweet stretched his mouth into a tight smile.

"Did you ever get together with them?"

"Why would I want to do that? To reminisce over old times? Not my cup of tea, Sheriff."

"It seems you might be inclined to do so, given your preoccupation with all things military," Cubiak said.

"I'm not the sociable type. Not the kind to maintain friendly relations with old army buddies."

"You were at the funeral."

"As a show of respect."

"But you had no contact with them after your service days."

"I didn't say that."

"No direct personal contact, perhaps. But I have reason to believe that sometime in the 1950s you sent Jasper Wilkins a photograph taken during the Aleutian Campaign, a photograph of the three veterans in a landing craft."

Tweet tried to shrug. Cubiak had struck a nerve.

"I may have, Sheriff. I don't remember. That's a long time back. There were one or two times I culled my files; if I had a name, an address, maybe I'd send something along. Hard to keep track of all the men I met over the years. And what if I did?"

Cubiak ignored the question. "You said you were a combat photographer."

"Yes."

"The Aleutian Campaign was largely ignored both during and after the war. It was Iwo Jima . . ."

"Iwo Jima." Tweet shuddered. "Nearly seven thousand Americans

191

killed and another twenty thousand wounded. When it started, there were twenty-two thousand Japs on the island and when it was over, there were two hundred and sixteen left. I don't think any of those men who died there went to hell. They'd had a bellyful of hell already. Five weeks of it. Men die in war and to them it doesn't matter if they're on sand or ice when they breathe their last. But while our men were slogging through mud and snow up north, the brass hadn't decided yet which arena was more likely to capture the imagination of the American people and ordered extensive coverage of both. Turns out, the South Pacific islands provided a better photographic backdrop than the Aleutians. Difficult to focus in the fog or get glory shots of guys huddled in parkas, freezing their asses off."

Cubiak wiped the sweat from his forehead. "Did you know Christian Nils?"

This time Tweet ignored the question. "Too warm in here for you, Sheriff?" He hit a switch on the arm of his chair and rolled forward. "This way," he said, steering toward the door. It opened automatically and Tweet headed down the hallway. "This all started as a hobby," he said, indicating the posters on the wall. "After the war, I was in the unique position to come across war memorabilia before it became memorabilia and had the good sense to start picking it up early. A lot of men just wanted to forget. They didn't care to be reminded of what they'd seen or done. To many soldiers this stuff was nothing more than junk. I was collecting for years before I realized that I was a 'collector' and before any of this had any real value."

In the foyer, Tweet activated a side door and led Cubiak into one of the private rooms, a library outfitted with leather couches, fireplace, vaulted ceiling, and three walls of built-in bookcases. Tall bay windows faced west toward Green Bay and Tweet took up a position in front of them, his back to Cubiak. "Christian Nils," he said finally. "Yeah, I knew him, too."

"Was Nils a homosexual?"

As much as possible, Tweet jumped in his seat. "Nils? Not that one. Mr. Macho was he."

"And the others?"

The retired reporter was silent for a long time. "You seem to be the one who should be telling the story, Sheriff," he said finally.

"I have a general sense of it but I'd like for you to fill in the details. I assume you know the specifics because I suspect you of using that information to encourage Huntsman and his pals to supplement your expensive avocation and rather comfortable lifestyle."

"I had nothing to do with their deaths."

"I'm not implying that you did."

"I never threatened to expose them."

"No?"

"I simply allowed them to make use of my services as a business consultant."

"For a hefty fee, and after letting them know that you possessed certain information unfavorable to them."

"As you wish."

"Did you ever do any actual work for them?"

Tweet spun his chair around. "In fact, yes. I handled several projects. Everything on the up-and-up."

"From your perspective. The law might take a different view," Cubiak said.

Tweet's face grew hard. "Let's get one thing straight. I did nothing wrong. They were the culprits. Huntsman, Swenson, and Wilkins. If anything, I protected them. Don't make me out to be a monster feeding on the trio of innocents. They were the guilty ones."

"Guilty of what?"

"They were in the coast guard, and during the war their primary job was to get the soldiers onto land and then safely back to the ship. That was their responsibility. Only they didn't bring Nils back. Nils was wounded and they left him on some godforsaken pile of rock and ice to die. They claimed there wasn't room in the boat, that Christian insisted they take the others first and then come back for him. But there was room, and with the storm hitting they knew there was no chance in hell for them to go back. In their version, Christian was a hero, and so were they."

"They must have had a reason for what they did."

Tweet scrutinized the sheriff. "You're what? Forty-something?"

"Yeah."

"Were you in the service?"

"Marines."

"And you think you know what it's like for gays in the military?"

"I have some idea."

"You have no idea. The world is much changed, Sheriff. We are talking 1943, when a homosexual was considered less than a normal human being. If you were outed, you were dishonorably discharged from the military. And then when you came back home you were ostracized. You had little chance of finding a decent job, and if you had one, you could be fired. You could be jailed for deviant behavior or tossed into a mental institution. You might even be on an FBI roster or a list maintained by the local police. The State Department considered homosexuals to be security risks and had its own file filled with names. If you were foolish enough to order a homosexual publication by mail, the U.S. Post Office would keep track of your address. And if the local thugs got word, they'd harass you, beat you up, maybe even cripple you or kill you.

"I'm in this chair because of Parkinson's but long before the disease got me, I spent seven months in the hospital recovering from a broken back and two broken legs. The men who attacked me were never arrested. And that happened in New York, a place where a homosexual should've been able to hide amid the great wash of humanity. Here? In a place like Gills Rock, they had no chance. Deceit was their only option. They had to hide; they had to pretend; they had to create an elaborate cover. I salute them for pulling it off. Wives. Successful businessmen. Civic leaders. Wilkins even having a kid! An exemplary public life to shield the truth."

"You must have thought Huntsman pulled off the biggest coup, marrying Nils's widow."

Tweet hesitated. "To be honest, I had trouble with that. Taking care of the boy was one thing, the honorable thing, putting aside all that came before. But for Big Guy to marry Ida? That was pushing it a little too far. Unless he did it as a penance, wearing a reminder of his sin like sackcloth and ashes." Tweet paused again. "But I doubt it. Huntsman was an arrogant son-of-a-bitch who'd do anything to protect himself."

"Even killing a friend."

"Nils was from the same small town. Whether he was a friend or not, I don't know. War can bring out the worst in a man, and Nils was pretty much an obnoxious jerk who couldn't shut up. Got on everybody's nerves. Probably just his way of dealing with being scared. You gotta remember, we were all just kids. We were all scared. Waiting for something bad to happen. If you've seen it, you know."

Cubiak let his silence speak for him.

"Some guys go numb. Some hyper. Huntsman and his friends faced a double threat and maybe dying wasn't the worst of it. You fall in battle, you get a medal posthumously. The other thing, maybe you get killed for that as well, but there's no medal." Tweet's tone was sharp and bitter.

"And Nils found them out."

"Yeah, he did. Big Guy convinced him to keep quiet but he assumed he couldn't trust Christian to keep his word. Maybe while they were all still in the service—the men turned their backs on a lot just trying to stay alive—but once they got home?"

"Sounds like you had a ringside seat to what went on." The perennial fourth man, Cubiak thought.

Tweet snorted. "I won't deny I was there when Nils crawled into the wrong tent. Poor sap knew nothing of life beyond how to screw his wife, catch fish, and drink. Never got a joke; half the time didn't know what the men were talking about when they got on to the raw stuff. It was actually kind of funny; I don't think he understood what the hell he'd stumbled on. He just knelt there, his knees inside the tent, his feet outside in the muck, with a deer-in-the-headlights look on his face, kind of quizzical, you know. 'Hey, fellas,' he said. There was some quick shuffling and a little nervous banter. Huntsman pulled him in and fed him a line about getting hold of some bad hootch. Claimed that we'd drunk too much and blanked out. And a good thing he'd come along because it brought them all back to their senses. Nils didn't say anything at first, which was odd because he was one of those running-off-at-the-mouth kind of guys. He just leaned back on his haunches and listened. Then I saw this twitch in the corner of his mouth and I knew that he'd figured it out. He got kind of jumpy for a second but then he calmed down again. He even went along with the story about the bad liquor, said he'd heard other guys saying the same thing."

"Did Huntsman believe him?"

"I don't know. I didn't. Nils realized he was on to something. Maybe he figured he could use their fear of being found out to his advantage. Only it didn't work out that way, did it?"

"The next morning, the army was ordered to take Amchitka. Nils was part of the invasion force. The air force softened things up with a couple of bombing runs, but then the weather turned. Nastiest kind of storm you can imagine. What the natives call a williwaw. Went on for nearly two weeks. Enough to drive a man mad. Snow. Fog. Waves the size of houses. Everything churning upside down. Landing craft capsized or thrown into the rocks. One of the destroyers ran aground outside the harbor and had to be abandoned. Men sick. Men drowned or stranded on sheets of ice and mud.

"Enter the coast guard. Search. Find. Rescue. Total chaos and half the time you can't see a fucking thing for the fog and the dark. Not a lot of light up there in winter. I documented as much of the incident as I could. No time to think about anything. To be honest, I don't even remember seeing any of those three, and when it was all over I was shipped out."

"Which means that when you left, you had no idea that anything untoward had occurred."

"That's about the size of it. I ended up in the South Pacific and then went to work for *Stars and Stripes*. Several years after the war, I was assigned a story about the coast guard's role in the conflict. I remembered the Sturgeon Bay contingent from my days in the Aleutians and contacted the local commander for follow-up on the men who'd served there. That's when I heard the story about Huntsman and the other two and their heroic attempt to save Nils. I had no reason not to believe it. When I went through my photos looking for pictures to go along with the piece, I found the photo of the three of them in the rescue boat. Something didn't sit right with me, and the more I thought about it, the more I realized that their version was a lie."

"The boat wasn't full. There was room for Nils."

Tweet nodded.

"What about the other men on the boat, the ones who were rescued? They'd know the whole story."

"They were army, probably from all over the country. I recognized two of them and both were killed later. Of those who survived, there's almost no chance in hell they'd ever heard the version of the story circulating up here."

"So there was virtually no one to dispute their story. But surely, someone must have noticed as the rescuers arrived . . ."

"It was complete chaos, Sheriff. There were rescue boats going and coming, and a couple hundred injured or stranded men being pulled off the rocks. All anyone cared about was getting the soldiers safely onboard. I was on deck documenting the action, and even I couldn't swear to anything. It was my camera that captured the truth."

Behind Tweet, the lowering sun burned bright orange over the water. As if sensing the spectacle, he spun back toward the window. "I tried to forget about it but you know how these things are; they sit and fester. I knew what had become of Nils and wondered about the three of them. Eventually I poked around and discovered they were doing quite well. Huntsman had started his plumbing business. Swenson was operating a charter fishing boat, and Wilkins had a dairy farm and a small cheese factory."

"What happened after you sent the photo to Wilkins?"

"Nothing. I kept in touch—you know, Christmas cards for a couple of years running—gave them time to get better established. When I figured they were in a position to help out a fellow soldier, I sent a letter renewing our acquaintance along with a proposal offering my consulting services. At a very reasonable fee, I might add."

"Did you allude to the photo?"

"I never needed to. They were intelligent men. They understood the situation."

"To anyone who cared to ask, this was strictly a business arrangement between their enterprises and yours, Great Lakes Office Support and Pepper Ridge Associates?"

"Correct."

"With regular increases in the retainer."

"The cost of doing business rarely goes down." Tweet scowled. "What I don't understand is how you found out about it."

"Wilkins's son, Marty, told me about the photo. He'd opened the envelope by mistake."

"He understood what it meant?"

"Not at the time. He was just a kid. He gave the photo and the note to his father, but he knew it upset Jasper and he never forgot about it. After his father and the other two died, he got to thinking things over and started adding up the pieces."

"And left it with you to wrap up."

Cubiak shrugged. "You admit to sending the photo but still claim you never met up with them?" he said after a minute.

"Sheriff, for years they didn't even know I lived in Wisconsin. Don't look so surprised. I had reason to believe they killed Nils, someone they'd known since they were kids, to safeguard a secret. I would have been a fool to trust them with my life."

"Then how did you communicate?"

"When I sent the picture and later initiated our business association, I was living out east. After I left *Stars and Stripes*, I took a job in Milwaukee and made arrangements with a friend to route all correspondence through him, so the letters were always postmarked from New York or wherever he happened to be at the time. He traveled a lot. Then with email, the subterfuge became unnecessary."

"And payments were made to a bank in Chicago?"

"Yes. One with branches around the country. For years, as far as Big Guy and the other two knew, I could have been anywhere. Eventually, I discovered Door County and like so many people decided to move here. When I bought this house, I made a big splash about relocating my business to the island."

"You didn't worry about them harming you?"

"By then we were all old men, and I was sick. It didn't seem to matter so much. If anything, it seemed we were waiting to see who'd check out first." Tweet chortled. "I was invited to the ceremony for the cutter, you know. In fact, the chief had arranged to borrow one of my coast guard uniforms and a few other items as well. Turns out there aren't very many men still living who were in the campaign, so, you see, I would have been a bit of a celebrity along with Huntsman and his cronies. I was looking forward to the day, wondering what it would be like for them to sit on the dais with someone who knew the real story of their Aleutian heroics."

As he spoke, the sun dropped from view, like a ball toppling off behind a ledge. The room dimmed and then slowly brightened as a set of antique table lamps lit automatically.

"I'd like to see the photo," Cubiak said.

Wordlessly, Tweet rolled to a tall bookcase and pressed his hand to the fluted casing. A shelf filled with John le Carré spy novels opened, revealing a hidden wall safe. Inside was a brown envelope. He handed it to Cubiak.

"You'll have to undo the clasp . . . ," he said, holding up a palsied hand.

Cubiak pulled out a grainy black-and-white photo and held it under one of the table lamps. The enlarged image was full of shadows. Three men stood along the gunwale, looking up, their faces blurred by falling snow. Behind them six soldiers wrapped in blankets huddled on benches, with room for more. "I can't see any of the faces clearly," he said.

"You don't have to." Tweet rode up to the sheriff's side. "That's Huntsman," he said, pointing at one of the men standing. "See the zigzag on his left shoulder? He tore his jacket the week before and sewed it up with fishing line he got from one of the locals. He'd learned from his mother, a seamstress. We razzed him about it because he did such a neat job. There's no question that it's him. He knew it. And he knew that I knew it, and that this photo proved it. There are only two other men in coast guard uniforms in the boat." He tapped a finger on each. "It can't be anyone else but Wilkins and Swenson."

"I assume the negative is in the safe?"

"Oh, it's safe all right, but it's not here."

"You're a cautious man."

Tweet held out his hand and Cubiak returned the photo.

"How many prints are there?" the sheriff said.

"Three. This one. The one I sent to Wilkins. And one that was in a bundle of material I donated to the Sturgeon Bay Coast Guard Station."

Cubiak raised an eyebrow. "Why?"

"Why not? It was just one of dozens of photographs I packed up for them for the archives. Maybe I like to take chances. Maybe I thought it was right that the official documents contain evidence of their duplicity, even if no one knew what it meant."

"When did you do this?"

"Last summer. The chief posted a request in *Stars and Stripes* asking for photos and such to be donated for the ceremony. I'm sure he amassed a lot of material. It was a crapshoot, what would be put on display and what wouldn't."

"You wanted to tempt fate—see if someone else picked up on the significance. What if one of the three saw it, what then? Your game would be up."

Tweet shrugged. "So what? I'd gotten all I wanted. I reached the point where the money wasn't important anymore. Besides, they were getting on, and when they died the deals would have come to a halt anyway."

"Several cartons are missing from the station archive room. Did you know that?"

"What do you mean missing?"

"Gone. Misplaced or stolen. Three of them ended up in Walter Nils's garage. His son, Roger, took them. The boy had his own reason for wanting to discredit Big Guy and the other two. There's nothing to indicate that he came across this particular photo or recognized Huntsman—how could he? Nor that Walter saw the photo and understood what it meant. But Ida might have. A lot of dreg gets past the censors in letters home from the field. It's not inconceivable that she knew about the patched jacket. What if Roger had found the photo and showed it to her?"

"He didn't need to."

"What do you mean?"

Tweet returned to his place by the window and stared out at the darkening water. After a long silence, he started to talk. "Ida Huntsman is one of the finest women I've ever known." His voice was soft.

Not sure he'd heard right, Cubiak moved closer. "You knew Ida?"

Tweet's head bobbled. He seemed to be struggling to keep his eyes open. "She was a volunteer reader for a local program for invalids. I had a relapse last fall and was bedridden for several months. I let the doctor talk me into signing up for the program, and as luck would have it, I got Ida."

"Did you know who she was?"

"Not initially. I'm not sure if she used her surname when she first came or if I just didn't catch it. She had a lovely voice and was very kind. She'd bring cookies from Smithson's Bakery and we'd share a pot of tea. I started looking forward to her visits." Tweet snorted. "Me! I never liked women but she was special. I asked her where she was from. 'Gills Rock,' she said. I was better then, sitting up in the chair, and we were here, in this room, by the windows like now. I asked her to tell me her name again. When she did, I started to tremble. She worried that I'd gotten chilled and went and brought a blanket and tucked it around me. I remember her hands, the pink nail polish, and as she was helping me, it all came back. Nils, the war, the whole sordid mess. I felt a visceral hatred for Huntsman, not just for what he did to his fellow soldier, a man he'd grown up with, but what he'd done to hurt this woman."

"You told her?"

"Not immediately. She'd seen some of my collection, of course, and wanted to know if I'd served and, if so, where. We talked a lot about the war and when she found out I'd been in the Aleutian Campaign, she asked me if I'd known Nils and what it was like for him and the others."

"You showed her the photo?"

"I showed her dozens of pictures from the islands. That one included. She recognized Big Guy from the shoulder patch and asked if I remembered when the photo was taken. I figured she had a right to know. Now I'm not so sure. I wonder if I didn't cause her more pain."

Cubiak studied Tweet. "I saw you at the funeral." Then as now Tweet was in a wheelchair. "Can you walk?"

The old man smirked. "Am I ambulatory? Not in the way you'd define it. A few steps maybe but only on a really good day. You're not thinking I flew up out of my chair and played gallant knight to the lady fair?"

"I consider all possibilities." Cubiak pointed to a dagger on the desk. "What's something like that go for?"

"That's a personal item and not for sale. But a couple of weeks ago, I sold a similar one for two thousand."

"Your entire collection is worth, what? Half a million?"

"Conservatively."

With that kind of money, a man could pay for a lot of dirty work, Cubiak thought.

A choppy sea rocked the *Can-Do* on the return ride. Nightfall came fast on the water and the sheriff drove cautiously, alert to the occasional shoreline light and fighting to prevent the prow from being pushed off course.

Only after he tied up at the marina and got behind the wheel of the jeep was he able to relax and think about what he'd learned that day.

Tweet's photo seemed to support Marty's theory that his father and the other two men had lied about their attempted rescue of the injured Christian Nils. If not, why would the three men succumb to the reporter's soft form of blackmail? For decades they felt it necessary to hide their sexual orientation but Tweet's threat had nothing to do with that issue.

Had Tweet suffered a sting of conscience after telling Ida the story and arranged the murders of the men he'd leeched off of for years?

Marty Wilkins had reason to want to see the men hurt, but enough to kill them? He said he came back when he got his mother's message; but what if he was lying? What if he'd come back earlier for his own reasons? He could easily have tampered with the heater and then put things right afterward.

Walter Nils also had motive. He claimed he acted on behalf of his son but what if he stumbled on the photo in the box of stolen archives and drew his own conclusions? Or talked to Marty, who already had suspicions about the importance of the picture? Maybe the two of them were in on it together. Walter's story about stuffing the vent with leaves could be a red herring, something he trumped up to draw suspicion away from Roger.

Indeed, Roger. The angry young man saw his life ruined by a series of events put into motion by his own grandfather. Could he have overheard Marty and Walter down in the garage while he sat upstairs in the loft, photo in hand, and listened as the two bitter men pieced together a drunken, whispered story of treachery and deceit?

Then there were the ladies.

Agnes freely acknowledged killing her husband. If she'd murdered the others as well, why not admit her guilt?

The three widows had spent the evening together and could easily have driven back to the cabin in Ida's car and confronted their husbands, avenging years of lies. But how? Even more important: were the women capable of killing?

Under pressure to pay off Tweet, the three vets copied his methods to create their own money-gouging plan. "Everything on the up-and-up," Tweet had said. Huntsman, Swenson, and Wilkins would probably use the same argument to defend what they'd done. In the end, enough money flowed through the pipelines to support the comfortable, even lavish lifestyles of four separate households. Maybe one of the local men being bilked finally had had enough.

When Cubiak opened the back door to his house he knew he had left the dogs for too long. The kitchen stank; the floor was filthy; the puppies were soiled. It took him nearly two hours to clean up. At ten thirty, he sat down on the couch with a bottle of beer, still thinking.

FRIDAY
MORNING

Fussing with the pups, Cubiak forgot the time. He was late getting to work, and when he arrived he was puzzled to find Lisa's chair empty and the lobby strangely quiet. The sheriff fumbled for his keys. At home he had been preoccupied thinking about Tweet's photo and the effect it might have had on Ida and hadn't bothered with coffee. If his assistant didn't bring any in, as she often did on Fridays, he'd either have to go back out or settle for the sludge that dripped out of the canteen vending machine. Maybe Lisa had coffee and was caught in traffic. That could happen, if the new bridge was up.

Still, where was everyone? he thought as he opened the door to his office.

The light flicked.

"Surprise! Happy Birthday!" Amid the cheers, Lisa stepped forward with a platter of frosted cupcakes. Rowe handed him a cup of coffee. Before he could respond the small crowd began to sing.

Cubiak faltered. He'd forgotten the day. In his former life, Lauren never forgot. His last birthday with his family, she'd baked a dozen chocolate cupcakes, and then she and Alexis had serenaded him in the kitchen behind twelve blazing candles.

A thousand years ago.

The serenade left Cubiak nodding his thanks and shaking hands with the staff. Lisa gave him a hug and a cupcake with a candle. He hoped it wasn't chocolate.

"I made carrot cake. Is that okay?" she said.

"It's perfect." He blew out the flame.

The party lasted the time it took for everyone to eat one cupcake. Rowe helped himself to a second and lingered.

Left with the sheriff, he pulled a sheet of paper from his pocket. "Not much of a birthday gift, I'm afraid," he said, flattening the page on Cubiak's desk. "These are the results from yesterday. I made a couple of graphs, one for each round of testing. Time passed, here"—he pointed to the baseline of the top chart and then tapped the vertical component—"and measurement of CO here."

The charts clearly showed that the carbon monoxide readings in the cabin were higher when the vent was filled with leaves than with insulation, but overall, the levels were surprisingly low. Even after four hours, neither produced enough dangerous gas to be deadly.

"The pieces of Styrofoam kept falling out. A couple of times, I had to pick up the stuff from the ground and shove it back in."

Rowe had moved to the window, and in the natural light Cubiak noticed a faint red line running across the young officer's brow.

"What happened to your forehead?"

The deputy rubbed the crease. "Still there, huh? I thought it would be gone by now. It's from the gas mask. I put it on plenty tight. Didn't want to take any chances."

Rowe retrieved his coffee from the desk. "What's this all about anyway? I thought those two confessed? One of them must have done it."

"Maybe, but your results cast serious doubt on that notion."

Rowe bent over the charts again. "Well, if Walter or Roger didn't kill those guys, what happened? You think maybe we need to take another look at the space heater? Hey, what if our experts weren't really that expert—or they're the ones who did it!"

"Motive?"

"Who knows? It could be anything. Gambling, like you said at the start."

Back to square one, Cubiak thought.

The sheriff knew he wasn't back to square one, not exactly, but he was still far from a definitive answer. He was sure he'd missed a vital clue, something he'd heard or seen, a small detail that by itself lacked significance but was crucial to understanding what had happened at the Rec Room. After finishing with Rowe, he headed to the nearby county park to walk and think.

The park ran alongside the shipping canal that connected the waters of Green Bay and Sturgeon Bay to Lake Michigan. Before the late 1800s when the passage was dug, ships had to sail around the peninsula to reach the lake. The canal cut more than a hundred miles off the trip. It also severed the land connection between the peninsula and the rest of the state, technically making a large part of Door County an island, a distinction generally ignored. Cubiak liked the park. Even during the height of the tourist rush, it was largely underused and offered a quiet, easy escape from the office.

That birthday morning, the bright sun infused the day with spring-like warmth. As he strode east toward the lake, he started to replay the conversation with Rowe but found himself overrun by the sentiment that had welled up earlier. For a few precious moments, Cubiak opened the part of his heart where memories were stored and stepped back into the life he'd known with his wife and daughter in Chicago. Love. Pain. Loss. The emotions overwhelmed him, and then slowly they settled into a peaceful calm that he tucked away once again.

A loud whistle blew. A man hailed from the deck of an approaching barge. Cubiak returned the greeting and watched the vessel recede down the waterway. Alone again, he gazed into the cloudless sky and then to the narrow blue waterway and gravel path that ran side by side, cutting parallel lines through the nascent green landscape.

Something about the colors and shapes held Cubiak's attention.

Without meaning to, he began to recall various objects and people he'd encountered during the previous two weeks. As the impressions came to him they formed a mental pastiche, and he gradually realized that everything he was remembering was connected to the deaths at Gills Rock. He closed his eyes and let the collage expand, drawing in details from the deep recesses of memory. What had he missed earlier? What had he seen but failed to comprehend? If he conjured up something significant now, would he grasp the importance of it?

Cubiak ran through events, from beginning to end. Still nothing. He opened his eyes. Once before, standing at the base of the wide bay outside Huntsman's home, he had looked to the water for answers and come up empty. This time, standing alongside the ribbon of water in the canal, he felt himself being pulled toward a resolution. What he was looking at reminded him of something he'd noted earlier that day at the office, something he'd seen before.

He went back to the first morning: the phone call from Rowe, the ride up the peninsula, the people he'd met and talked with. And there he came to the missing link, the clue for which he'd been searching. The key to the deaths of the Three of a Kind, the seemingly negligible detail, had been evident the day the men had been found dead inside the old cabin. He'd noticed it shortly after he reached the Huntsmans' homestead, but until this morning, he hadn't realized its relevance.

There was no doubt that Huntsman, Swenson, and Wilkins had been murdered; that Agnes was not the culprit, though she was guilty of her husband's vengeful shooting; and that gambling had not played a role in the tragedy.

Finally, he understood the MO, the motive behind the crime, and the identity of the killer.

With a heart full of regret, Cubiak turned his back on the splendor of Door County and retraced his way to the jeep.

FRIDAY AFTERNOON

20

Cubiak waited for the warmest part of the day before heading north to Gills Rock. He was in no rush, and when he got to Ephraim, he stopped at Smithson's Bakery for pecan rolls. The village was saturated with sunlight and nestled into the hillside like a cat on a warm radiator. Signs of spring suffused the quaint little town and followed him up the peninsula, but they did nothing to lighten his mood.

At the Huntsmans' place, Ida was digging in a patch of black dirt near the house. Ramrod straight and dressed in a red plaid shirt and baggy brown work pants, she leaned into a pitchfork and broke the dense earth into loose clumps.

She must have heard the jeep because as he approached she looked up, her face flushed with exertion beneath the brim of a floppy straw hat.

"Sheriff, what a pleasant surprise." Her words belied the strain in her voice. "Getting ready to put in the radishes. Too early yet for the tomatoes. So much to be done now that the weather's finally turned," she went on, ignoring the bakery box in his hands.

"I brought something for coffee, if you'd like to take a break."

Ida tossed aside her canvas gloves. "Of course."

"We could sit in the gazebo, if it's not too cold for you."

"Not at all. I washed the table and chairs yesterday, so they're clean. And the coffee's on. It'll just take a minute for me to freshen up."

They were being polite, circumspect.

While he waited for her to return, Cubiak angled two chairs toward the sun and pulled the table close. A soft breeze rustled the surface water, and overhead gulls floated like plump, luminescent pillows. In the tranquil setting, Cubiak readied himself for what he was about to do.

Ida reappeared without the hat, her hair neatly combed, and a dash of pale pink on her cheeks and mouth. She set down the tray and handed him a platter for the rolls. For several minutes they busied themselves with the small chores brought on with the presence of food. Cubiak took his time arranging the pastry on the dish; he was stalling and felt that Ida was doing the same as she fussed, pouring the coffee into yellow mugs.

Finally he set down his cup and turned toward her. "I have come to you with news that will be hard for you to hear," he began.

Following his example, Ida lowered her coffee to the table.

"Both your son and your grandson have claimed responsibility for the lethal level of carbon monoxide in the cabin that killed your husband and his two friends," he said with all the gentleness he could muster.

She made a sound like a seal's bark. "That's absurd! They both loved Big Guy. Everyone did."

"We both know that's not true, Ida. Far from it, I'm afraid," he said after a moment. "Perhaps it's time for the charade to end."

Ida started to protest.

"Allow me to tell you a story," Cubiak said, interrupting her. He rested his arms on the table and looked out toward the sun-glazed water. "It begins many years ago when you were still living at the other end of the county and struggling with your own harsh circumstances. It's a story—a true story, I'm afraid—about three boys who grew up together in an isolated fishing village." He couldn't help but glance back in the direction of Gills Rock. Ida did the same. "As youngsters," he went on, his eyes still on the tiny village, "the three were close in ways that boys are, but as they grew older the friendship developed in ways they didn't understand and that made them feel increasingly out of step with their peers. They knew what their families expected of them and realized that what they wanted conflicted with the strict morals and narrow viewpoints imposed by their community and, in fact, by the larger society as well."

Cubiak turned his attention toward Ida. She was pale and rigid and unable to meet his glance.

"They were still kids when the Japanese bombed Pearl Harbor. Within months they enlisted in the coast guard, all three on the same day, all three lying about their ages. There's a lot of fervor when war starts. Nobody knows what to expect. It seems glamorous and exciting— a chance to get out of your small town and see the world and do something for your country. I'm sure, like everyone, they thought the fighting would be over in a couple of months. And if they thought of danger, it was probably as something distant and romantic, like dying together when their ship was sunk by enemy torpedoes. They were good men but young and naïve. Living on the base they could get away with certain things, but after they shipped out circumstances changed. Suddenly they were confined in close quarters day and night, and the situation became perilous. They probably took risks. Let's assume they did, because we know that they were found out. The first man who stumbled on their secret became complicit and posed no threat. There was at least one other, maybe more, but this other man, the one who posed the greatest threat, didn't survive the conflict. The three friends made it through the war and came back as heroes with their secret intact. Once home, they slipped into the roles needed to blend in. It wasn't hard, at least from the outside. They knew what was expected and as long as they played along they could live in the two different worlds they'd created. They married but lied to their wives about war injuries that prevented sexual intimacy."

"Please, Sheriff, get to the point."

"Once they established their ruse, they had to maintain it. They assumed leadership roles in the community and their church, even as they pursued occupations that allowed them to work alone and in isolated circumstances. This made them answerable to no one much of the time and allowed them to do as they pleased and involve others as they wished."

"Why are you telling me this?"

"Because there's a part of the story I don't think you know. One of the men who eventually came into the circle was an athletic coach. By then the three childhood friends were successful businessmen. As part of their largesse, they established a program for young boys, a wrestling program."

Ida gripped the arms of the chair. "Oh my god, they didn't . . ."

"No, they did not. Pedophilia is something quite different. The program itself was a good thing for the community but there were ripple effects that they couldn't control."

"Go on," Ida said, barely above a whisper.

"Marty Wilkins came to see me last week."

"Marty." Ida tensed. "Someone did something to Marty?"

"The coach."

Tears welled in her eyes. "Oh, that poor boy. That's why he went away?" she said after a moment.

"Yes. Vinter threatened to blame him if he told anyone and to expose his father and the other two. Marty figured no one would believe him. He'd only end up being run out of town and ruining his father's reputation. Rather than take that chance, he left home."

The breeze had stiffened, and Cubiak saw that Ida was shivering. "Perhaps we should go inside," he said.

She didn't protest and walked meekly at his side, his hand at her elbow. In the yellow kitchen he helped her to a chair and brought her a glass of water. At the stove, he put on the kettle for tea. Ida seemed suddenly worn down and fragile; if she was aware of him scouting through the cabinets, she did not protest. He found the pink cup and saucer on a low shelf, and when he set the tea on the table, she reached for it eagerly.

"You added sugar," she said with a quick uptick to her mouth. "I like sugar in my tea." She held the cup with two hands and drank until it was half empty. "There's more to this story, isn't there? More I need to know."

Cubiak had settled in across the table. At her signal, he continued. "Sadly, yes."

"Coach Vinter?" Ida tightened her brow in concentration and then slumped into the chair. "Roger!" she said and looked to Cubiak for confirmation.

He nodded and she began to cry.

Cubiak slid the napkin holder closer. To give her a private moment, he busied himself fixing more tea. When he sat down again, her eyes were dabbed dry and her ramrod posture had returned. "I knew something was wrong. He was such a good boy." Ida moistened her lips. "So it was just like with Marty. The same thing all over."

"Essentially, yes. Vinter told him he thought it ran in the family and drew the line all the way back to Big Guy. Roger knew Terrence and his friends had recruited the coach and he figured they knew what he was doing, so he blamed them."

"Did they?" She choked on the question.

"I don't think so. There's nothing to indicate that they did. But Roger wanted to punish them. Last fall when he traveled with the team, he sent anonymous notes to the Sturgeon Bay coast guard chief hoping to discredit them and force the cancellation of the ceremony. After he dropped out, he got a job painting the station and stole some of the archive material. He realized he couldn't stop the event but figured he could make it harder for the coast guard to honor Big Guy and the others. The *Herald* article put him over the edge."

"But you said Roger tried to kill Big Guy. How? What did he do?"

Cubiak told her about the pellets, Roger's change of heart, and Walter's part in the events of the fateful evening. "To understand the whole story, we have to go back to the beginning. To the war. To Charles Tweet. And to Christian Nils. You know Tweet's version, of course."

Ida turned a ghostly white.

"I went out to Chambers Island yesterday."

"Of course." She pulled a napkin from the holder and neatly folded it in half. "Nils knew about them, too."

"That's what Tweet says."

"And he didn't approve." She folded the napkin again.

"No. Very much so, no."

"They *knew* him. And they left him to die." Ida tossed the napkin aside and stared out the window at the water. "Why? He was harmless, as innocent of the world's ways as they."

"War strips away a man's innocence."

Ida reeled on him. "You sympathize with them?"

"I'm just trying to understand what they did and why. War makes men desperate to survive. They were practically still kids themselves. They panicked and probably in that moment saw Nils as the enemy."

"They didn't know what he would do!"

"They made assumptions."

"They killed my husband to protect their own skins."

"They failed to save him. It's not the same."

"It is to me."

"Christian might have died anyway."

"We'll never know though, will we?" Ida got up and paced the tidy kitchen. "They made themselves out to be heroes. I believed them! Everyone did. I married Terrence partly because I had no options but also because I felt I owed him something for trying to save Christian. All those years." She made a barking, braying sound. "Then Tweet showed me that horrible photo. I felt as if I had been shat upon."

214

"You could have gone to the chief in Sturgeon Bay and told him the truth."

"I had no proof. You couldn't distinguish faces in the photograph. The only clue was the patched jacket and that wouldn't mean anything to him."

"It would to Walter."

"The patched jacket was part of the family folklore, one of those things that gets mentioned around the table at Christmas." Ida spoke listlessly, as if in a trance. "Except he couldn't have known about the photo."

"I'm afraid he might have."

Ida stumbled to the table and dropped into a chair.

"Tweet included the photo in a bunch of pictures he sent to Gary Dotson, tempting fate as it were. Walter went through some of the stuff Roger took. If the photo was in there, he might have seen it and decided to avenge you and his birth father by stuffing the vent with leaves during the Friday night card game."

Ida frowned. "I thought the squirrels did that."

"That's what Walter wanted everyone to think."

"But you said Roger confessed, too."

"He did. He plugged the vent first but then he changed his mind. Once Walter got him to own up to what he'd done and to what had happened with Vinter, he took matters into his own hands. He already knew about Marty and decided things had gone on far too long. He acted out of guilt and remorse for what happened to Roger."

Cubiak gave Ida a few moments to take in what he'd told her. Then he added, "But their actions didn't kill the three men. I had my deputy check it out. Filling the outside vent with either Styrofoam or dried leaves doesn't cause enough carbon monoxide to back up into the cabin to be lethal."

Ida's blue eyes flashed. "Then they're both innocent. They can't be charged with murder or even attempted murder if no one died as a result of what they did."

"It doesn't work like that in Wisconsin. State law says that if a person intends to kill and takes steps they think are needed, then they've committed the crime, whether anyone dies or not."

"That's absurd. A good lawyer is all they need."

"There could be mitigating circumstances. It might also help if the person who actually committed the crime confessed."

"You've as much as said it was an accident."

"I said clogging the vent didn't kill them. Something else happened inside the cabin, and I think you know what."

Ida feigned amusement. "Are you going to tell me another story?"

"I'll give you the condensed version. Tweet showed you a copy of the photo. You recognized the three, and after he told you when and under what circumstances he took the picture, you understood the implication. You may have decided then to take your revenge but you needed to wait for the right occasion. That Friday evening was ideal. The *Herald* article, the drop in temperature, the three men celebrating together and getting drunk and careless. You said you didn't have a key to the cabin. But for the sake of the story, I'm presuming you did and that you let yourself in. You had your rifle with you and confronted them at gunpoint. You told them you'd seen the photo or maybe you even got a copy from Tweet. Let's say you did and that you showed it to them and forced a confession out of them. You knew how the damper worked, so you closed it and turned the heater on high. Then you stood there and watched while they suffered and died. As a final sign of contempt and perhaps to confuse matters, you laid the three jokers on the table. When you were finished, you opened the damper again. On your way out you closed the curtains and then locked the door from the outside with your key, leaving Terrence's key in the lock on the inside."

"Sheriff, if I'd been in there and doing all those things like you said, I'd have died from the carbon monoxide along with them."

"Not if you were wearing a gas mask. That morning when I talked to you, I noticed a red crease across your forehead. I thought it was from a hairnet. My mother used to sleep with one and sometimes her brow was lined like that in the morning. You were sitting in there" —he motioned toward the living room—"looking out at the water, probably planning when you were going to take the boat out to ditch the mask and the key. My guess is that if we could drain the bay, we'd find them both at the bottom, if they're not buried in mud or if the current hasn't pulled them out into Death's Door or even the lake by now."

Cubiak poured more tea, leaving Ida to consider what he'd said.

"Roger confessed to the graffiti on the shed. That must have taken you aback but it also gave you the idea to go one step further and deface the boat. You wrote the letter as well, suddenly suggesting the possibility that a bunch of reckless kids or someone with a grudge could be responsible."

"If what you say is true, would you blame me?"

"Grief makes people do things they wouldn't normally consider. I learned long ago not to judge people's motives when they've lost someone they love. But there is a difference between right and wrong, and you and I both know it."

"So did they." Ida pulled her cup close but didn't drink. "What if that part of your story is correct? That I went in with my rifle and told them I'd seen the photo? They would have asked how, and when I told them about meeting Tweet, they would have realized that if he was willing to tell me he'd probably be willing to tell others as well. They must have figured it was just a matter of time before the real story came out. Then what if they confessed and begged for my forgiveness? Which I would never have given. I would have told them that and then, satisfied that at last I knew the truth, I would have walked out—not just out the door but out of Terrence's life, and he knew it. The other two realized their wives would do the same. They were finished. Rather than endure the shame the truth would bring, they took the cowardly way out, which, ironically, preserved their status as heroes."

"They closed the damper, and afterward you came back and re-opened it?"

"According to my version of the story, yes."

"But you wanted them dead."

"They killed Nils, the only man I ever really loved. They killed my son's true father, a man who would have loved his child as a father should. I wanted justice."

"At any price?"

"Is any price too high to pay?"

Yes, Cubiak wanted to tell her. Life had taught him that much. But he knew she would not be swayed. Had she told him the truth? He hadn't considered the possibility that events had unfolded as she'd described, but it made sense. She'd gotten her revenge and given them an honorable way out. She had no way to prove that her version was true but he had none to substantiate his.

"What time was it when you went to the cabin?"

"It was about two. I figured they'd still be up, so I set an alarm for myself when I got back from Olive's."

If the three were alive when Ida surprised them at the cabin, then Roger hadn't inadvertently harmed them. And if things had gone down either as the sheriff imagined or as Ida suggested, the men would have been dead long before the predawn hour when Walter arrived and tucked the dried leaves into the vent.

"What about the mark on your forehead?"

Ida raised her brows and looked at him as if he were a simpleton. "Women do wear hairnets, Sheriff. I have a drawerful that I can show you."

Cubiak finally left, worn down from the exchange with Ida. Had he intended to arrest her? He wasn't sure. He had no proof that she had murdered her husband and the other two men and had told her as much. Maybe hers was the correct version, that after she'd forced an admission of guilt from the three for killing her first husband, they'd taken their own lives rather than face dishonor. If she confessed, would a judge find her guilty or would she be accused of trying to divert suspicion from Walter and Roger? He hadn't arrested Roger, either,

218

though he'd allowed Ida to assume the boy was in custody. How much discretion did he have in the matter? Some would say none but that was a naïve answer; an officer of the law often relied on personal discernment in making an arrest. There was a line, however, and Cubiak knew he was standing with one foot already planted on the other side.

From Huntsmans', Cubiak drove through Gills Rock and turned onto the twisty portion of the road that led to The Wood. He could have turned around and headed down the peninsula away from the memories. But he no longer possessed the will to resist what he knew he wanted. The Wood was gated shut. Maybe Cate wasn't staying there. Maybe she wasn't coming for the wedding. Half a mile farther, around a soft curve he slowed and eased onto the narrow shoulder across from the house where Cate's late aunt and uncle, Ruby and Dutch, had lived. Caught in the afternoon sun, the house glowed against the backdrop of cedars. Smoke pulsed from the chimney and a faint light shone from one of the front rooms. Desire urged him to cross into the yard; fear locked him in place. He craved nicotine and reached toward the dash for a pack of cigarettes. Nothing was there. Did Cate still smoke? he wondered as he lowered the window and inhaled air scented with burning wood and fresh pine.

A whistle shriek startled the sheriff from his reverie. The ferry had docked and in a few minutes a cascade of cars would tunnel through the forest past him, the drivers casting curious glances at the vehicle parked alongside a lonely stretch of road. Perhaps Cate would emerge as well and see him there, if she hadn't already spotted him from inside the house. Chagrined, he made a sharp U-turn away from her.

Workers were putting the final stakes into the corners of a large tent on Bathard's front lawn when Cubiak pulled up. Under the high peaked roof, another crew arranged two dozen round tables in rows for the next day's dinner and celebration. Sonja's catering crew had taken over the kitchen while the rest of the house pulsed with a flurry of activity involving flowers and strings of white lights. The sheriff found Bathard in the boat barn, sweeping the floor to a flow of simple, haunting music.

"Scheherazade?"

"Cornelia's favorite." Bathard listened a moment and then gave the broom a quick shove. "The only way I could find to make myself useful," he said.

Uncharacteristically the coffee pot was not on. The coroner lifted a glass of whiskey off the counter and proffered it toward his visitor. "Liquid courage. Want some?"

And uncharacteristically, Cubiak said no.

While the doctor worked the push broom across an already clean floor, Cubiak provided a condensed version of his conversation with Ida.

"Well, it is possible, you know," Bathard said.

Cubiak nodded.

"What are you going to do?"

"Is Ida invited to the wedding?"

"Yes. Sonja's mother was friends with her and the other two; they're all on the list."

"If she shows up, I'll talk with her again. If she doesn't come, I'll know that I misread her. Where's Roger?" Cubiak glanced around as if expecting to find the boy lurking in the corner.

"Last I saw him he was helping unload chairs from the truck."

"Good. I need to talk to him, too."

"Roger's a fine lad."

"I know." Cubiak hesitated and then pulled back the door. "Until tomorrow then."

Neither man had mentioned Cate.

The sheriff intercepted Roger carrying a double load of chairs into the tent. "When you're finished," he said.

The boy scowled but five minutes later he joined Cubiak on the lawn. The sheriff walked him to the fence, where they looked down on the rocky shore and bay.

"How's everything going?" Cubiak said.

"Doctor Bathard said I could help tomorrow. He said he'd pay me but I think I owe him more than that for letting me stay here. He's even asked me to keep watch on the place while he and Sonja are gone on their wedding trip. He said he doesn't like the term 'honeymoon.'"

Suddenly the boy turned toward the sheriff. "Why haven't you arrested me? You know I did it."

"The one thing I know for certain is that you did not kill those men."

"What do you mean? I didn't clear out the vent well enough, and they all died."

"Not by your hand."

Roger scrubbed his hands over his face. "Then I'm innocent?"

"Not necessarily, although a good lawyer could probably get you off."

"I don't understand."

Cubiak explained the law's intent.

"Then you have to arrest me," Roger said and stuck out his hands.

"I will"—Cubiak watched the color drain from the boy's face—"unless you agree to do what I say."

The boy tensed.

"I'm trying to make a deal with you."

Roger fell back against the fence. "You're letting me go?"

"No. I'm trying to help you. If you promise that you'll stop hanging around with that gang in Fish Creek and go back to school, I won't take the matter any further."

"I fucked up. They won't take me back."

"They will. I'll see to it. If not Eau Claire, someplace else."

"Why?"

Because a boy growing up without a father—or with a lousy father—has the odds stacked against him? Because, as Bathard noted, Roger was a good lad? Because an arrest on the charge of murder—even if it was thrown out, which it would certainly be—would dog him for life?

Cubiak shrugged. "Because you got a lousy deal and I think you deserve a chance to prove yourself. Just remember this. What you did could be considered a felony and there's no statute of limitations on that. You screw up and I come after you."

The sheriff let the young man absorb the full import of what he'd said. "Deal?"

Roger extended his hand. "Deal."

WEEK THREE: 21
SATURDAY

Cubiak studied his reflection in the full-length bedroom mirror. The deep charcoal suit he'd bought for the occasion, the first he'd purchased in two decades, made him presentable enough, he thought. If only he could remember what to do with the tie. He adjusted the ends and then closed his eyes and allowed memory to carry him through the steps of the one useful skill he had learned from his father: How to produce a precise, four-square knot. Right over left, under, over again, then up and around, through the loop and down. "Best done without looking. Concentrate on the wrists," his father had instructed.

Cubiak woke early that morning, determined to be in a good mood for Bathard and Sonja's wedding. He completed a full three-mile run listening to a concerto of birdsong and fed the dogs to Mendelssohn's Italian Symphony. Happy music. He ate a breakfast of crisp bacon and fried eggs standing up so he could watch a migrating flock of gray geese circle the lake and the family of cardinals, the young males vividly red, at the backyard feeder. Life renewing itself; nature opening itself to the promise of tomorrow. No looking back, ever onward. Primed by a pot of black coffee, he showered and then dressed for the ceremony. New suit, pressed; old shoes, polished. He'd even unearthed a bottle of musky aftershave from the back of the linen closet.

If he'd owned one of the despised clip-on ties, he could have made it out the door without having to confront his first depressing hurdle, memories of good old Dad. Funny, he thought. His father hadn't dressed up often—for church on Christmas and Easter and the occasional funeral. Yet as a boy Cubiak had never wondered how the old man had learned to produce the perfect knot or why he was so particular about the result. Maybe the silky feel of the fabric on his rough hands provided a brief reprieve from harsh reality and carried him into a fantasy life where the butler would announce that the car was waiting instead of the usual carping "Hurry up. We're gonna be late" from his mother in the kitchen. A concert of bickering.

But the old tunes had to be silenced, especially that morning. Again Cubiak studied the image in the cloudy mirror. The knot was passable. He tightened and tugged it under his collar. In the kitchen, he scratched Butch on the head and ran a hand over the mound of snuffling puppies asleep in the middle of the floor. The little ones had progressed to solid food, and their dish as well as their mother's was licked clean. Cubiak poured fresh water and filled the food bowls halfway and left a note for his neighbor Nagel to do the same when he came later to check on the dogs. Nearly to the door, Cubiak doubled back and turned on the radio so the animals could have something to listen to while he was out.

The day was all sunshine and warm air perfumed with fresh pine. The wind had died during the night and the lake rested quietly against the shore. In the distance, a long, starched pleat of white clouds stretched above the horizon beneath an expanse of sky clear and blue. As Cubiak popped the glove box and reached for his sunglasses, his mood faltered. The jeep felt empty. He wondered if he should swing by and pick up Natalie. But he knew that was futile. He was early and chances were she wasn't ready.

He backed down the gravel drive burdened by the realization that it was his own fault he was driving solo. If he'd been smart he'd have agreed to go with Natalie. If he was brave, he'd have called Cate and invited her to join him. But he was neither; he was simply alone on a solitary path through the sun-speckled north woods, thinking of Lauren and their wedding day. Wondering if Bathard was thinking of Cornelia.

He drove too fast. When he arrived at the white clapboard church, the doors were closed and the parking lot empty. After a moment's hesitation, he accelerated to the corner and turned toward downtown Sturgeon Bay. The main drag was flanked by streetlights hung with new spring banners: Door County Does It Better. Blue lettering was silk-screened onto pastel-colored canvas: pinks, yellows, and greens that reminded him of Alexis holding a basketful of Easter eggs. The past lapped at the wheels of the jeep like a vast ocean beckoning him in. The water was warm, comforting, and familiar.

The jeep's fuel tank was three-quarters full, but Cubiak detoured into the gas station. He needed the mundane routine, the normal ordinary activity, of filling the tank to keep himself rooted on solid ground. As the pump clicked, he glimpsed the badge on his belt and remembered who he was—what he was. A church bell clanged and he remembered where he was supposed to be.

On his second arrival at the chapel, cars lined the streets and the lot. He pulled into one of the last spots and eased out of the jeep, allowing himself to be caught up in the bonhomie of the people who'd come to witness the marriage of a retired doctor and a former schoolteacher.

Madeline and Sofia ambushed him as he came around the corner. The two junior bridesmaids wore tea-length ecru dresses and carried straw baskets filled with blue hydrangeas. "You get to escort us in," Sofia said, jittery with excitement.

Assaulted by memories of his darling Alexis, Cubiak tucked their slender arms into his, adjusted his long stride to match theirs, and marched them up the stairs. Bathard and Sonja were inside the church foyer, greeting guests. Like the twin girls, they looked happily dazed and slightly old-fashioned, he in a light gray suit and she in a lemon yellow linen dress and bolero jacket.

Cubiak bussed Sonja's cheek and shook hands with Bathard. The melancholia he had detected in the doctor the previous day had disappeared. "Perhaps I failed to mention this, but I'd be honored if you would say a few words at the luncheon," Bathard said as he gave Cubiak the rings.

"Of course." A toast. Cubiak was the best man. He should have realized. There was still time; he'd think of something.

Cubiak arranged his face and again offered his arms to the bride's granddaughters. In step with the music, he led the girls down an aisle lined with candles and peace lilies.

He looked for Cate and found Emma Pardy and her husband in a middle pew. Natalie was next to them. A sandy-haired man sat to her left. Had Natalie brought a date? Cubiak colored, recalling his earlier plan to stop for her.

Ida, Olive, and Stella were lined up together in the last pew, occupying the rear of the church just as they had the front row at their husbands' funeral two weeks prior. The trio reminded Cubiak of the brevity of life. Sonja's daughter and son-in-law were in the first pew, like bookends at the opposite end of the small chapel. They made him think of hope and faith in the future.

Sonja's fraternal twin sister, a minister, would marry the couple. Dark, short, and reserved, she was the opposite of the bride in every obvious characteristic. Still, she nearly bounced through the brief ceremony and recitation of the vows. A commitment to love and respect, to cherish and honor. Then the pronouncement of marriage. A kiss. Applause. Cubiak clapped enthusiastically but he felt detached, as if he were looking down from the ceiling.

Still alone on the drive from the church to Bathard's house, he fumbled for a meaningful phrase or quote with which to honor the newlyweds. As the guests filed into the tent, Cubiak recalled a bit of wisdom he'd garnered from one of his high school teachers, a taciturn Jesuit who had enjoyed confounding his students with quotes from Kant. "A famous philosopher says we shouldn't focus on making ourselves happy but upon making ourselves worthy of happiness," Cubiak said, raising a glass in honor of Bathard and Sonja. "I can't imagine any two people more worthy of happiness."

After lunch, Natalie followed him outside. "You might take your own advice," she said as they stood shoulder to shoulder, pretending interest in Bathard's rose garden.

He grunted.

"Too bad Cate's not here. I was hoping to see the two of you together."

"You were?" Her gentle candor and lack of sarcasm left him defenseless.

"Sure. You think I don't know that all the time we've been seeing each other you've been waiting to see what happens with her?"

Cubiak winced. The truth stung.

"I've known Cate most of my life. She's not your type. You're not going to be happy until you get over both her and your guilt about Ruby." Natalie swiveled toward him. "Look at me. I know about her and about your wife and daughter, too. And I am so sorry that you had to suffer such loss and pain, but you can't hang on to the past forever. Not if you want to be worthy of happiness. And I think you do." She held his gaze a long moment and then turned and walked away.

He wanted to follow her, to tell her that it wasn't that easy. The past was part of him. He wasn't hanging on to it; the past lived inside him. Cate would understand, he thought. Like him, she had a history of loss.

Eventually the sound of music drew Cubiak back to the tent. Most of the guests were still seated, talking among themselves or listening to the string quartet that played Mozart. Cubiak wandered through, stopping to greet people he knew, smiling at those who turned a friendly face in his direction. The three widows shared a table with two other women. Olive caught his eye and he nodded politely but feigned a need to keep moving. He'd told Bathard that if Ida were at the wedding, he'd talk to her but he wasn't ready for that yet.

The coroner stopped him near the doorway.

"A very nice toast. Apropos for everyone, I would think," he said.

Cubiak shrugged. "So I've been told."

Bathard started to say something more when Sofia and Madeline latched onto his elbow.

"Time to cut the cake," they said together. As the girls tugged the doctor away, Madeline glanced over her shoulder. "Come watch, Uncle Dave."

Uncle Dave! Cubiak saluted. "I'll watch from here," he said. After the first slice was plated, he circled to the drinks table. He was surveying the crowd, still looking for Cate, when Ida approached.

"Sheriff."

"Ida."

"Such a lovely couple," she said, accepting the glass of champagne he held out.

"They are."

"To happiness." She raised her glass, and they drank together.

"If you have a moment . . . ," she said and began walking toward the door.

Cubiak picked up another drink and followed her out, wondering what more she had to say. She was at the fence, watching a handful of sailboats struggle to catch a whiff of wind. He came up alongside, rested a foot on the bottom rung, and waited.

"I've lived here all my life and I'm still fascinated by the water. Do you sail, Sheriff?" she said finally.

"No. Not yet. I'm going to learn."

"You'll like it."

Suddenly she grabbed his arm. "Thank you, for helping Roger. He came up last night and told me everything. That was very humane, very kind."

"It's up to him, really."

"Oh, he'll be fine, I wouldn't worry about that." Her grip tightened for a moment and then relaxed. "You don't believe me, do you?"

"About Roger?"

"No, about that night and what I told you happened."

"I'm not sure."

"Are you going to arrest me?"

"I haven't decided."

She turned back to the water. "It can't be easy. I apologize if I'm making your life difficult."

It's not you, he wanted to tell her. It was him. He had a duty to the law.

"I'm going to fight for Walter. I'll hire the best lawyer I can to defend him. After the trial—the acquittal—I'm selling the business and going away for a while. I've always wanted to take a cruise up to Alaska, and see the Grand Canyon, as well."

"Will you come back to Gills Rock?"

"No. I'll sell the house and find something else, but here on the peninsula. Assuming I'm not in jail."

"And if I arrest you?"

"I'd kill myself," she said with no hesitation.

The response startled Cubiak. "That's pretty hard to do while incarcerated."

"But not when you're out on bail." She looked at him. Her eyes flashed, whether in amusement or taunting, he couldn't be sure. "I'm an old lady, Sheriff. No one would be surprised if I keeled over. Especially faced with the shame of being accused of murder."

"You're blackmailing me."

"I'm telling you the truth. Just as I did yesterday. I didn't kill them. I wish I had."

Cubiak had heard those exact words before. Where? From whom? He remembered Olive, inebriated and defiant in her chic living room.

"You were all in it together," he said.

"The three little Indians? Hardly. I was the only one with a justifiable motive."

"Is that how you see it?"

"What was it you'd have me do, turn the other cheek? If Christian hadn't been wounded, they wouldn't have been able to leave him—he'd have fought to survive. To come back. He knew I was pregnant. I did what I had to for Christian."

"What if Terrence rejected your suggestion?"

"I knew he wouldn't. To a man like Big Guy, life was all about pride and saving face. He would do anything to avoid disgrace. He proved that by the way he lived."

"And the others?"

"Eric and Jasper? Those two! They stopped thinking for themselves years ago. It was always 'Big Guy this' and 'Big Guy that.' And how could they refuse? They sold their souls to the devil the day they agreed with his plan to abandon Christian."

Ida took a quick breath and continued. "They had no choice but to do as I said. If word got out that they were gay, there'd be plenty of gossip, but people are more tolerant about that kind of thing now and after a while they'd have put it out of their minds. But deserting a childhood friend, leaving a soldier to die? That's unforgivable."

A burst of applause rose up from the yard, drawing their attention to the lawn where the string quartet had regrouped on a wooden floor outside the tent and begun to play an old-fashioned waltz. In time with the music, Bathard twirled Sonja across the platform.

Ida moved a hand to the music. "Do you dance, Sheriff?"

"No," he said. Lauren had suggested they take lessons. Why had he refused?

"You should learn. Christian danced," she said, pivoting back toward the water.

"There is something else," Cubiak said when the music faded. "Has it occurred to you that you could be wrong about them leaving Christian? What if the truth is that they didn't find him? Or that he'd already died and they simply fabricated the story to make heroes of them all."

She seemed to shrivel at the suggestion.

"I'm sorry, Ida. I had to ask it."

The music started again. A fox trot or cha-cha, he didn't know the difference.

Ida fingered the gold chain around her neck and pulled it free of her dress, revealing a small cross. She held it out for Cubiak to see. "This was my wedding gift to Christian. When he enlisted, I made him promise to wear it always. I thought it would keep him safe from harm. He'd never have taken it off if he thought he was going to make it. He gave it to Terrence to give to me because he thought his friend was telling him the truth, that there was no room in the rescue boat."

She tucked the necklace back into place. "I gave the three of them a choice. Which is more than they did for Christian."

"And you can live with that?"

"They lived for years with the knowledge that they'd murdered a man. I can live out my remaining time knowing that I gave them an option."

"Disgrace or death." Cubiak hesitated. "Will you tell Walter?"

"When this is all over, I think so. He grew up feeling like he never was good enough for Terrence; the truth will free him from that lie."

"And Roger?"

She smiled. "Roger acts tough, but he's all mush inside. And he's so young. I think the truth would break him. Later, when I'm gone and if you're still here and still sheriff, you can make the call."

"You trust me with your secret?"

Ida took his arm. "I suspect you are a man with many secrets," she said.

As they slowly progressed across the lawn, Cubiak felt her strength ebb. Twice she faltered. Near the tent, she stopped and lifted her face toward him. A lifetime of weariness was worn into the pale flesh and the blue eyes dimmed with a quiet resignation. "Well, Sheriff?" she said.

Cubiak knew he had no proof that Ida had done anything to harm the three old vets the night they died in the cabin. He'd offered one version of events and she'd countered with another, equally plausible. If he repeated his story, she would deny it and which of them would a judge and jury believe? The only tangible piece of evidence that supported his scenario was a blurry photo of an event lost to history and the murk of war, and he didn't have a copy. He also had no proof to support or deny the possibility of suicide. If they had taken their own lives—either as a result of Ida's actions or because of some long-lingering vestige of remorse—no one would ever know. Fact and circumstance indicated that the deaths were the result of an unfortunate accident. And if that were a lie, then it was just another fabrication attached to a long list of lies. If anything, there seemed to be some element of poetic justice that three lives built on a foundation of deceit should end the same way. Even Walter's admission of attempting to harm the men could be plea-bargained into a slap on the wrists. And Roger, by the sheriff's own hand, had been given a pass. He had a duty to the law but he'd already sidestepped that on Roger's behalf.

Ida trembled. Cubiak squeezed her arm reassuringly.

"I find it touching that you and Olive and Stella came to celebrate the wedding so soon after the tragic incident that claimed your husbands' lives. I'm sure Bathard and Sonja and all the other guests feel the same."

Ida grasped his hand and planted a quick kiss on his cheek. "You are a good man," she said.

Soon after Bathard and Sonja drove away, the party started to break up. Natalie and her escort followed Pardy and her husband down the driveway. The three widows left in Ida's car with Olive behind the wheel. The outside bar had been dismantled, and as the remaining guests headed toward their vehicles, Cubiak wandered into the kitchen looking for the last of the champagne.

The musicians were eating at the table. Roger brushed past him toward the door.

"You leaving?" the sheriff said.

"Yeah. Got some business to take care of."

Cubiak questioned the boy no further. Roger was on his own.

A streak of ashen pink lit the horizon when Cubiak left the house. Dusk was settling over the peninsula, and overhead in the great wash of charcoal sky, a single star glistened. Anxious about the pups, he barreled east toward the lake, but at the highway junction he made a sudden turn north toward Fish Creek. He told himself he meant to check on the loitering situation outside the Woolly Sheep, but he knew that the real reason behind the detour was Roger. Despite the boy's promise and Ida's assurance that her grandson would keep his word, Roger's quick departure from Bathard's house and the excuse that he had "business" to tend to made Cubiak wary. Had he made a mistake in trusting the boy; and if he'd been wrong about Roger, had he erred in believing Ida as well?

Cubiak hit the slope into Fish Creek at fifteen over the limit and rode the brake hard down the hill. On the nearly empty streetscape around Founders Square, the motley crew outside the Woolly Sheep stood out easily. The sheriff crawled forward. Inside the brightly lit shop Kathy O'Toole rearranged skeins of yarn on the rear shelves. Cubiak drove up onto the curb opposite the store, not so conspicuous that he'd draw attention from the half-dozen tourists wandering the area but close enough for Timothy and his five cohorts to see him. Cubiak checked the clock on the dash: 8:10. He'd give them another ten minutes and then shag them away.

Besides the leader, Cubiak recognized four of the loiterers. The other was a new recruit who looked barely sixteen. Tim's girlfriend and the other girls were notably absent. Roger also was not with them.

The punks were smoking and talking but Cubiak couldn't make out more than an occasional curse word. Pop cans and bags from the local burger joint littered the ground. Cubiak wished one of them would crack a beer so he could run them in for underage and/or public drinking but figured they were too smart for that. At 8:15, Timothy hauled himself off the bench, gave fist bumps to a couple of his pals, and started ambling up the street toward the corner municipal lot. The others followed in his wake; one of them even stooped to pick up a discarded bag and toss it into a wire trash basket. When they were out of sight, the shop lights dimmed and the sheriff drove away.

As soon as he turned into his driveway, Cubiak noticed the lights through the kitchen window. Had his neighbor turned them on? A dark car stood in the shadows alongside the garage. Had Nagle traded in his brown truck and stopped by on the way from town rather than just walk across the road? And why so late? He said he'd feed the dogs at six and it was nearly nine. Could the car belong to Tim or one of his pals? Until then Cubiak hadn't considered the possibility of retribution for his stand against the troublemakers. At the thought of a welcoming committee waiting inside, the sheriff took a small handgun from the glove box and dropped it into his pocket.

Keeping to the grass, Cubiak crept up to the house. The porch smelled of dogs and fresh coffee. There was no evidence of forced entry into the kitchen but he heard voices inside. He tested the knob. It yielded easily. Cubiak turned it the rest of the way and kicked the door open.

Butch barked.

"Hey. You're back."

Cate sat on the floor across the room. She wore a black turtleneck and jeans and leaned into the wall, her long legs crisscrossed lotus style. Two of the pups chewed the leather strips that hung from the cuffs of her black boots. Another slept in her lap. The fourth was at the water dish.

"How'd you . . . ?"

"Evelyn lent me his spare key. I stopped this morning to give him and Sonja my best wishes. He told me about the puppies and said he thought it might be all right for me to come see them."

"I thought maybe you'd be at the wedding."

She shook her head. Her hands and face were tan; her hair was deep brown and hung straight to her shoulders. She frowned at the open door. "It's getting cold. Would you mind?"

"Sorry." Cubiak pulled the door shut.

"I've never seen you in a suit. You look nice."

Almost apologetically, he glanced down at his new clothes, trying to remember what he'd worn to Ruby's funeral, the last time he'd seen Cate. "I was best man," he said, as if that explained things.

"Evelyn said he'd asked you. Was it a nice wedding?" She shifted her attention away from the sheriff and began stroking Kipper.

"Very nice."

"I'm happy for both of them."

"Why didn't you come?"

Cate looked up suddenly. Her gaze was penetrating, the same look that had pierced him from the page of the *National Geographic*. "I thought it might be too distracting. You know how people are."

He nodded. Her presence would have conjured up memories of the nightmare the county had been through only two years prior.

Cubiak took a step forward. "I . . ."

"Please, don't. I know what you're going to say and it's not necessary. It wasn't your fault. None of what happened was your fault." Cate hesitated and lowered her gaze. "Or mine."

At the door, Butch yelped and danced a nervous jig, her nails clicking on the hard floor. "She needs to go out," Cubiak said, feeling cowardly but grateful for the reprieve as he followed the dog onto the porch and then into the yard. The moon was rising over the horizon. The night was still, as if the wind was holding its breath. Cubiak gulped in the cold air. Why hadn't Bathard told him Cate was back? Had she asked the coroner not to say anything because she wanted to surprise him, or because just a few hours earlier she hadn't made up her mind about seeing him?

Cate was still on the floor when he came inside. He scooped up one of the pups and slid down alongside her. Cate smelled like sea breeze.

"That's Kipper," he said, indicating the pup in her lap. "This one's Scout. The two at your feet are Buddy and Nico."

"I didn't know you were a dog person," she said.

"I'm not."

"I see."

He started to move toward her, but she pulled away from the wall and turned to face him. They were inches apart but it felt an enormous distance. Kipper stirred. Cate stroked the pup gently. "You've done a fine job so far."

"I've had help from the vet."

"Who's that?"

"Natalie Klein."

"Ah, Natalie. She's good."

They lapsed into silence and then spoke at the same time.

"Can I have one?"

"I've missed you."

Cate bent her head, her face hidden by her hair.

Cubiak closed his eyes. He'd spoken too soon, acknowledged a reality he'd kept hidden even from himself. "Yeah, sure. Why not?" he said after a moment. "But with your travel schedule . . ."

"It won't be so bad anymore. I've cut back. And I thought that maybe when I take an assignment, you could dog sit."

"You're moving back?"

"I already have."

Cubiak felt his color rise. "That's good."

Buddy and Scout rolled into a single, squirming ball that demanded their attention.

After a few moments, the pups fell away from each other, and Cubiak held out his hand to Cate. When she took it, he rose to his knees and pulled her up. With Nico and Kipper cradled between them, they melted into an awkward hug. When he tried to lift her mouth toward his, she burrowed her face into his chest. He heard her say something but the words were muffled.

"What?"

"I missed you, too," Cate said, leaning away from him.

Their eyes locked.

"No guarantees," she said.

"There never are." Cubiak drew her close and kissed the top of her head. For him, for now, this was enough.

ACKNOWLEDGMENTS

Like so many writers, I work in isolation but I could not do my work without the help and kindness provided by others. My gratitude extends to many:

To my daughters, Julia and Carla, who continue to offer their support and encouragement as well as their criticism, suggestions, and hands-on assistance.

To the women of my writers' group, B. E. Pinkham, Jeanne Mellett, and Esther Spodek, who enthusiastically read and critiqued every word of the novel.

To my early readers, Norm Rowland and Barbara Bolsen, whose candid reviews of the initial draft helped shape the final manuscript.

To Max Edinburgh, who read the completed work aloud to me—twice—giving the words a voice other than my own and thus offering an invaluable and sometimes humbling perspective.

To Rod Polacek, who shared experiences from his days of high school wrestling.

To Raymond Zielinski, who patiently tutored me on the complex process of repairing a wooden sailboat.

To Wayne J. Spritka, the former officer in charge of the Sturgeon Bay Coast Guard Station, for providing important factual information and escorting me on an extensive tour of the facility. Historic data was gleaned from several works: *The United States Coast Guard in World War II* by Thomas P. Ostrom; *The U.S. Army Campaigns of World War II*, vol. 6, *Aleutian Islands*, prepared by George L. MacGarrigle for the U.S. Army Center of Military History; and *Yank—The GI Story of the War* by the staff of *Yank*, the army weekly.

To Alex Skalka, my late father, who served in World War II. Though he seldom talked of his experiences, his stories made it clear that war was ugly and a far cry from the glamourous adventure portrayed in many late-night television movies.

Finally, my sincere thanks to the staff at the University of Wisconsin Press, including Raphael Kadushin, Sheila Leary, Carla Marolt, Sheila McMahon, and Andrea Christofferson, for cheering me on through the second book of the Dave Cubiak Door County Mystery series.